MW01137306

LADY IN WAITING

SHANDI BOYES

Edited by
MOUNTAINS WANTED PUBLISHING
Illustrated by
SSB COVERS AND DESIGN

COPYRIGHT

Editing: Mountains Wanted Publishing
Proofreading: Carolyn Wallace
Cover: SSB Covers and Design

DEDICATION

To the crazy girl, Sheridan.
You know who you are!

Shandi xx

ALSO BY SHANDI BOYES

Perception Series:

Saving Noah

Fighting Jacob

Taming Nick

Redeeming Slater

Saving Emily (*Novella*)

Wrapped up with Rise Up (*Novella - should be read after Bound*)

Enigma:

Enigma of Life

Unraveling an Enigma

Enigma: The Mystery Unmasked

Enigma: The Final Chapter

Beneath the Secrets

Beneath the Sheets

Spy Thy Neighbor

The Opposite Effect

I Married a Mob Boss

Second Shot

The Way We Are

The Way We Were

Sugar and Spice

Lady in Waiting

Man in Queue

Couple on Hold

Enigma: The Wedding

Silent Vigilante

Bound Series:

Chains

Links

Bound

Restrained

Psycho

Russian Mob Chronicles:

Nikolai: A Mafia Prince Romance

Nikolai: Taking Back What's Mine

Nikolai: What's Left of Me

Nikolai: Mine to Protect

Asher: My Russian Revenge

Nikolai: Through the Devil's Eyes

RomCom Standalones:

Just Playin'

The Drop Zone

Ain't Happenin'

Christmas Trio

Falling for a Stranger

Coming Soon:

Skitzo

Trey

PROLOGUE

A roaring buzz draws me back to consciousness. The thrumming of my heart in my ears is painful and raw—as if I am submerged in three thousand feet of water. The same can be said for my chest. It feels like an elephant is sitting there, squeezing the air out of my lungs as effectively as they were robbed of oxygen earlier tonight.

My mouth moves as I attempt to speak, but not a hum escapes my lips. I feel woozy and frail, like I haven't slept in a week. Pain scorches my veins when I slowly crack open my eyes. The sky is pitch black. Even the moonlight has withered away. I wish it were too dark to see anything because I would sell my soul to the devil not to see this.

"Luca," I croak out in a sob, my broken heart resonating in my tone.

He doesn't respond. He remains motionless in the driver's seat of his beloved Jeep Wrangler soft-top. It was a gift from his father on his sixteenth birthday. He loves it more than anything—except me. He has stated that many times the past three years. That's why the circumstances of our night are so hard for me to understand. This isn't Luca. The man sitting lifeless next to me isn't Luca.

He's the goofball. Our school's star quarterback. *My soulmate.*

I squeeze his hand that's still clutching mine. It takes all my strength to give him the three squeeze routine we do every time we silently declare our love for one another. *I* (squeeze) *love* (squeeze) *you* (squeeze).

Usually, he'd squeeze my hand back four times, the "too" at the end of his declaration requiring an additional squeeze. This time, he doesn't respond. His hand stays perfectly still.

"Luca, please."

My appeal is in utter desperation. The smell, the dark pools of blood staining his light gray t-shirt, and his head hanging low brings our night smashing back into me. We fought. That isn't unusual; we are worse than an old married couple. We bicker over things not worth fighting about because we are as stubborn as each other. My father has often predicted we would either smother each other to death or murder each other in a violent act of hatred.

Luca went for the latter.

He couldn't see past his pain, past the disbelief surrounding him.

He lost his faith in me.

"I'm so sorry, baby. So very sorry. I should have tried harder. I should have kept plugging away until everyone saw the real you." *I should have been honest with you from the very beginning.*

I weave my fingers through Luca's dark hair, stained with sweat, before tracking them down his jaw. Our impact with the tree trunk stole the last of our light, so I am unable to see his glistening green irises. It's probably for the best. I prefer the memories in my head than the image presented before me now.

"You will always have my support, Luca. *Always.*" My tone holds the same conviction as it did leading up to our crash.

My lips quiver when I lean across the mangled wreckage separating us to place a final kiss on Luca's cheek. "I promised to love you until my final breath. I'll kept my promise. Fly free, baby; your secret is safe with me."

With a majority of the damage on Luca's half of the car, I can exit the passenger seat without any hindrance. Every step I take away from the wreckage is done with an immense amount of pain. Although I am covered with cuts and bruises, the majority of my pain centers around my heart. It's broken. Shattered. Never to be repaired.

My brain feels seconds from exploding, but I still dive for the bushes edging the roadside when sirens break through my pulse shrilling in my ears. I should be aiding in their endeavor to help Luca, but if I do that, I can't keep the promise I made to Luca over three years ago. I let him down tonight. It will *never* happen again.

When bright lights break over the horizon, I thoughtlessly crank my neck backward. It's a stupid thing for me to do. The cracked windscreen and twisted metal of Luca's Jeep send me scampering backward until I land on my ass with a thud. First responders rush to his crumpled car, praying there are survivors amongst the debris of shattered glass and bloodstained metal.

Their prayers are in vain. There are no survivors.

Luca isn't the only one who lost his life tonight. I did as well.

CHAPTER ONE

Three years later...

Bright pink feathers fall to my feet as I dart offstage. My corset covers the risqué parts of my body, but with the minuscule folds in my stomach sitting a mere inch under my chest, I can't suck in an entire breath.

I want to say my mad dash off the stage is because I want to shred this corset off my body, but, unfortunately, that isn't the case. Just like three years ago, the vibe tonight is off. The clients at Substanz still exude excitement; the dancers are glammed to within an inch of recognition, and Tarren's new routine is out of this world, but no matter how hard I strive to ignore the niggle warning me that something isn't right, it won't budge. It's as strong as the strips of leather pushing my lungs into my throat.

"Boisterous crowd tonight." Dwain unravels the feather boa from my neck before twirling me away from him. His big, strong hands make quick work of the threads holding my lungs hostage. "Never seen you so eager to get offstage before. What's the deal?"

I wait for him to yank out the last strip from the back-breaking outfit before spinning around to face him. Since he's nearly seven feet tall, my neck strains to peer into his almost black eyes. Dwain is a bouncer at Substanz Cabaret Club. He is what the dancers and I call a perfect "3B": big, beautiful, and black. He started at Substanz around the same time as me, going on three years now. He's in his late twenties and has not an ounce of hair on his head, but he has all his teeth.

Dwain is adamant we add on the last reference. For some reason, a mouth full of chompers is more important to him than chiseled cheeks and a strong, defined jawbone. It's fortunate for him he has all three. His molten smirk sends the girls into a tailspin, but not one has taken him home. The girth of his fingers would snap some of the dancers in half, so imagine the massacre other regions of his body would incite?

"Rae? You still with me?" Dwain asks, breaking me from my ruminations.

I halfheartedly nod. "Yeah, sorry. Got a little carried away by my thoughts."

His deep murmur rumbles through my chest. He knows what I'm thinking without a word seeping from my lips. This is a prime example of why I'll never jump aboard the Dwain *snap them while they're sleeping* Train. He knows me too well.

Nobody knows me. The cabaret dancer who shakes her ass in a seedy club is a myth, a metaphor, a girl you'd never take home to visit your parents. She isn't the real me. She's the shield I use to keep myself safe—*to keep myself sane*. If I don't occupy my thoughts, my mind wanders. A nomadic mind never ends well.

I've changed a lot the past three years. At times, I barely recognize myself. But Dwain sees past my glittery chest, big eyes that promise trouble, and mega-watt smile. He has a gift for reading people for who they are—not how they present themselves. He reminds me a lot of my daddy, just in a younger, more ravishing, darker-skin version.

My theory is proven dead accurate when Dwain mutters, "You can talk to them, you know? No matter how bad things are, you'll always be their little Rae of sunshine. It's a parents' job to view their children through rose-colored glasses."

I roll my eyes before pushing off my feet. "Not happening, Dwain. As far as my parents are concerned, I'm on the final stretch of a paid scholarship, and you're the dorky hall monitor who saves my virtue every weekend by forcing me to study instead of attending frat parties." *They also believe Luca died an honorable man, and I intend for it to stay that way.*

Dwain's hefty chuckle is barely heard over the jazz blaring from the speakers above our heads as he follows me through the underbelly of Substanz. This humble abode was once my place of solace. It was the place I used to escape my worries in a positive, somewhat glamorous way.

Now, it feels sleazy and grimy.

Its revamped aura is accredited to the new owner who flew in on his broomstick with a vision of greatness. Unfortunately, a majority of his ideas depended on the dancers taking off their clothes.

Cabaret performances ooze sex appeal, but Jayce doesn't want glitzy routines that dazzle the mind and spirit. He wants skin, boobs, and bump and grinds that stimulate the areas between a man's legs instead of the ones between his ears.

Within six months of Jayce taking over the helm, Substanz went from a family-friendly environment to the dancers being shunned on the street by disgruntled single women who cite our "unachievable standards" as the reason they can't get a date. Their legs haven't seen a razor since the nineties, but Jayce's unbendable rules of the dancers not gaining more than four pounds after being hired are to blame for everything.

With a grumble about ill-informed people, I dash for the curtains separating backstage from the dressing rooms. Halfway through, the quickest flash of a smirk stops both my heart and my feet. A handsome man with wisps of blond hair sticking out of a low-hanging cap stands at the end of the corridor. He's in a restricted area—an area reserved for the staff of Substanz.

I lift my eyes to Dwain, who has also spotted the stranger. Unlike me, he isn't taking in the man's cut jawline, tempting body, and sultry smirk with agitated excitement. He looks concerned. I'd even go as far as saying frazzled.

The unease pumping out of him sends my pulse racing. "What is he doing back here?"

I'm not worried about my safety. Dwain could snap Hercules in half without breaking a sweat. I'm concerned about what the stranger's sneaky glances are doing to my insides. My stomach is flipping more now than it did during my gymnastic routines in high school. I haven't felt like this in years. . . not since I was intro-duced to a thirteen-year-old Luca.

"I don't know." Dwain's deep timbre relays his eagerness to find out. "Jayce mentioned something about foreign investors earlier this week. What do you think? Investing his inheritance in a seedy club to combat his mommy issues? Or are his preppy boy features hiding a tiny wiener?"

Dwain's snappy comment strips the worry from my gut, allowing the butterflies inside to take flight without hindrance. I should have realized he isn't scared. Nothing scares Dwain—not even the furious stink eye of my little sister, Raquel.

My eyes shift from Dwain to the mysterious stranger when the heat of his gaze captures my attention. With his head slanted to the side, the man peers at me from beneath the brim of his cap in the same manner he did earlier tonight. He isn't the least bit deterred by Dwain's rapidly forming anger.

He should be—very much so. I blame him for nearly stumbling three times on stage tonight. Although I couldn't see his eyes, his all-encompassing glare worked my inside muscles as effectively as my outside ones when I strutted across the stage. Half of his god-crafted features were hidden from my view, but that didn't leash my curiosity in the slightest.

His mysteriousness adds to his appeal, giving him a *you may never get out of this alive* vibe. It was so invigorating, I performed my routine on half of the stage: his half. That's why I darted off as I did. My lungs were demanding oxygen, but not all their deprivation was from my air-pinching corset. Most of it rested on the unnamed gentleman.

If only I could see his eyes, then I'd know which team he belongs to. A person's eyes are the gateway to their soul. They reveal a person's heart, spirit, and the reason they seek solace in sordid locations. Not all clients at Substanz come to get their rocks off. Some are just lonely. That's how I stumbled upon my line of work almost three years ago.

"Hmm." Dwain's rumble—as deep as Earl Brown's murmuring and as scrumptious as Garth Brook singing a love song—returns my focus to him. "Remember Celeste's side business?"

"No way. . . Do you think?" My voice is higher than my brows.

For almost two months, Celeste offered additional "services" for clients at Substanz. When Jayce caught wind of her illegal operation, he didn't fire her as expected; he wanted in on her scheme. The boutique massage parlor a few miles from Substanz has expanded to a six-figure entity the past three months. They don't relieve any of their clients' strains. . . unless they're sexual kinks.

"I think your radar is a little askew tonight, Dwain. He doesn't need *help* to relieve tension. Why shell out funds for something he can get for free?"

Dwain's eyes drop to mine. "So if he asked you on a date right now, you'd accept?"

"I didn't say that—"

"Uh-huh. My point exactly," Dwain interrupts. "I saw him gawking at you all night like you were the only girl on stage. There were over thirty dancers vying for his attention. His eyes never left you. He wants it." He rubs his hands together like a rhubarb pie is sitting in front of him. "He wants it *soooo* bad, he's willing to pay for the privilege."

The instant I spot his furling lips, I recognize his game plan. "This isn't a good idea. He won't take kindly to being swindled." The worry in my voice reflects the country twang I've struggled to conceal the past three years.

"He can't be swindled if he has no intention of cracking open his wallet. If he has merely mistaken backstage as an exit, he'll go on his merry way when I point him in the right direction. But if he thinks Substanz is an escort service, he'll pay for his stupidity before I toss his ass to the curb."

Dwain lowers his eyes to mine. They have the same effervescent edge they always have, just with a more cunning, bloodthirsty glow. "What do you say, Rae-Rae? Fifty-fifty?"

"Seventy-thirty." My words are barely heard over my heart thumping in my throat. I should not be negotiating. My gut has been in knots all day, warning me to remain cautious, but I've got a tuition check due at the end of the month. I can't miss this payment, or four years of study will go down the drain.

When Dwain glares at me, I give him the same pathetic mantra I repeat every time I enter the parking lot of Substanz: "Only those who fight for what they want truly achieve it."

"Uh-huh. That's why I'm fighting. I've got future baby momma nest eggs to save up for." I know he's joking. He's been as dateless as me the past three years.

When Dwain's stance remains strong, I bring out the charm. I want to say I thrust my chest high and graze my teeth over my lower lip, but unfortunately, Dwain isn't a sucker for big breasts and raunchy smirks. He desires what all handsome man crave: he's a booty lover.

"Sixty-forty and you buy me dinner," Dwain grumbles when my dip to gather a loose feather from the floor propels my scarcely covered backside into his peripheral vision.

My back snaps straight in an instant. "With how much you eat, I'm getting short-changed," I snarl under my breath, though it's just to cover up my notice of the stranger's discomfort.

He's doing a good job pretending to glance at the flyers disgruntled wives pin to the noticeboard every Sunday after church, but I heard his sharp breath when I dipped low. Just like I saw the briefest shuffle of his feet to ensure his view wasn't blocked by Dwain's impressive girth. He's eager alright. I just can't fathom if it's for what Dwain assumes or something entirely different. If I were to trust my gut, I'd say it's the latter, but after a few years of bad decisions, I don't trust my intuition as much as I used to.

Dwain's deep sigh rustles my shoulder-length blonde hair. "Come on, Rae. Look at him. He's more than eager," he murmurs, spotting the same signals as me. "If I don't approach him soon, he'll bust a nut just looking at you, then we both leave tonight with only our measly hundred dollar paycheck in our hands."

I wish he were lying, but he's as honest as his tone. With my refusal to do my routine topless added to my constant decline of Jayce's many invitations to join Celeste's private services, my paycheck went from two to three hundred a night to not even a hundred. Men are stingier with their money when they're not shoving it between a set of breasts.

My heart drums against my ribs as I contemplate Dwain's suggestion. I've been busting my ass the past term to earn the tuition money needed for me to graduate, but can I do this, can I pretend to sell my body to make coin? Even though it's a hoax, and at no time will services be rendered for payment, my worry remains high. The last time I agreed to a ruse like this, I lost more than a few hundred dollars.

"Sixty-forty," Dwain negotiates, believing my delay stems from wanting a bigger slice of the pie. It isn't. It's horrid memories. "But you have to send the extra ten percent to Ms. Sweet Thing. She's starting out in a big city. She needs a boost."

"I think she'd prefer your eyes off her ass the next time she visits," I snap, my mood as thinly-guided as my morals.

Dwain holds his hands in front of his body while remaining as quiet as a church mouse. His demure stance serves him well. I am less likely to lash out when my target is subdued. Furthermore, if I were truly concerned at his appreciative ogle of my sister's backside, I would have shut down his interests months ago. Dwain is a good guy, but even if he wasn't, Raquel can handle herself. Our momma taught us well. We are as smart as we are beautiful.

I shouldn't baby Raquel, but it's hard. She's my little sister—only by a year, but still younger than me. My involvement wouldn't be so dramatic if she wasn't as eccentric and over the top as me. For two country girls, we grew up glam. We bedazzled everything: our jeans, shirts, and boots. Even Daddy's belt buckle was covered with so much rainbow glitter, the ranch workers nicknamed him Sparkie.

I miss home. I could go back at any time, and my parents would welcome me with open arms, but I don't want to be a lady in waiting. I want to rule the world. It's the reason Luca and I packed up and left town the week following graduation. We wanted an adventure. We couldn't achieve that in Milam County, Texas.

Shaking my backside is how I make ends meet now, but once I've cruised through law school, passed the bar with flying colors, and established myself as the number one business lawyer in the state, cow dung, 3 AM milkings, and world domination will once again be on the agenda. But instead of milking the cows and shoveling their poo, I'll protect the Ma and Pa co-op's like my family's estate from being sold to foreign investors.

"Fifty-fifty, and you take Raquel and me out for dinner next time she's in town." For the first time tonight, my voice reveals my determination.

I didn't leave Luca trapped in his mangled Jeep for no reason. I did it so I could give back a smidge of the love my parents have bestowed upon me the past twenty-two years. If I'd been found in the wreckage with Luca, I would have been forced to lie under oath. If my lies were exposed, my childhood dream of becoming a lawyer would have been destroyed, and I would have reneged on the promise I made with Luca on his sixteenth birthday. We were young, neither of us truly knowing what we were promising, but nothing will stop me upholding my end of our agreement. I lost my life three years ago. I refuse to give up my soul as well.

Dwain agrees to my suggestion without words by heading for the blond man. His giant steps slow when I say, "Not a food truck meal. I want real food—at an *actual* restaurant."

Since I can't see his eyes, he answers with a throaty murmur. It's one of those southern drawls that makes me think of bow-legged men with sexy stubble and mouthwateringly wide shoulders. It's as far away from Dwain's Dominican ethnicity as you can get.

As Dwain approaches the unnamed lurker, I roll my shoulders. My breasts no longer feel perky since they aren't stuffed under my chin, and my mood is teetering, but fingers crossed my mile-long legs will make up for their lagging counterparts. I don't see this being an easy hustle. This unknown man is attractive, but I doubt he has a trust fund. His suit doesn't scream wealth and superiority. It fits him as if it was tailored for his slim waist, banging guns, and rigid stomach, but it's the latter three qualities responsible for my light-headed response—not his Hugo Boss knock off.

His aura, on the other hand. . . you couldn't put a dollar amount on it. He's confident, self-assured, and would have absolutely no issues bending me over his knee to spank the sass right out of me. *It's a pity our plan is a ruse. He could have been a lot of fun.*

I shimmy my shoulders, snapping myself out of my uncharacteristic thoughts. I don't date. I haven't in years. I merely gobble up attractive men, storing them in my memory bank like calorie-laden sweets before dispersing the energy in a non-ladylike fashion.

What does my mother call my toys? "Gimmicks designed to make men feel less inferior."

I call them gyrating saviors. If it weren't for my vibrating bunny and his wickedly naughty friends, I'd still be splayed on the back seat of Jamie's truck, waiting for him to locate my G-spot. Instead, I pointed it out for him, taught him what to do and precisely how to do it. He left feeling fabulous, believing he was the first to bring me to climax. He was the first man, but it wasn't my first orgasm. Country girls who wake before the sun have a lot of time on their hands for experimenting.

I'm pulled from my thoughts when a pair of intense, pene-trating eyes peer at me. Even with his gaze hidden by the brim of his cap, I can feel the blond's anger radiating off him. The flare of his nostrils indicates he isn't impressed with Dwain's suggestion, much less the tight clench of his jaw. I'm so confident he won't fall for our trick, I physically balk when he reaches for his wallet instead of sprinting to the quickest exit.

The veins in my neck thrum when he snags five one hundred dollar bills from his leather pouch. My heart rate isn't speeding up because of the impressive amount Dwain negotiated; it's from the stranger's pulse-quickening glare pinning me in place. He has a knife-like stare, slicing through my perception as readily as his handsome face dampens my panties. It's a warning glare, one I've witnessed only once before in my life. It was delivered by Luca a mere hour before his death.

My lips pucker as if I am going to be sick when Dwain pockets the man's money in his bomber jacket. I should be pleased our scam worked, but haunted memories keep my excitement at bay.

I take deep breaths to settle my flipping stomach when Dwain seizes the man's shoulder in a firm grip to drag him toward the concealed exit. I almost feel sorry for the handsome stranger, but the fact he assumed I'd accept payment for services stops me. He may be handsome, but that doesn't excuse poor morals. Maybe next time he'll think twice before treating a classically trained dancer as if she's a hooker.

CHAPTER TWO

I issue the stranger a final sneer before pivoting on my heels to enter the curtain separating backstage from the underbelly of Substanz. Just before I break through the thick material, a deep "oomph" sounds through my ears.

Jackknifing back, my heart launches into my throat. Dwain is buckled on his knees, holding his gushing nose with his large hand. His attacker is standing over him, wordlessly cautioning him a bloody nose will be the least of his problems if he budges an inch.

Before my hazy brain can decipher what's happening, the blond man removes a set of cuffs from his belt. His brisk movements reveal that our ruse wasn't just foolish; it was life-altering. He's a federal agent. If the gold eagle on the top of his badge isn't enough of an indication, the bright blue FBI print beaming from his leather wallet is a clear sign.

"You have the right to remain silent. Anything you say. . ."

The blond's words trail off when someone grabs me. I'm dragged through a thick curtain without a squeak escaping my lips; I'm too stunned to do anything. Dwain isn't being arrested by a half-witted cop who would accept a bribe. He's being taken into custody by an agent from the Federal Bureau of Investigation.

This can't get any worse. If I am arrested, I cannot go to law school; I cannot sit the bar, and I will not save my parents' property from liquidation. This undoes all the good I've achieved since Luca's death. It will unravel everything.

"Unless you want to be arrested, keep your head down and your legs moving." My savior's voice is deep, protective and laced with secrecy.

"My. . ." My quivering words end when the man clutching my wrist snatches my purse from my dressing station before taking a sharp left.

How did he know which one was mine?

Bitterly cold winds smack into me when we exit the secured side entrance of Substanz. It was the door Dwain was heading for before he was detained. We glide down the blackened sidewalk, a rusty awning keeping us concealed from the helicopters hovering above our heads.

The scene is frantic, matching ones I've watched many times on *Cops.* Clients race for their cars parked blocks up so their wives don't grow suspicious of their nightly routine. I do the same thing, but more to hide my secret life from the dean of my college and the one or two people from my study group hoping to weasel their way from study companions to friends. *I wonder if they'd still like me if they knew about my double life?*

As riot officers circle the premises, ensuring everyone inside Substanz remains trapped, I raise my eyes to my suited companion. "They have us surrounded. We can't get out."

He brushes off my worry with a smirk. "It isn't what you know, Regan. It's *who* you know."

My feet stop as my heart rate rockets sky-high. "How do you know my name?"

I haven't been called Regan in years. Since venturing down this sordid path, I've gone by the nickname my father calls me when I give him sass. Everyone at Substanz refers to me as Rae. No one here knows my real name — not even Dwain.

"I'll explain everything the instant we get out of here. But we need to dodge your arrest first. Okay?" His question doesn't match the sternness of his tone.

He stops dragging me across the cracked asphalt when an armed agent steps into our path. The riot officer's shield is lowered, hiding his face, and his weapon is pointed at the unnamed man's chest. He looks peeved. Rightfully so. He did break formation to approach us milling about in the far back corner of the parking lot.

"Henry said to say hello." I glare at the dark-haired man clutching my waist. Is he certifiably mad? We're about to be arrested—now is not the time for niceties.

Feeling the heat of my gaze, the stranger lowers his eyes to mine. Their intensity has my throat drying up. Not because I'm in fear for my life, but because their unique gray coloring is diverting the moisture in my body to a more *needy* region.

With a wink acknowledging he noticed my whitening tongue, the stranger returns his focus to the armed agent. "Which way?"

"Go west for half a mile; the trek is steep. When you see an old set of railroad tracks, wave your arm in the air three times." The agent steps closer to us, ensuring we can hear him through his face shield. "Three times only. Do two, my guy will shoot you. Four—"

"He'll shoot me. Got it," the gray-eyed man interrupts. "What's the deal?"

He nudges his head to the line of men and women kneeling outside of Substanz. The agents haven't segregated the groups from the longtime clients who spend more time here than their homes to the one-off visitors who couldn't contain their curiosity for a moment longer. They're all being treated as criminals.

I finish scanning the ashen faces for Dwain when the agent answers, "Don't know. This isn't Henry. He only got word of our sting while we were in transit." Although I can barely see the agent's eyes, I'm certain they are on me when he adds, "Why take her with you? She'll slow you down."

"She's got something I need." The dark-haired hottie chuckles when I take a step back, apparently humored by my desire to flee. "Thanks for the knock to my ego, sweetheart, but I'm not here for your body."

His term of endearment seems off. He has wise eyes and an affluent taste in clothing, but his lack of wrinkles reveal he isn't much older than me. He may even be the same age, so a term my grandpa regularly uses doesn't suit him.

After thanking the guard for his assistance, the unnamed man curls his arm around my waist and forces my legs forward. Since we're moving away from an assembly of people who could sweep my every wish out from beneath my feet, I let him.

Approximately five minutes later, we reach a hole cut into a chain link fence separating Substanz from the adjacent property, which is covered in a thick underbrush and weeds. The scene is as chaotic as ever, but with the focus centered on entrance and exit points, our escape goes unnoticed.

I eat my words when a deep, profound voice yells for us to

freeze only seconds later. Without fear, my unexpected superhero dives through the fence, ignoring the repeated demands for us to stop or he'll shoot.

"Watch the edges; they'll shred your skin to pieces." His deep voice strains when he pulls apart the steel to ensure my skin remains unnicked.

The ruffled skirt of my corset shreds when I haphazardly fall through the hole. I'm not usually so rash, but the stranger's confidence is making my head swim. Besides, if my dreams go up in smoke, at least I can say I didn't go down without a fight.

After interlocking our fingers, the stranger races us toward the blackness of the night. We barely make it six steps before the frightening ricochet of a bullet freezes me. My abrupt stop only pauses the strangers' flee for barely a second. He's smarter than me. He doesn't stay standing at the edge of a meadow field, making himself a prime target. He uses the overgrown weeds to conceal himself.

Only once the unnamed man's profile is hidden from view do I spin to face the consequences of my actions head on. My legs wobble as I struggle to stop tears from slipping down my face. I worked at Substanz as it was the only way I could continue the ruse Luca and I began years ago—the one that made my parents believe I had a scholarship.

My parents are wonderful people, but they couldn't afford to send me to college, much less Raquel only a year later. The hoax Luca and I plotted wasn't ideal, but it was better than seeing my family's dairy farm divided and sold to land-hungry investors. Within hours of telling them I had a scholarship, the for sale sign was removed from a parcel of land our family farm needed to survive. Without land, we can't grow Lucerne hay. Without feed, our cows go hungry. Hungry cows don't produce good quality milk. My family ranch would have gone under in months, if not weeks.

I swallow the bile burning my throat when I notice who is approaching me. It's the man from the corridor in Substanz—the one Dwain hoped to play for a fool. He's standing on the other side of the fence, seemingly conflicted about whether to climb through the hole and chase me down, or use his weapon.

He must decide on the latter when he warns, "If you run, I'll have no other option but to shoot you." He sounds as conflicted as me, like his decisions aren't his own. "Don't make me do that. Come back on this side of the fence and face your choices in a respectable way. I can help you, Rae. You just need to pick the right side of the law."

My earlier wish to see his eyes grows rampant. His pledge of assistance sounds authentic, but with the low hang of his cap sheltering his eyes, I can't reach a sound conclusion.

"Are you arresting me for prostitution?" I bite on the inside of my cheek, annoyed at the snivel in my tone. I am stronger than this.

After a roll of my shoulders, I quote, "State laws were implemented to target offenders conducting the prohibited act of engaging in sexual conduct with another person in return for a fee. I didn't touch you, so you have no basis for arrest."

I expect my extensive criminal knowledge to stump him. It doesn't—not even for a second. "Prostitution laws also target those agreeing or *offering* to engage in sexual activities in return for a fee. Solicitation is as criminal as the *act* itself." The way he sneers "act" leaves no doubt to his feelings on the matter.

Incapable of giving up without a fight, I retaliate, "We weren't soliciting you. We were playing you. Dwain stupidly thought you were interested in me, so we decided to test the theory. Big mistake, apparently!"

"The only mistake you made was petitioning a federal agent for sex—"

"We didn't know you were an agent! Duh!" The immaturity of my last word should shock me. Unfortunately, it doesn't. I'm notorious for being childish when the odds are stacked against me. Tonight is clearly no different.

Realizing my argument isn't getting me anywhere fast—*except to jail*—I switch to a tactic I haven't used in an extremely long time. I hit him with straight up honesty. "I work at Substanz as a cabaret dancer. Nothing more. I wouldn't have sex with you even if you paid me."

I snap my mouth shut, praying it will hoist me out of the massive sinkhole I'm digging. I said straight up honesty, so acting like he has a dog's ass for a face is the most dishonest thing I've pretended the past three years, and I've had some doozies.

"That was a lie. I'd have sex with you even without an exchange of money." His growl quickens my words. "But in saying that, there was never any intention for us to exchange bodily fluids. I don't do attachments. With attachments come lies, and with lies come heartache. I've had more than my fair share. I don't want any more."

The stranger sighs. Since I can't see his eyes, I can't decide if it's an annoyed sigh or a frustrated one. With his weapon still honed on my chest, I'll assume it's the latter.

When the stranger's silence becomes too great for me to bear, I plead, "Please, I am begging you. I can't be arrested." The prayer in my voice is unmissable. "This won't ruin my weekend, month or year. It will destroy my entire life."

For the first time tonight, I seem to get through to the stranger. His voice sounds genuinely dependable when he assures, "If tonight's exchange was merely a misunderstanding, you have no reason to fear stepping back onto this side of the fence. Much to the dismay of every woman in this town, cabaret dancing is not illegal. You won't face charges if all you did tonight was earn an honest living."

"That's all I was doing. I swear to you," I pledge.

The agent steps closer to the fence, unshadowing half of his face. It adds to the sweat slicking my skin. "Then tackle the issue head-on, Rae. You don't appear the type to back down without a fight. Prove to me what I saw the instant I spotted you is true. Show me your fighting spirit."

My reluctant step forward is sliced to half its natural stride when a curt voice snaps, "Don't."

It's the same voice that told me to keep my head down and feet moving to avoid arrest. I thought his dart across the dew-covered ground left me high and dry. I had no clue he'd return to rescue me for the second time tonight.

"Look at him, Regan. He won't shoot you." He keeps his voice low, ensuring the federal agent can't hear him. He assumes my silence is because I'm contemplating his promise—not plotting a way to evade him.

"His gun is pointed at my chest," I murmur, certain the gray-eyed stranger isn't seeing things clearly since he's several paces behind me.

A rustle of air hits my neck, making me imagine the stranger briskly shaking his head. "Truly look at him, Regan. His gun is to the left of your chest. His finger isn't on the trigger. He has no intention of taking you down."

I take a step forward. I'm not giving in. I'm merely authenticating the stranger's assumption.

He is correct. The agent's gun is veered just left of me, and his trigger finger is straight and un-cocked.

My pulse thrums through my body as an incalculable number of questions bombard me. *Am I the cause of the indecisiveness in his tone? Is his inability to direct his weapon at me the reason he seems more reluctant now than he did when Dwain approached him? Will he let me flee without protest?*

My first two questions go unanswered. My last doesn't require a lengthy deliberation. He's an FBI agent, and I am a cabaret dancer who solicited him for sex. The only way we will ever get cozy is when he's circling cuffs around my wrists.

As if he heard my unspoken words, the unnamed man suggests I make a dash for it. I shake my head. "I can't. You don't know what we did to him. He'll shoot me."

When I remain frozen in place, the man steps out of the low-hanging tree sheltering him from the agent's view. The agent's attention snaps to him so fast, I'm certain his neck will feel the effects for weeks to come.

"Are you an idiot? What are you doing?!" My scold is barely audible over the agent's repeated demands for the man to raise his arms above his head.

Although he does as requested, his eyes remain locked on mine. "Now we've only got two options. You either run with me or I die. The choice is yours, Regan."

"If he has no intentions of shooting me, why would he shoot you?!" I stop badgering him with my *you're such an idiot voice* when the crook of a finger steals my words. The agent's trigger finger is no longer straight and flat. It's curled in a soul-stealing way.

Shit.

"On the count of three, I'm going to run. You either run with me or watch me be carted out of this field with a bullet hole in my back."

"I can hear you, you know," the agent growls, pissed we're talking about him as if he isn't here, much less the only player holding a gun.

The gray-eyed stranger smirks as he mockingly states, "I know."

He charges for me so fast, the agent barely has a second to blink, much less yank back his trigger. His theory that the agent has no intention of gunning me down is proven without doubt when his dash behind my back coincides with the lowering of the agent's gun.

"Need more proof?"

Not waiting for me to answer, the gray-eyed man steps out from behind my shoulder. The instant he's unblanketed from my body, the agent curls his finger around the trigger of his gun. When he steps back, placing me in the firing line, the agent's finger goes as straight as a board.

The unnamed man's husky laugh is barely audible over the hammering of my heart. With the unusual range of emotions hammering me, I can't declare if it's a good flutter or a bad one. If I had to choose, I'd say it's a bit of both. I hate that we're in this predicament, but this is the first time in a long time my heart has thumped this way. Luca was the instigator of any trouble we got into, so he was the one left answering for it. I'm not saying I'm totally innocent, but compared to Luca's antics, I appeared to be a saint.

The stranger's minty breath fans my earlobe when he whispers, "On the count of three, I'm going to spin and run. If you come with me, we'll be scot-free. If you stay put, I'll be dead."

I don't get the chance to protest before he counts down, "Three. . . Two. . ."

"Rae, don't," the agent warns when my feet shift an inch to the right. "I can protect you. I can keep you safe. You just need to trust me."

The honesty in his tone makes me believe his pledge of protection, but apart from my dad and brother, there has only been one other man who gained my utmost trust. He is buried under six feet of dirt. He took my secrets to his grave—just as I will his.

For that alone, I turn and sprint when the stranger screams, "One!"

With my brain on the verge of shutting down, I focus on one thing and one thing only: keeping my body aligned with the man two feet in front of me. The closer I stay to him, the less likely he'll be bitten by a bullet.

I hear the agent chasing after us, shouting my name on repeat, but I also smell freedom. It's there, right over the railroad tracks. I just have to keep running like I did the night Luca guided his car toward a massive tree trunk.

Did you know if you sprint fast enough, the entire world blurs? That's what I do to forget haunted memories. I run until the tears streaming down my face are replaced with sweat, and running home is the last thing on my mind. I run until my legs give out, and my toes bleed as heavily as my heart did that fatal night three years ago.

I run and run. Then I run some more.

The stranger waves his arm in the air three times when we cross a railroad track. A dark blue sedan skids to a stop in front of us two seconds later. When the suit-clad man gestures for me to enter before him, I shove him into the backseat with a grunt. Can't he sense the danger surrounding us? The agent is so close, his hot breaths are quivering on my neck. They're the reason my heart is battering my ribs even more than my overworked lungs are struggling for air.

I dive into the car with barely a second to spare. The driver floors the gas pedal, leaving the agent standing on the road edge with his gun pointed our way, but his bullets intact.

I'd like to say my heart is in the same condition. Unfortunately, I can't.

CHAPTER THREE

My feet are planted shoulder-width apart, and my aim is perfect; I just need my head to get the memo that my target is a criminal. She chose evil over good, the villain over the hero. She chose him instead of me.

So do your fucking job, Alex! Shoot out the goddamn tire!

Pain rockets through my right cheek when I peer down the barrel of my gun to line up the back left tire. One bullet and my pursuit will be over. The sedan will flip, most likely injuring the assailants inside. That shouldn't be an issue. If they weren't fleeing a crime scene, they wouldn't get hurt. But her, for some fucking reason, I can't hurt her.

Have you ever wondered what would happen to an angel if she visited hell? Would her feathers wilt under the heat? Or would she be protected by a bubble of goodness too strong for the most profound sins to penetrate? Those were the questions that popped into my head when I spotted Rae on the stage for the first time weeks ago. She was smiling like every other dancer, but her smile wasn't to entice money. It was genuine and unique, a smile that revealed she'd survive the depths of hell without a single feather being singed.

She's the reason I stalled our sting the past month. I was sent into Substanz undercover to determine if they were the operative responsible for the shipment of illegal firearms and drugs from Africa the past year. The only illegal thing I spotted was an excessive amount of cleavage. . . until I was approached on my way out.

I should have walked away. I should have pretended Dwain's offer wasn't as insinuated, that he was simply asking if I enjoyed the show enough to tip generously, but the motion-activated camera in the button of my shirt ensured I couldn't ignore his proposal.

My superiors witnessed what I witnessed. They heard what I heard. I had no other option but to act on the oath I swore. Substanz may not be running drugs and guns, but they are overseeing another illegal operation: prostitution.

Things have certainly changed since I left the academy. My first assignment was a sex trafficking ring run by a Russian association on the West Coast. None of the women looked like Rae. The life in their eyes had vanished within a week of being "recruited," and their skin was blemished with bruises and scars.

Only one girl's eyes held the same esteem as Rae's: it was Katie, a pretty redhead with milky white skin and big doe eyes. I fought my superiors for months to let me break cover to save her from the lifestyle that was slowly killing her, but they always offered the same argument: "One woman's life will never be more valuable than many lives."

I understood what they meant, but the plea in Katie's eyes couldn't be felt through surveillance images. Their impact in person could take down the strongest man. I nearly succumbed numerous times. The only reason I didn't was because I am not a man. I am an agent. My job comes before anyone—even the dancer who stole the air from my lungs with a can-can kick and bright smile.

Exhaling sharply, I return my focus to the task at hand. With the dark sedan's dangerous speed gaining them an impressive advantage, it will be a long range shot for me to take them down, but my marksmanship skills are the best the academy has seen. I'm confident I've got this.

As my finger creeps back on the trigger, a blur of blonde captures my attention. I adjust my vision, sharpening it so profoundly, the rare speckles of black mottled through Rae's green irises can be seen from a distance. She's staring straight at me, begging me not to shoot.

I remind myself that she's a target, a criminal, a person who sells her body for profit, but no matter how loudly the facts are screamed at me, nothing forces me to squeeze the trigger. Even with my wallet being five hundred dollars lighter, I believed her when she said she only works at Substanz as a dancer. The way she holds herself backs up her claims, let alone the honesty in her eyes. I don't know the premise behind her ruse tonight, but I trust my gut. It has never let me down. That singlehandedly has me lowering my gun.

Regrettably, I'm not the only agent in pursuit.

"Don't fire!" I scream, waving my hand in the air to alert the agent dressed head to toe in riot gear to stand down. "They're civilians."

Agent Dane relaxes his stealthy stance before raising his face visor. I knew who he was before he revealed himself. If the tattoo on his hand didn't give it away, I can smell his taco-laced breath from here. I swear, from the day we met as freshmen in college, I've seen him consume a minimum of three tacos a day.

Dane and I were recruited to the agency straight after graduation. His laidback attitude has hindered him climbing the ranks as rapidly as me. Not that he minds. He believes everyone can achieve greatness no matter how slow their pace is.

I'm taking the reckless, steep track. He's choosing the safer, more boring option. Although I doubt he'd have an issue taking my place if the Bureau discovered I let two suspects flee without using my exemplary weaponry skills.

After housing his weapon, Dane lifts his icy blue eyes to mine. Our eyes, cut facial features, and identical height often have us mistaken for brothers. It's only Dane's inky black hair keeping the rumors at bay. I do have a brother in the agency, just not anywhere you'd suspect.

"If they're civilians, why are you injured?" Dane drops his eyes to my right ear.

I run my hand across the area he's glaring at. Air hisses between my teeth when I discover a thin but deep gash running from my right temple to just below my earlobe.

"It's barely a scratch. When I heard rustling in the bushes, I dove through the fence to check it out," I murmur like it's not a big deal. "Must have cut myself. Doesn't hurt."

For a man trained to lie, I'm shit at it. An average man would hear my deceit a mile out, let alone one who knows me better than family.

"Let the medics take a look at it. We don't want anything happening to your pretty little face. Barbie will get upset if she discovers her main squeeze isn't made out of plastic." The deep hum of his voice is hindered by laughter.

My eyes roll skywards before I give him a curt nod. Nothing he's saying is new to me. He was the one who started the Ken doll rumors at the academy. Sometimes I wish I were made out of plastic, then I wouldn't face moments like today. You can't feel conflict if your insides are hollow.

I trained for years to ensure I see nothing but the truth when I look at someone. Criminals are criminals regardless of their gender, age, looks or social status. It shouldn't matter if my heart had an elongated beat at my first glance into Rae's eyes or that the music dulled to barely a buzz when she smiled. A criminal is a criminal. That's it. No further deliberation required.

After scrubbing my hand down my face in frustration, I trudge back toward the flashing lights on the horizon. It's time to face my actions like a man instead of the coward I portrayed tonight.

My brisk pace slows when Dane calls my name. When I spin around to face him, he gives me a smirk. It's more of an *I'm your brother even without the blood* smirk than one of a rival. He's not peeved about my advancement in the academy. He's proud.

He throws a chunky field laptop into my chest before jabbering, "If you're leading with the civilian story, you better wipe her from the data first." He drops his eyes to my chest, his brief scan halting at the exact button housing my hidden camera. "Wipe my roguishly handsome face while you're there, will ya? I don't want my measly paycheck sliced even more. . ."

His lopsided grin lowers half an inch as the width of his pupils double. He stumbles forward, his face whitening with each jagged step he takes. I stare at him, stunned into silence. He's acting as if he's been. . . *Oh fuck.*

"We've got shots fired on Mulberry Hill," I roar into my radio before grabbing Dane by the scruff of his shirt to drag him behind a thick tree on the edge of the roadside. Because he's in the process of dropping, we exit the clearing extremely fast. "An officer has been hit. I repeat, officer down; send medics!"

Blood splatters Dane's chin when I push my hands on the massive stain oozing out of his vest. He must have been shot with a high caliber weapon as the bullet shredded his bulletproof vest. It's left a hole the size of a penny in the upper left quadrant of his stomach.

"Come in heavy. Looks like a sniper." My demands are remarkably strong for how hard my heart is hammering. "Bullet is a through and through. Wound is puckering."

My crew replies but Dane's garbled moan drowns them out. His battle cry is warranted. I am tugging his vest off so I can inspect his wound more diligently. Although I hate hurting him, if I don't act quickly, he'll suffer more than a tinge of pain. He'll feel nothing.

The situation worsens when I remove Dane's vest and shirt. He's bleeding profusely, meaning either an artery has been nicked or the bullet entered and exited his liver. Neither scenario is good.

"We need to get you to the medics. They'll never make it here on time."

Dane grips my hand, impeding my calculation of the steps from our location to base. Since his throat is filling with blood, his welling eyes have to speak on his behalf. He doesn't want me risking my life to save his.

"If I don't get you down that mountain, you'll bleed out. It won't be pretty, and it will hurt like fuck, but I'm not letting you die up here. You're coming down that hill with me, Dane."

When I attempt to throw him over my shoulder, he puts up a protest. Considering he's minutes from death, his strength inspires me.

"You either come willingly, or I'll drag you down that fucking mountain by the scruff on your chin," I grunt through the pain shredding my chest in half.

I know his issue. I know he's worried I'm putting myself in the line of fire to save him, but if I don't get him to a medic within minutes, he *will* bleed out. This isn't a possibility. It's a fact. I already lost a part of myself on this field tonight. I'm not losing him as well.

Dane locks his eyes with mine. His pupils are so massive, I can't see any specks of blue. "K-K-Kristin."

"No!" I shake my head so rapidly it grows woozy. "If you want to tell Kristin something, you tell her your goddamn self."

Kristin is Dane's high school sweetheart. They married not long after we graduated college, and they had a baby girl only four months ago. She's the apple of her daddy's eye. I'm not going to let anything stand in my way of getting him back to his wife and daughter. If I'm taken down during the process, so be it. It won't be the only stupid thing I've done tonight.

Feeding off the adrenaline roaring through my veins, I yank Dane up by his arms. His helmet falls to the ground with a clatter when I heave him over my shoulder, landing next to my beloved 69ers cap. I wore that cap tonight as it's my lucky charm. It has never let me down. *Had,* I mentally correct.

The amount of blood seeping into my suit jacket is all the evidence I need to know I've made the right decision. For every second passing, Dane's likelihood of survival diminishes. I have to get him to a medic, and I have to get him there now.

"We're coming down. Cover us. Shooter is on a rock face northwest of base," I advise my superior officers.

My radio crackles before I hear, "Hold back. We have no marksman in place."

"I can't hold back. If I hold back, he'll bleed out." Devastation dangles on my vocal cords.

"Hold back, Agent Rogers. This is not a suggestion; it's an order. . ." The rest of my supervisor's reprimand is lost when I yank my radio receiver from my ear.

I've broken enough rules tonight to have me removed from my position, so what's another bout of defiance?

I fire three shots in the direction I believe the sniper is lying in wait before charging down the mountain. I'm not advising him of my location, I just need him ducking for cover long enough for me make it to the stand of trees three-quarters of the way down the valley.

We make it halfway to cover before pain shreds through my left knee. I continue racing to the tree line, using the harrowing pain to fuel my determination. The bullet that tore through my knee feels like I'm being operated on without anesthetics, so imagine how intense Dane's pain is? I can't let him suffer like this. He's my best mate.

I make it another good hundred or so feet before my busted knee buckles under our combined weight. We collapse onto the dew-covered ground with a thud, the roar leaving my throat unlike anything I've ever heard. I'm not screaming in pain. I'm frustrated. Annoyed. Pissed as fuck at the situation we are in.

If I had just left when I failed to find evidence of an illegal operation, we wouldn't be hunkered down in barely an inch of grass, waiting to be slaughtered. But no, I had to listen to the irrational thoughts in my head. I had to see if Rae was as mesmerizing off the stage as she was on it.

I entered the backstage of Substanz as a civilian; I left as an agent.

While sheltering Dane's body with my own, I scan the area. I'm expecting a helicopter to hover down low and protect us before a stream of agents charge the rockface the sniper is sheltered behind.

I get neither of those things.

I get silence—and a reminder that one life will never be more valuable than many.

CHAPTER FOUR

"Call him off." My still unnamed hero leans over the seat to grip the driver's suit jacket. "Call him off before I shell your body with as many bullets as are raining down that valley!"

The driver smirks a mocking grin, revealing the decision on who lives or dies isn't up to him, before returning his attention to the horrific scene unraveling in heart-clutching detail. The agent who let us flee is a sitting target. He's hunched halfway down the grassy meadow, using his body to shelter another agent who is clearly injured. If the slump of his head isn't enough of an indication to his near-death state, the amount of blood pooling into the blond agent's suit jacket is the final nail in the coffin. He's moments away from death—if he hasn't already crossed over.

Incapable of watching the horror unfold for a second longer, I return my eyes to my backseat companion. I want to plead mercy on behalf of the agents, but words are eluding me. I'm so stunned by tonight's events, I can't separate fact from fiction. There has only been one other time I've been stumped like this: the night of Luca's death.

Unfortunately, not all my confusion stems from his accident. It comes from the events that occurred before we climbed into his Jeep, screaming at each other at the top of our lungs. I wanted something Luca couldn't give me, but instead of showing me how I could have both my wish and him, he stripped away any possibility of it ever coming true. He took himself away from me.

When my eyes lock in on my mysterious stranger, I realize he hates this turn of events as much as I do, but he's also at a loss on how to stop it.

After a few seconds of silent deliberation, he secures a cellphone from his suit pocket. For his sophisticated suit and high-end haircut, I wasn't expecting him to pull out a relic. His cellphone is dated—perhaps even as old as me.

A small trickle of hope seeps into my veins when the gray-eyed man roars down the line, "This wasn't our deal, Henry. You guaranteed I'd get her out safely, not cause a bloodbath." A groove embeds between his dark brows. "There's a sniper gunning down agents in cold blood. . . No. . . Why would I bring in my own crew?"

Relief washes over his face a mere second before he hands the driver his phone. I swallow the bitter taste in the back of my throat when the driver nods three times, hands back the stranger's phone, then steps out of the car. He heads for the trunk like a man on a mission.

I feel like I've stumbled into a crime show when he removes a long-barreled assault rifle nestled between the spare tire and the jack. He sets up a tripod on the now-closed trunk before screwing the rifle into place.

After a quick adjustment of the scope, he fires one bullet. It's swift and precise, and as quiet as death itself. Oblivious to my gaped jaw and bugged eyes, he dismantles his gun, places it back in its rightful spot, then joins us inside his car.

Without a word spoken, he continues our trip. Stunned at his nonchalant response to the loss of life, my gigantic eyes drift to my backseat companion. He shrugs, a little lost.

Even though I am on the verge of coronary failure, my heart rate settles when my eyes return to what could have been a valley of death at the bottom of the hill. The blond-haired agent is back on his feet, hobbling toward the concealed entrance of Substanz, dragging the unresponsive agent behind him.

CHAPTER FIVE

"A business proposal?" I flop onto my bed in my dorm, still as stunned as a mullet. "Two federal agents were shot, one severely, all to issue me a business proposal?"

The man who introduced himself as Isaac halfway through our hour commute to my college dorm offers me a handkerchief. I almost rib him about his old-fashioned ways before an image flashing before my eyes makes vomit charge up my esophagus. It's the lifeless flop of the dark-haired man's head when his fellow agent dragged him to safety. It brings horrid memories rushing to the forefront of my mind of another time I witnessed the same thing.

"Did he die?" I choke out, my words barely audible as I struggle to hold in the scarce bit of nutrients left in my stomach. "Was another man killed because of me?"

The mattress dips when Isaac sits next to me. "Nothing that happened tonight was your fault. It was a wrong place, wrong time scenario."

I glare at him, calling him out as a liar without words. When he fails to hear my unspoken accusation, I say, "If I didn't run, the agent wouldn't have followed me. If he hadn't followed me, a second agent wouldn't have backed him up. If he didn't back him up, he would have never been shot. How is this not my fault?"

Before Isaac can answer me, the shrill of a cell phone sounds through my dead quiet room. Thank goodness my roommate is in Tuscany with her parents, or how would I explain getting home at one in the morning with two suit-clad mafia-looking men in tow?

While striving to ignore my heaving stomach, I eavesdrop on Isaac's conversation. I don't know why I bother. He communicates with nothing but grunts and groans.

My brows join together when an unexpected chuckle joins his unscripted conversation. "I understand. Pleasure as always." He snaps his relic phone shut before his gray eyes drift to mine. "Both agents will survive their injuries."

I exhale a relieved breath.

It's quickly withdrawn when Isaac says, "But. . ."

He remains quiet, building the suspense.

"But. . .?" I encourage, hoping to move him along.

He keeps me hanging long enough for sweat to bead on my top lip. "The agent we interacted with in the field was wearing a wire. My source believes he has images of us on his device."

I groan. It was either groan or cry; I went for the less pathetic one. I'm beyond relieved the agents aren't receiving a visit from the grim reaper any time soon, but if we were caught on surveillance, everything we just went through was a woeful waste of time. I'll still face charges, but instead of them centering around prostitution, they'll add evasion, conspiring to commit a crime, and god knows what else into the mix.

I don't want that. The only time my face should be splashed across the headlines is when I am revered as the best business lawyer in the country, not because I tried to sell my snatch to an undercover operative before I slipped his net with the help of a mafia-affiliated man and his disobedient lacky.

The inane beat of my heart triples when Isaac chuckles, apparently amused by my screwed-up-with-panic face. I'm glad he can find pleasure in my discomfort, but I am anything but overjoyed.

When he continues laughing, I sock him in the stomach. "Why are you laughing? Nothing happening is funny!"

He shrugs, not believing me.

When I glare at him so firmly, steam billows from my ears, he asks, "Have you ever watched *Rugrats*?"

"Am I an American? Of course I have," I snap back, my tone snarky.

His smile grows, replacing some of my annoyance with giddiness. My teetering moods can easily be excused. Isaac is an extremely attractive man. Unique-colored eyes, a panty-wetting face, and the strength to carry me up three flights of stairs when a panic attack rendered me a wheezing idiot guaranteed him a spot on the Top Ten Most Handsome Men list I've been compiling since high school.

He didn't even bat an eye when my dinner was ejected in an awfully unladylike manner. He just held my hair out of the firing zone before cracking open a window to lessen my queasiness. In different circumstances, I would have assumed his chivalrous act was a ploy to get into my panties. But for some reason unbeknownst to me, I know he isn't acting. This is who he is. He's a protector. An alpha male. The very definition of the virile man I usually gobble into my spank bank for future examination.

If my mind would stop veering to the handsome blond agent who created more moisture in my sex than my eyes with his gallant effort tonight, I could come out of this situation a winner. It's a pity my body knows whom it wants, and it doesn't mind sidestepping equally attractive obstacles until it gets him.

My god—I can still smell the testosterone pumping out of the agent's pores when he raced across the field with another agent on his back. His back was against the wall, but not once did he give in or cower. He tackled the issue head-on, his fight one I wish Luca could have imitated. If he fought with one-tenth of the grit the agent did tonight, he would be sitting beside me, squeezing my hand like Isaac is.

"Can you open the window? There's too much maleness in this room. It's suffocating me," I mutter, blaming the heat of three bodies in a small space for the moisture gliding down my cheeks.

When the unnamed man does as asked—*for once*—I shift my focus back to Isaac. He has spotted the tears slipping down my face, but thankfully, he acts ignorant—for the most part.

"What does a cartoon have to do with our faces appearing on *America's Most Wanted?*" I ask, hoping to get our show back on the road. "I'm sure TV execs won't display our mugshots during preschool time-slots."

That hurt just to say. Bye-bye dreams of becoming a lawyer. Hello four by four concrete cell. Maybe I should change my name to Bertha? It's more befitting of a trailer-living momma with fifteen kids and a husband called Billy.

A quivering breath parts my lips when Isaac brushes away my tears with a sweep of his hand. For how swiftly he removes them, it appears as though their arrival frustrates him as much as me.

Confident my cheeks are moisture-free, he assures, "We won't be featured on *America's Most Wanted*."

His tone is confident, but it doesn't lessen my worry in the slightest. "They don't just have me fleeing a crime scene, Isaac; the surveillance images contain *other* illegal stuff." For a woman known for her smarts, I sound like a moron.

For the first time tonight, Isaac's smirk morphs into a genuine smile. "My contacts handled *all* aspects of your time at Substanz. As far as anyone is aware, you've never stepped foot in the place, much less operated your little side business from its core."

My spine straightens to a rod, the anger burning my veins sufficient to remove any residual moisture from my eyes. "I'm not a prostitute!"

"Never said you were," Isaac rebuts, smirking. "Although next time, I recommend not swindling an agent for a bonus."

"We didn't know he was an agent." I'm five seconds from stabbing myself in the throat for how whiny my voice sounds. "We thought he'd be easy prey."

"Did your dad not teach you anything? If you look hard enough, you'll spot a sucker in every crowd. He was giving off plenty of signs. None of them screamed 'sucker.'"

The ridicule in his tone shocks me. "What are you saying? You knew he was an agent all along?"

Isaac nods without pause. "In under a second."

Spit flies into the air when I make a *pfft* noise. "Whatever. Even an in-depth search of someone's private life leaves some stones unturned."

My mouth falls open when Isaac denies, "Not all the time. I know you very well, and we've only just met."

My eyeroll ends midway when Isaac nips my attitude in the

bud by saying, "Regan Myers, graduated top of your high school class, which wasn't hard considering there were only seventeen other students in your grade."

I punch him in the arm like we're old friends, unappreciative of the candor in his tone. Even if it's true doesn't mean it's laughable.

Isaac continues, "You grew up on a dairy farm in a little town in Texas. Your parents were high school sweethearts who married only a few weeks after their twenty-first birthdays. You were supposed to take a gap year to backpack Europe, but after a financial blunder saw a forty-five percent share of your family's ranch transferred to foreign investors, you went straight to college, where you've remained the past four years, working your tail off in the hope of graduating early."

His eyes flicker like he's reading my life history in the stalker dictionary inside his head. "Did I miss anything?"

I twist my lips to hide their quiver. "Just a few things."

When his brow arches in hushed confirmation, I say, "I was crowned Miss Moo Queen my senior year. I had two boyfriends; both were morons, hence my love of battery-operated company. And my dog's name is Isaac."

Isaac throws his head back and laughs, assuming I am being funny. I'm not. "Woof woof. You're a miniature chihuahua." I toss a photo frame from my bedside table onto his lap.

I nearly punch him for a second time when he laughs even louder upon spotting Isaac's fangless growl.

"He kept biting the cows. They retaliated," I disclose, smiling my first genuine smile in nearly three years.

Isaac's eyes lift from my furry companion to me. "Did he learn his lesson?"

I shake my head.

"Then his name suits." He places the frame back in its rightful spot before twisting his torso to face me. "Even when their opponents are ten times their size, Isaacs never stay down. That's why I arrived at Substanz tonight: to lessen the big guy's kick."

He jerks his chin to the business proposal he handed me earlier. "I've been watching you for a while, seen the hard work you put in, and that's why I want you to be a part of my empire."

Usually, I'd be freaked at a guy admitting he has stalked me, but Isaac doesn't give me the creep factor. He's stern, has a way with words, and looks killer-fabulous in his three-piece suit. "Creep" is not a word I would *ever* use to describe him.

"I'm not planning to study criminal litigation. My focus will be fixed on business mergers and acquisitions. Nothing against you, but from what I saw tonight, I doubt my skill set could be useful to your *business*." My voice dips toward the end of my comment. "You are here for my knowledge, aren't you?"

This time around, when he chuckles, I don't hold back my retaliation. I punch him so hard, my knuckles throb. "For a guy who looks suave, you need to up your suaveness. This is the third time tonight you've insulted me."

My stern tone halts Isaac's laughter. "I insulted you? How?"

"First, you didn't glance at my ass in my practically non-exis-tent leotard when I dove through the chained fence. Second, your hands stayed far away from my womanly curves when you carried me upstairs. And last, but not at all least, you laugh at the thought of us getting naughty without our clothes on. My ego hasn't been this bitch-slapped since Lenny Moron declined my invitation to dance because his mom told him only good girls go to heaven, and supposedly, there were no spots for me since I like sticking my tongue down boys' throats!"

Isaac nearly laughs again, but my vicious glare stuffs it back into his throat. "Do you want to know why we haven't gotten 'naughty'?" His tone is smoother than his wrinkled brow.

I nod, desperate to discover if I lost my mojo somewhere between Substanz and here. That's the only plausible excuse for his shortage of interest—surely! I don't have tickets on myself, but I don't lack confidence either.

I stop seeking blemishes in the mirror when Isaac explains, "One, as much as the female population disagrees, men's eyes don't pop out of their head as they do in cartoons. Your fine ass was the first thing I noticed about you. Doesn't mean I tripped over my tongue on the way out, though."

His reply makes me smile.

"Two, you just witnessed the shooting of three men."

I nearly correct him that it was only two until he quickly reminds me of the sniper his sidekick took down.

"And three. . ." He leans close, aligning his unique-colored eyes with mine. "Cormack has often told me to go fuck myself. I never thought it was possible until I found you."

I angle my head to the side, more confused than ever. "Huh?"

"You're driven. Beautiful. Don't stay down when shoved in the gutter." He glides his hand down the front of his body. "You're just missing some *vital* organs."

I fake a gag. "So you're saying I'm you, just with female bits?"

"Yes," he answers without delay.

"As in, like a sister?"

Isaac purses his lips. "If I had one, I guess so?"

"That's disgusting." This gag is for real.

After taking a few seconds to settle my flipping stomach, I lift my eyes to Isaac. "Drive like mine doesn't come cheap. If you truly want me to become a part of your empire, hit me with your best offer." When he attempts to interrupt me, I continue talking, stealing his chance. "But cut the bullshit. We dodged enough landmines tonight; I'm not up for a second run through the gauntlet."

Knowing my time at Substanz has ended should render me meek, but unfortunately for Isaac, my daddy is the bartering king of our town. His love of negotiating was one of the many things he passed down to me: that and his adoration of wickedly mouth-burning wings.

"My contacts had Dwain released from custody without charges—"

"Yes, that's true. But we discussed his release during our drive. That means it's not a part of our current negotiation," I interrupt.

The glare Isaac gives me would make grown men quiver in their boots, but it excites me more than it scares me. Not sexually. The more I think about it, the more what he said rings true. We are very similar. He reminds me a lot of my younger brother, Ayden, just in a more mature, refined way.

"There's a compensation package included in our agreement." He flips over the contract until it stops at a figure well above the standard pay rate of a twenty-two-year-old up and coming law student. "I require exclusivity. You cannot work for anyone but me. The amount cited is negotiable, although you don't seem the type driven by money. If you were, you would have been offering your services tonight for real. There's a lot of money in the prostitution market."

Half of what he is saying is true. I'm not driven by money, but the needs of my family are. "Before I can agree to anything, I need you to be aware I'll require three years' salary in advance. I also have no conflict with your exclusivity clause as I can't work for you, attend law school, and maintain a fulltime job at the same time. It isn't possible."

I expect Isaac to glower, laugh, or at the very least, pack up his shit and leave. He does no such thing. He just snaps his fingers together two times, wordlessly demanding his companion bring over the suitcase he's been clutching the past two hours.

"Cash or check? I prefer cash." Isaac snaps open the suitcase, exposing bundles upon bundles of hundred dollar bills. Noticing my shocked expression, he adds on, "This is the correct amount to save your family farm, isn't it? I had my accountant run figures last week. He assured me this was correct."

His smirk reveals what his mouth failed to acknowledge. He knows I had no intention of my wages going toward my schooling. I would use them to save my family ranch.

"Is the amount correct, Regan?" Isaac asks, his tone lowering with understanding.

"It looks about right," I stammer, shocked and overwhelmed by the circumstances of our night. Not just our exchange, the entirety of everything.

The answer to my prayers is presented before me, but I can't wrap my head around it. Nothing has ever been easy for me. I still have three years of law school to trudge through before I can contribute to my parents crippling business. . . *don't I?*

"Why me?" I ask before I can stop myself.

For the first time tonight, Isaac looks conflicted. Even his shrug isn't as defined as usual.

"There are hundreds of students in my predicament, so why me? A man as handsome as you would only need to smirk at Bella, and she'd work for you for free. She's the top student in our program. She would be a prime candidate for you."

"I want a fighter," Isaac deadpans.

I huff, relieving the air from my lungs as rapidly as his confession stole the wind from my sails. "You saw the way I froze tonight. I'm not a fighter."

"I disagree." He tugs a manila folder out from beneath a bundle of bills before adding on, "The fact you survived this makes you a fighter in my book."

Tears burn my eyes when he flips open the manila folder, exposing the source of my nightmares in horrifying detail. My lungs saw in and out as I fight through the heaviness clouding me. The memories bombarding me hit as hard as Luca's Jeep when it smashed into the tree trunk. My throat is still raw from the silent screams I released when he was pulled from the wreckage mere seconds before he was covered with a thin white sheet.

I peer at Isaac with watering eyes when he asks, "Why didn't you tell anyone what happened that night, Regan? Your family would have been there for you if you had given them a chance."

He isn't judging me; he's merely confused. I understand. I'm still baffled by my actions all those years ago, so how can a stranger be expected to comprehend them? Luca was eccentric, dramatic, and severely suicidal. I didn't want his name tarnished by what he had done. I wanted people to remember who he was, not an illness he couldn't overcome.

For that reason, and solely that reason, I used the darkness of the night to escape the accident scene. I've never told a soul I was in his car when its excessive speed was instantly stopped by an old oak tree that now bears his name. My secret will remain with me until the end of time. I loved Luca, and nothing said or done will ever change my opinion on that. He was sick. His actions weren't his own. I am not going to let a lapse in judgment undermine our relationship.

I swipe at a rogue tear rolling down my cheek before reconnecting my eyes with Isaac's. "If I accept your proposal, my first suggestion will be for you to find a new PI. This one is extremely ill-informed."

I toss his manila folder back into the suitcase as if it's nothing but idle gossip.

Even knowing I am lying, Isaac nods. "Does that mean you're accepting my offer?"

Images of Luca's smile when we devised our scheme years ago flash before my eyes, causing my lips to inch high. He was so pleased with my decision to become a lawyer, he sent a text message to every resident at Colendale. It was his way of shouting it off the rooftops.

His pride forces me to say, "As long as your offer doesn't interfere with my studies and family, I'll abide by it."

Isaac remains quiet, intuiting there's more to my demands.

He's right.

"But, if you *ever* mention Luca's accident again, or so much as breathe his name in a derogative snarl, I will not only quit, but the return of any advance payments will be null and void." I lick my dry lips, praying a bit of moisture will help deliver my last set of words. "Those are my terms. You either agree, or we go our separate ways."

I hold out my hand, ignoring the way it's shaking. I need this more than Isaac will ever know, but that doesn't mean I'll be walked over. If Luca's death taught me anything, it was that nothing good comes easy. You have to work for it.

I expect Isaac to take a moment to consider my provisions, so you can imagine my surprise when he simply shakes my hand. "This is the reason I chose you, Regan. The people who remain loyal during the bad times are the ones most deserving of the good times. This is just the beginning for you. How far you take it will only be determined by you. Don't dream for success—"

"Earn it," we say at the same time.

CHAPTER SIX

Five years later...

She arrives at the same time every morning. Unlike five out of the seven days last week, her hair is pinned away from her face. She has on the same tight pencil skirt she wears every day, the same smattering of blush on her cheeks, and the same fire-engine red lipstick on her lips. Even the sprays of perfume dotting her neck are in the same spot.

For a woman whose presence excites every soul in the room, she moves blithely through the populated restaurant. It doesn't matter if she's pounding the pavement on the isolated streets of Ravenshoe during her daily 4 AM run, or entering a restaurant full of money-hungry investment bankers and their trophy wives, she's forever noticed.

Men want to bed her. Women, although jealous, admire her. It never falters.

I adjust the tilt of my newspaper when Rae reaches a table at the back of the restaurant. My eyes consciously scan the print even without my brain taking in a single word. Months of rehabilitation strengthened my ability to undertake covert operations. Even the slight limp a bullet to the knee caused my frame doesn't dampen my effort. I've watched them every day for weeks, and not once has their focus shifted to me.

I thought I was imagining things when I spotted Rae entering a restaurant two months ago. My mind has often strayed to her since our fatal night in the field five years ago; I was beginning to wonder if I was hallucinating. She glided into the restaurant as casually as she did now, her hair tousled from the breeze, her nipples stiffening from her braless state. She was utterly oblivious to the numerous field agents scattered throughout the restaurant. Her focus was on the same target we had our sights set on: Isaac Holt.

I haven't spoken Rae's name in over half a decade. It's for the best. With the surveillance images I obtained at Substanz corrupted by re-runs of *Rugrats,* I had no evidence to back up my theory that the owner of Substanz was running an illegal prostitution ring. All I had was my recollection of events and my photographic memory.

My head was woozy with sedatives when I sat down with a sketch artist, but the image she created of Isaac was so compelling, a positive match was found in the FBI's Facial Analysis Comparison the following morning.

We had our man. He just happened to have an alibi — a solid one.

I argued until I was blue in the face that Isaac Holt was the man responsible for Dane's life-altering injuries. No one listened. They believed a criminal over one of their own. Their inability to see the truth should have had me handing in my badge, but for some fucked up reason, I couldn't resign. I trusted the system and was confident one day we would get our man. I was right.

Isaac popped up on the FBI's radar a little over twelve months ago. His fascination with an underground fight ring run by notorious members of an organized crime syndicate was the start of his demise. We've had operatives on him the past six months. They've yet to stumble upon a shred of evidence that will convict him for life. I'm sure it isn't far away, though, even more so since I've been brought in on the case.

I am supposed to be watching Isaac, but I can't help but wonder if I should pay more attention to those associated with him. Isaac is pedantic about dotting his i's and crossing his t's. Justly so. He has a lot to lose. Those under him don't.

I dip my chin in silent agreement to the waitress offering to refill my coffee.

"How was your breakfast this morning, sir? Up to your standards?"

My lips curl at her formal salutation. She's not doing it because I am her superior and she's being respectful. She's hinting at her submissiveness, begging for a chance to display the naughty girl hidden behind her sultry smile and hourglass figure. It isn't just years of studying body signals awarding me this knowledge. It's the flirtatious winks I've seen her bestow on Isaac numerous times this week.

She's hoping the generous swell of her breasts and cute smile will have him overlooking the fact she's a brunette. She's regrettably mistaken. I've only ever seen Isaac converse with timeless, captivating blondes with dazzling smiles and legs that stretch for miles—women who look remarkably similar to Rae.

Sickened by a daytime nightmare, my eyes jackknife back to Isaac's table. Upon discovering it's empty, I abruptly stand to my feet. While throwing bills onto the table, I scan the area. Blue eyes, brown eyes, even a few handfuls of mismatched ones reflect back at me, but I fail to find a single pair of steel-gray eyes. I don't even spot the ones that have graced my dreams many times the past five years.

"Do you have a back entrance?" I ask the waitress, who startles from my curt tone.

"There's one at the back of the kitchen. . . but no one uses it!" She shouts her last sentence to ensure I can hear her over my feet stomping the floors as I charge for the swinging kitchen door.

"Did a man come through here? Black suit, short hair, stands about this tall?" I hold my hand to just above my left brow.

A Taiwanese man in a white chef's jacket and checkered pants shrugs. "Every male patron in this restaurant matches your description."

Although annoyed by the candor in his tone, I understand it. "What about a female? Blonde, approximately five-nine. Dazzling green eyes, satiny hair that sits in waves between her shoulder blades, and timeless features. She's wearing a light pink fitted shirt and a tight black skirt."

The man's eyes light up. "No, but if you find her, can you give her my number?"

He lands against a pair of stainless steel fridges when I side-step him. There was plenty of room for me to maneuver around him, but his snippy comment couldn't go unpunished.

Humid winds smack into me when I exit the restaurant at the speed of a rocket. My eyes stray left before dragging to the right. Even with the alleyway less congested than the sidewalks of

Ravenshoe, there are enough people milling around, it takes me several tedious minutes to scan each of their faces.

When manual facial recognition fails to find either Isaac or Rae, I recruit an old technique every agent uses at least once in their placement.

"Have you seen this man?" A lady with a wrinkled face and lipstick-covered teeth shakes her head when I show her Isaac's license photo.

I move on to the next person.

The crackle of a receiver interrupts my interrogation of the sixth Ravenshoe local. "You lost him again, didn't you?"

Mindful I don't want to look like a loon talking to myself, I pivot to face a solid brick wall before answering, "No. He's just. . ." I inwardly curse a hundred times before finalizing my lie, ". . .using the restroom."

"Uh-huh." The supervisor of my department, Theresa Veneto, huffs down the line, "I didn't think Isaac was a *pee in the alley* type of man."

My profanity isn't silent this time around.

After wiping the annoyed expression from my face, I spin around. As the uncomfortable creep of my body hairs announced, Theresa is standing behind me. She's leaning on a dumpster, her lack of fanfare unsurprising.

Theresa is attractive; she just has a massive stick lodged up her ass. If you're willing to set aside your morals for a couple of hours, you'll be her new best friend. But if you aren't fucking her, antici-pate being handed every shit, underhanded project she can find. I was interim leader of my previous department. I've worked for the Bureau for over six years, and excluding my little blunder five years ago, I've never received a record of conversation or been reprimanded by my superiors.

Years of dedication means sweet fuck all to Theresa. She wants every agent under her licking her boots—*or a few inches higher*. Refuse that, refuse advancement. I can't spell it out any simpler than that.

When Theresa glares at me, demanding an answer to her silent interrogation, I say, "He was there, then poof, next minute, he was gone." My tone is as pathetic as my excuse.

I am a confident, alpha male who has no qualms being friendly with the ladies, but this is different. Theresa isn't a woman you sleep with then sneak out while she's napping. She'd pin your nuts to the noticeboard at headquarters if you so much as failed to seek permission to use the restroom. It isn't just her ball-stringing demeanor informing me of this; it's many painstakingly detailed stories. Not rumors. True life stories from reliable sources.

My focus snaps back into place when Theresa pushes off her feet to stalk my way. She has the bloodsucker walk down pat, lithe and soundless. "So what distracted you this time? Or should I ask, '*who* distracted you this time?'"

Her penciled brows shoot up high when I remain quiet. I have a million thoughts streaming through my head. None are suitable for my superior.

The chances of holding back my retaliation are lost when Theresa advises, "I'm assigning you a new target."

I try to speak, but she continues talking, beating me to the task, "Don't fret; your time will be *well* occupied. I'll even let you have first pick." She throws three color-coded folders into my chest. "Barbie. The Hulk. Or Harvey Dent? What's your flavor?"

The reason for her superhero nicknames comes to light when I open the folders. The Hulk reference is for the man we've surveilled with Isaac numerous times the past few months. His name is Hugo Jones. He's practically a ghost, his file as scarce as mine. He doesn't even have a Facebook page.

Harvey Dent is the man often referenced as Isaac's college roommate/best friend, Cormack McGregor. His file is significantly more established than his roommate's. His wealth is as substantial as Isaac's, but his family lineage has saved him from the FBI's scrutiny. *For now.*

The last file—the Barbie one—belongs to Rae: aka Regan Myers. Her file has the standard information you'd expect to find in any all-American girl's record. I read it with interest, acting as if I haven't perused it before. Her parents have been married for decades. She went to a standard run-of-the-mill school, kept her grades up enough, and received numerous offers of attendance to various colleges. She chose NY State. She has two siblings. Raquel is twenty-six years old and has recently relocated to the Ravenshoe area, and her younger brother, Ayden, is set to graduate Lennington College in a few months' time.

"Who's priority?" I ask Theresa, pretending I haven't already chosen my target.

When I attempt to hand her back the file, she slices her hand across her body. "I've had agents on all three for months. I doubt you'll unearth anything useful."

"Had or have?" I question.

When Theresa's eyes snap to mine, I strive to wipe the riled expression from my face. My attempts are borderline.

"Had. Is that an issue for you, Agent Rogers?" Her snappy tone tells me she didn't miss my irritation.

I half-heartedly shrug. "Not at all. Just wanted to make sure I wasn't treading on anyone's turf."

She drags her aviator glasses off her razor-sharp nose. "I don't care if you stomp on their prize gerberas. You have a job to do. If that requires you to trim your pubic hair, launder a goddamn suit, and lie down in a bed of fleas, you do it! Do you understand me?!"

Her reply pisses me off, but I dip my chin all the same. "Yes, Ma'am," I reply, acting like the good little soldier I am supposed to be.

Pleased with my cowardly ways, Theresa puts her sunglasses back on then saunters away from me. I wait until there's a good distance between us before yanking my receiver out of my ear and throwing it to the ground. I'm acting like a two-year-old, but it's better than magnifying my anger with violence.

I stop kicking up dust with my dress shoes when a snarky voice shouts, "And Alex?" Theresa waits for our eyes to align before saying, "Her favorite flowers are sunflowers."

She smirks, ensuring I can't miss the words she didn't produce. She knew which candidate I was going after without a word seeping from my lips. That's why she called Rae "Barbie," as everyone knows Barbie is defenseless to Ken's charm.

CHAPTER SEVEN

"Hold the elevator."

My Saint Laurent Opyum black pump darts out to stop the elevator doors snapping shut without a thought crossing my mind. Country girls are already quick-witted, but the hustle and bustle of city life the past decade has doubled my perceptiveness. If you snooze in a town like Ravenshoe, you lose. I'm not exactly sure what eludes you, but it must be significant for how finicky the locals are about staying on top of things.

I like Ravenshoe. Isaac is transforming it from an unknown town to a metropolis, but nothing can replace the smell of fresh cow dung in the morning. It's amazing the things you miss when you no longer have access to them. My mom's southern cooking. My father's fake rooster call when the rooster stopped waking me up. *My cell phone.*

I sigh loudly at my last one. While darting to an appointment, my heel got stuck in a grate. In my endeavor to keep up with the thousands of residents pounding the pavement, yanking my foot out made my cell phone fly from my grip. I fumbled, cursed, then fumbled some more to save it but to no avail. Even if it hadn't slipped between the steam vents, its brutal connection with the ground rendered it a lost cause.

"Thanks," my new riding partner praises before stepping into the confined space.

A peppery cologne filters through the air from his brisk spin to the control panels of the elevator. "What floor?"

I peer past his shoulder, certain I pushed my desired floor when entering. I'm unable to see the panel past the broad span of his shoulders. "Fifty-three."

"Ah, the penthouse. I should have known."

The mirth in his tone has my brow rising. "What floor are you going to?" I nudge his hip with mine, moving him far enough away from the dashboard to see he has selected floor thirty. "The thirties aren't too shabby."

I sound as if I have a plum in my mouth. My response is accurate. Apartments in this building go for the high six figures, if not occasionally dipping into the millions.

"The west wing has nice views of the skyline at night. What section are you in?"

I bite the inside of my cheek. The only way my question could have sounded more seedy is if it were delivered with a pigeon call. I'm not striving for a date. My stance on the dating scene hasn't changed since my teen days. I'm merely intrigued at my elevator companion's inability to look at me while speaking. I know he's watching me. It isn't just the heat of his gaze; I can see his baby blue irises peering at me in the brushed stainless steel panel of the elevator dashboard.

"I can't give an opinion on the views. I don't live in the building. I'm just here visiting a friend," he eventually answers.

"Oh." I'd like to issue a more confident reply, but I'm a little lost for words. I don't need him to be Pinocchio to know he's lying. I heard it in his tone. "What apartment number? The floors and apartment numbers are a little jumbled. They don't always match up."

I'm not lying. With the apartments growing in size with each floor, the numbering system is a little off. I've voiced my annoyance to Isaac many times. It isn't because I mind helping the lost residents of his building; I just don't believe in the whole Fengshui crap his latest designer is spouting. You create your own luck, not a frog with a coin shoved in its mouth.

"Ah. . . 34A?" The unease in the stranger's tone makes his statement sound like a question.

I shuffle my feet to take in his profile more diligently. Just as the generous cut of his cheekbone comes into sight, he twists his torso away from me. Suspicion runs rife through my veins. From what I saw, he has no reason to hide his face. Just his pouty lips spiked my heart rate, much less the quickest peek at his bright blue eyes. Even seeing only half of his face, I can confidently say he isn't ugly by any means.

"Are you sure your *friend* said apartment 34A?"

A beat of sweat forms on his nape as he replies, "Yep."

Short and precise. How most lies are delivered.

"I am carrying mace in my purse and perhaps a weapon that will have bodily fluids leaking down your leg before you realize you need to pee. If that isn't enough incentive for you to leave this elevator at the next floor, take a glance at my shoes. The heel alone is a perfect weapon to have your eye and brain becoming *extremely* friendly."

When the pegs of his white teeth become exposed in the dashboard, I remove a stiletto. After the week I have had, I'm not in the mood for games.

His smile disappears. "Hey, whoa. Come on. There's no need for violence—"

"Push the damn button for the next floor." My tone is brimming with heated warning.

"Maybe I was mistaken. Perhaps he said 44A?"

"There are no apartments in this building with the number four in them. The Chinese believe it's bad kosha as it represents death."

"Seriously?" He sounds more shocked than worried for his safety.

"Yes, seriously! Now push the button for the next floor. There are stairs on each side of the elevator." After taking in an illuminated twenty-three above the brushed steel doors, I say, "You only have six floors to climb. I'm sure it won't kill you."

"I—"

His words stuff into his throat when I raise my heel into the air in silent warning. If I could reach the dashboard without leaning over his body, I'd push the button myself. But since he's hogging the panel like Mrs. Vermont from apartment 12B does anytime she rides with me, I have no other option but to resort to violence.

"Five. . . Four. . . Three—"

"I'm not a child; you can't count down and expect me to jump to your command somewhere between two and one."

I continue counting down like he never spoke, "Two. . . O—"

"Alright! Jesus Christ!" He stabs the button for floor twenty-five six hundred trillion times before spinning around to face me. "Happy?"

"Uh-huh," I reply, my pulse quickening.

It isn't his rueful glare speeding up my heart rate. It's his deliriously handsome face. *My god.* Chiseled cheeks, a sculptured jaw covered by an unkempt beard, and blue eyes that are the color of the ocean. His blond locks are a little overdue for a trim, and the scruff on his chin should be immediately removed for the travesty it's hiding, but he couldn't be classified as anything less than perfect. This man isn't partially handsome; he's downright out-of-this-world gorgeous. His cocky smirk, thick arms, and Ragnar Lodbrok-inspired beard don't just have my mouth drying up; they have my stiletto falling from my grip.

My eyes follow its slow track to the carpeted floor. It dings and bounces three times before it comes to a complete stop. Not eager to fight without a weapon, I bob down to gather my shoe. I don't know if he's clambering for safety or being a gentleman, but our simultaneous dive for my stiletto results in our heads knocking together.

"Oww," I moan. "Your face is as hard as it looks."

Panic rains down on me when my hand darts up to my throbbing brow. I'm bleeding. Not just a slight trickle. A full stream of vibrant red blood is gushing down my eye. It makes being mugged the least of my problems, as you can't get any more frightening than death.

"Fuck," my elevator companion grumbles under his breath when he notices I'm injured. Ignoring the ding of the elevator announcing its arrival on floor twenty-five, he throws off his suit jacket, unfastens the buttons of his blue dress shirt, then yanks his undershirt out of his trousers.

The wooziness in my head intensifies. He doesn't just have a handsome face. He has an equally enticing body. Abs stacked on abs, a slim waist, and pecs that are thankfully missing the hair scattered along his sharp jaw—not that you'd be able to see it through the large tattoo on his right pec.

"Thank you," I mutter, slightly disoriented when he places his wadded-up shirt on the laceration on my forehead.

My brain is throbbing against my skull, but it has nothing on the manic pulse between my legs. I'm being inundated with a manly, virile scent, and there isn't a damn thing I can do about it. This is pure torture to a woman as domineering as me.

"I'm sure it's fine now. It doesn't even hurt," I lie, dragging his shirt away from my head.

Bile races up my throat when I spot how much blood has soaked his shirt. "Is that all mine?" My hand darts out to settle myself when my question arrives with a frantic rush of dizziness. "Woo. I'm a little woozy."

Who the hell's voice was that? I sound like a giddy drunk.

"I think you're concussed." The strange man peers at my wound with worry slashed across his features.

I'm fairly sure his assumption is right when I stammer out, "Concussed from being smacked with too much manliness."

I laugh at myself. *I'm fucking hilarious when I'm on the brink of collapse.*

"Alright, Rae. Time for a trip to the ER."

"Noooooo," I whine. "I hate the doctomorphors." That sounded nothing like it did in my head.

When the world moves beneath my feet without warning, I stumble forward. My companion catches me in his arms before the ground and I make kissy faces. After pulling me to his chest, he jabs his elbow into the security panel, redirecting our car to the lobby.

"If they give me a needle, I'm going to pierce your eyeball with my shoe."

It takes three floors to issue my warning, but it was worth the effort when my savior says, "Duly noted."

I nuzzle into his chest, wanting the mad beat of his heart to replace the thump in my skull. It's racing a million miles an hour but could lull me to sleep in an instant. It's already replacing the fuzziness surrounding me with a pleasurable, less flighty sensation.

"Excuse me," I mumble a short time later, my lips as uncooperative as my drooping eyelids.

I wait for the stranger's glistening baby blues to connect with mine before asking, "What's your name?"

Halfway out of the elevator, he stills, amplifying the crazy beat of his heart. It pumps three long, panicked beats before he answers, "Alex. Alex Rogers."

"Alex?" My tongue clicks my teeth when I test out his name. "Alex. Alex Rogers. I like the sound of that."

I giggle again, my impersonation of James Bond too hilarious not to laugh.

With Alex's steps matching the purposeful thuds of his heart, it's only a matter of time before I succumb to the blackness engulfing me.

CHAPTER EIGHT

"What was I supposed to do, leave her bleeding in the elevator with a concussion?"

. . .

Silence. Dead fucking silence.

. . .

"She has half a dozen stitches in her head because of me. Furthermore, my moral obligation to the public ensures I couldn't leave her."

. . .

More obsolete silence.

. . .

I drag my cell away from my ear, certain Theresa has hung up on me. It wouldn't be the first time.

The clock is still counting down. She just wants me to stew.

Fuck her and her black heart. Fuck the world. I feel like shit, the pain tearing at my chest as strong as it was when the doctors advised me Dane would never walk again. He was alive but paralyzed from the chest down. To him, death would have been the better option.

Regan's injuries are nowhere near as bad as Dane's, but that hasn't stopped guilt from gnawing at my chest. If I had continued watching her from a distance as I have the prior six weeks, she wouldn't be in the hospital, high as a kite on pain pills.

"You told me to get close," I mutter, using the only excuse I can find.

"No. I told you to monitor her. Not expose you are an agent," Theresa rebuts, speaking for the first time since I called her to update her on Regan's condition ten minutes ago.

I lick my suddenly bone-dry lips. "I told her my name. That's it. No harm has been done."

Theresa huffs, clearly peeved. "Then how was she seen so quickly? I know firsthand how the hospitals in Ravenshoe work. I delivered my son here. If you hadn't flashed your badge, she'd still be waiting on the hard plastic blue chairs lining the waiting room."

As I spin in a circle, my wide eyes take in the plastic chairs surrounding me. They are rigid and blue, just as Theresa stated. "You have an agent tailing me? Are you fucking insane?!"

"I have an agent on a *target*—not you. And this is your final warning, Rogers. Cuss at me one more time, and I'll write you up for being insubordinate."

My teeth grit. *I'll show you insubordinate, you fire-breathing motherfucking bitch!*

Before I can flush my career down the toilet, a sing-song voice calls my name. When I crank my neck to the voice, I discover a nurse in a blue uniform and stark white shoes. "Regan is awake and asking for you."

I cup the receiver of my phone. "Did she ask for me specifically or. . .?" I leave my question open for her to answer how she sees fit.

The nurse grimaces. "Not exactly. She asked to speak to the person liable for her plastic surgeon bill."

"Oh." –*That's it? A fuckin' 'oh'?!*— "Tell her I'll be there in a minute." *That's better. Stern, yet understanding.*

Well, I thought it was. The nurse's eyeroll weakens my assumption.

I wait for her to be out of earshot before returning my focus to Theresa. I should quit. I should tell her to shove her stone-aged antics where the sun doesn't shine. The only reason I don't is because of a pledge I made to Dane years ago. I told him I'd never stop hunting until the man responsible for his injuries is brought to justice. That man is Isaac Holt, and my ticket to him is holed up in an observation bay, waiting for me.

If it were anyone but Regan, I'd get pleasure knowing I'm the man responsible for taking down a member of Isaac's empire. But since it's Regan, a woman who confuses me as much as she excites me, I'll wait to crack open my celebratory drink until I have a more deserving victory. I want Isaac to suffer as much as Dane has the past five years, not the woman sheltering him from prosecution.

Although numerous reports have failed to link Regan to Isaac's empire, my gut assures me I am following the right trail. Regan knows Isaac—the depth of their friendship, and if it started before Substanz is unclear—but I'm certain she's the key to unlocking Isaac's deepest and darkest secrets. That's why I chose to investigate her.

Well, that's what I tell myself when snippets of doubt surface a hundred times every day for the past six weeks.

Ignoring my racing heart, I press my phone closer to my ear.

"You instructed me to use any means necessary to bring Isaac to prosecution. I'm following your direct order, Theresa. You've read the intelligence; you know Regan is our way in, but if I don't break through her wall of distrust, she'll stay as guarded as Isaac."

Theresa murmurs. It isn't a conclusive agreement with my statement, but I am going to take it that way.

"If you want your man, let me do my job. If you want to pull me from the case, pull me from the case. But for fuck's sake, give me a bit of breathing room. I aced the academy; I am singlehandedly responsible for the incarceration of thirty-one notorious men in a little over six years, but even Houdini couldn't break out of the restraints you've put on me. Give me half a chance, Theresa; that's all I am asking."

My pulse pounds my ears as I await her reply.

Thankfully, she doesn't keep me waiting for long. "Your leash is extremely short."

"A leash is a leash, as a spade is a spade. I won't let you down."

Stealing her chance to reply, I disconnect our call and return my phone to my pocket. I enter Regan's curtained-off room ten heart-thrashing seconds later. When jumping from one dragon to another, swiftness is the only option. It's just a pity I want to take this dragon for a ride instead of slaying her as I do Theresa.

Regan stops sipping water from a plastic cup when she notices me standing in the doorway. The thin stitches holding together the split our bump caused don't dampen her appeal in the slightest. The blood darkening her manicured brows enhances her green eyes, and the crinkle in her cheek proves some of her time in the emergency department was restful.

I'm not surprised by her eagerness to nap. I'm exhausted from all the tasks she undertakes every day, and I've only been shadowing her the past six weeks.

When a curious crinkle pops into her brow, I move to her bedside. "How are you feeling?"

She gestures to the nurse she's had enough water before her eyes stray to mine. She looks as if she's about to chew me up and spit me out.

My assumptions are accurate when she snaps, "I thought I said no needles?"

I shouldn't smile, but I do. You can't see what I am seeing. Her tiny—although still provocative—body is swamped by a hospital gown three sizes too big. Her face is stark white, and the faint tremble of her top lip is more cute than concerning. She's putting on a brave front even though she is petrified.

She's done similar the past six weeks. Her blank stares into space at precisely 10:03 every night when she thinks no one is watching, the mouthed promise she sends to heaven mere seconds later, and the way she runs every morning as if she's outrunning her fears reveal she's strong enough to hide her pain from the world, but not quite strong enough to completely erase it.

When Regan coughs, reminding me I've failed to answer her, I say, "You weren't given any needles."

"So how did this get in my arm?" She jangles her arm that has a cannula attached to it. It looks extra dainty since the enticing swell of her breasts is hidden by her hospital gown.

I twist my lips. "It's plastic; it doesn't count."

"A needle is required to insert a cannula into a vein, isn't it?" she murmurs fraily, proving the extensive smarts that had her graduating law school with honors doesn't extend to the medical field.

"Usually," I agree, stepping close to her. "But when I told them how much you hated needles, they shoved the cannula into your vein without one."

I praise the lord for my brilliance of thinking on the spot when I stump her. It's only for a second, but she's still stumped all the same.

Her gaped mouth doesn't dangle for long. "So they magically pierced a plastic tube into my arm?"

It's the fight of my life not to smile. She's extra cute when she's angry. Her top lip does this wobbly snarl thingy, and the fire in her eyes matches what you'd expect to see when she's in the midst of ecstasy. She's a fucking knockout—*even after being knocked out.*

After suppressing my guilt with a quick swallow, I continue my ploy of deception. "Other than your ability to blow spit bubbles in your sleep, no magic tricks were performed this evening."

Anger broadens from Regan's gut to her face, the mirth in my tone agitating her even more.

"They did cut you," I disclose, hating the look she's giving me.

Even being responsible for adding a scar to the most gorgeous face I've ever seen, I don't want to be on the receiving end of this look. She's not angry or embarrassed. She's disappointed. That guts me more than any amount of yelling ever could.

"Did they give me a needle?" she questions with an impressive gulp.

"No," I reply, shaking my head. "They used a scalpel."

I rush to her bedside when her gills turn green. She sways so uncontrollably, I'm glad the safety rails are upright, or I may not have saved her from tumbling to the floor this time around.

Her eyes look like silver balls going to war in a pinball machine when I ask, "Not a fan of scalpels either?"

She swallows harshly before shaking her head. This is true pain, one that can't be hidden by her bright smile and a go-get-'em attitude.

I wait until the sorrow in her eyes moves to sincerity before asking, "How's the head—*truthfully*?"

It pains her, but she grumbles, "Throbbing."

I gesture for the nurse to get her some pain medication before wetting a washcloth in the sink.

"Let me," I request when she attempts to remove the cloth from my hand. Not waiting for permission, I gently dab it on the angry bump above her brow. "It's the least I can do."

My last words were meant for my ears, but I clearly expressed them out loud when Regan assures, "This isn't your fault, Alex. I shouldn't have been so defensive. I've just been. . ." Her words are swallowed by a soft sigh.

"Been?" I prompt, not at all discombobulated that I'm forcing her to share something she wants to keep secret.

This is my job. Whether it occurs in the ER or a concrete cell with steel bars, this is what I do. I interrogate people. It's one of the reasons I love my job. You can learn a great deal about someone when they are placed in a hostile environment. I guess that's why I jumped into the elevator when I did. I wanted to put myself in the pressure cooker, to prove the inane thoughts I've had about Regan the past five years were just that—inane.

All I discovered is that years haven't matured me. I've been as reckless and idiotic the past six weeks as I was in the field five years ago.

Regan locks her massively dilated eyes with mine. She seems to be evaluating whether to tell me the truth or not. She reaches her conclusion quickly. I don't know if it's a good or bad thing.

Even more so when she discloses, "I think someone is following me."

My throat dries. "What makes you say that?"

"I don't know. It's just a feeling," she whispers with a shrug.

"How long have you been suspicious?" I try to remove the interrogation from my tone. It's a woeful waste of time. I am an agent as much as I am a man.

My father was an agent. His father was an agent. Even my younger brother is an agent. The only members of my family not associated with the Bureau are the ones missing dangly bits between their legs. That isn't by choice. My great grandfather was set in his ways, which means his father was set in his ways. . . Can you see the pattern emerging?

I secure my first breath in what feels like months when Regan stammers out, "Around five or six weeks." –*That's how long I've been tailing her*– "But before that—"

"Before that? There's a before?" I interrupt, my tone as low as my mood is nosediving.

Forgetting about the washcloth I'm holding to her brow, she nods. "Yeah. The first time was years ago." She sounds as if she's in pain. I don't know if the cloth nipping at her fresh stitches is the cause or painful memories.

There's only one way to find out. "You said the first time. How many others have there been?"

Regan screws up her nose as her eyes flicker. "Three or four," she casually murmurs, as if it's perfectly normal to be stalked.

"Three *or* four, Regan? There's no in-between. It's either one or the other."

I don't know why I'm scolding her. I'm not angry at her; I just have no better way to disperse the anger incinerating my veins to black ash. I either yell or go on a rampage. Yelling seems the more appropriate response for two strangers who only met hours ago.

"Jeez. Calm down, Elevator Man. The vein in your forehead is throbbing so fast, it looks seconds from bursting."

Regan laughs, aiming to ease the tension teeming between us. It works—somewhat. Her laugh suits her perfectly. It's husky and sweet, brimming with wicked naughtiness. It could only sound more pleasurable if it were happening because she's happy —not sad.

Once my anger has lowered from a boil to a simmer, Regan asks, "What did you say you did for a living?"

I smile, admiring her attempts to interrogate me. It takes gall to question anyone, much less a man you've just met. "I didn't. There wasn't a chance between you giving me my marching orders and us bumping heads."

She arches her uninjured brow, revealing she's well aware I hadn't disclosed my field of expertise.

"I work in accounting." My words are barely audible.

Lying has never been my specialty. My career requires the occasional mistruth, but I've never straight-up lied in my everyday life before. Although Regan shouldn't be included in the very small list of people I class as friends, the number of times she has entered my thoughts the past five years has placed her there.

I searched for her for months after the incident at Substanz. My investigation wasn't conducted on behalf of the FBI. Every tri-state visit, license plate scan, and hours spent scrolling thousands of images of women matching her description was done on my own accord. I needed to know she was okay—that she wasn't a byproduct of an industry she didn't belong in. That isn't something I'd do for anyone. I did it for Rae because I cared about her. *I still do.*

"Accounting?" Regan's spiked tone returns my focus to the present. "You're an accountant?"

"Yes, I'm an accountant." I say my words slowly, as if she's hard of hearing. It gives them an edge of honesty. Not much though.

I warned Theresa during my placement interview no one would believe the cover she selected. She said it wouldn't be an issue. She's an idiot. The only way I could pass as an accountant would be if my sole client was a steroids company.

When Regan's lips twitch as if she heard my private thoughts, I glare into her eyes, daring her to release the giggle she's barely harnessing. She reins in her laughter—barely!

Lucky, as the only brainwave I could summon to stifle her giggles involved my mouth sealing over hers. Since I'm currently on the clock, and kissing a target is a big no-no in my industry, that would end badly on all accounts.

"What about you? What do you do for a living?"

Regan's reply is interrupted by me carefully cleaning a smear of blood above her right brow. I don't know if her delay arises from me touching her wound or because I am touching her. I hope it's the latter.

"I'm a lawyer," she advises a short time later, her voice huskier than normal.

A whistle parts my lips. "A lawyer, eh? Sounds fancy."

Her grimace causes her brows to join. "Not really. I file acquisitions and takeovers all day long. It's quite boring, actually."

The honesty in her tone surprises me. I always envisioned the life of a mafia lawyer would be more dangerous than the monotony

Regan described. Maybe Theresa's intel is wrong? Perhaps Regan isn't Isaac's full-time lawyer?

Feeding off newfound hope, I remove the last traces of blood from Regan's brow, then toss the stained washcloth into the sink. "How's the throb now?"

"Better," Regan approves with a gentle nod.

She intakes a sharp breath when my fingers skim her uninjured brow before drifting down her cheek. I tuck a stray hair behind her ear, making out it was the reason for my impromptu touch. It isn't. I just couldn't wait a moment longer to see if her skin is as soft as it looks. For future reference, it's even silkier than I expected.

Regan has classic, unmarked beauty, but in an almost too perfect way. Her big green eyes are prominent on her porcelain skin, and her lips are a little large, but when you place them in perfect symmetry on her elongated face, she is beyond perfection. I think that's why I was so taken with her five years ago. She has such unique, soul-stealing features, you can't help but look again and again and again. It's fortunate I have her under surveillance, or the number of times I've scanned her photos the past six weeks would have me facing stalker charges.

I grow wary I said my last comment out loud when Regan asks, "Have we met before?" Her tone is high with guarded skepticism.

"I don't think so," I lie through twisted lips. "Are you from around here?"

Her eyes drift over my face, cheeks, and lips before shaking her head. "I'm a relatively new resident to Ravenshoe. You?"

"I arrived a few months ago. Not sure what I think about the place yet." Because my statement is honest, it comes out sounding that way. "What about you? Lifelong plans or a fly-in, fly-out visitor?"

"I don't know." The indecisiveness in her eyes weakens her laidback response. "The town has a lot of potential. Who knows what will come from it."

She isn't referring to Ravenshoe's landmarks. She has her sights set on something not made out of glass and steel. Something human. Someone whose ego shouldn't be inflating from the insinuation in her tone.

Before I can get our conversation back on respectable grounds, Regan tugs on the clump of hair on my chin. "This is new, isn't it?"

I swallow numerous times in a row. I was cleanly shaven the last time we interacted, but with every covert operation arriving with a new shaving routine, my facial hair is too unkempt for my liking. I feel like I'm vying for a part on *Vikings*. I just need to grow my hair a few inches longer, and I'd be set.

My throat feels like the Sahara in the middle of summer when Regan adds on, "You didn't have even a shadow the first time I spotted you. Your face was as smooth as a baby's bottom."

My brain screams for me to reply, but I'm at a loss. I have no words.

I snap my eyes to Regan faster than a rocket when she asks, "Did you ever accept the waitresses' advances? They seemed pretty eager."

My heart rate shifts from guaranteed coronary failure status when I secure my first breath in over a minute. I try to play it cool. "You dine at Taste?"

Regan mistakes the relief in my voice as surprise. She huffs under her breath before folding her arms across her chest. If she's hoping her prima donna routine will backhand my ego into submission, she's sadly mistaken. I like my women with backbones. It makes the switch of power in the bedroom even more rewarding.

Her tough stance relaxes when I say, "I saw you at Taste —*many times*. I just didn't want you to think I was one of the creepers you mentioned earlier."

"Oh, don't worry. I still think you're a creeper. You've got the whole creeper vibe down pat."

When I arch a brow, demanding proof of my supposed "creeper ways," she adds on, "No man with a jaw as firm as yours goes the messy beard route. Your aftershave costs in excess of a thousand dollars. Your suit, on the other hand, screams JC Penney."

Since she's directly on the target, I remain quiet. My aftershave was a gift from a childhood friend. She has acquired tastes. The suit is as far as my agent salary can extend. Unlike Isaac, I earn everything I have. I don't steal, cheat, and lie to better myself. I work for it.

Regan remains silent. Her demands don't need to be voiced to be heard. I end her silent interrogation by saying, "They say the smell makes the man. I was testing out the theory—"

"By sitting in a restaurant that charges one hundred dollars for two poached eggs and a sliver of salmon?"

I smile. She didn't just *notice* me at Taste; she monitored me as closely as I watched her. That's precisely what I ate for breakfast every morning while tailing Isaac.

"You forgot the rye toast. It's baked fresh every day. That alone is worth the expense." Nothing but pure cheekiness resonates in my tone.

Regan shakes her head, barely concealing her curling lips.

I wait for her to accept two tablets of Tylenol from the nurse and swallow them before asking, "Is that why you're unsure on the previous number of stalker incidents? Because you're skeptical about including me?"

Over our game of detective and victim, Regan rolls her eyes. I'm not willing to give in as easily. Three incidents, I can brush off. I watched her like a creep at Substanz five years ago. I was on the clock, but my behavior was borderline creeper. Theresa admitted she had agents following Regan before her case was assigned to me, and I've been actively shadowing her the past six weeks.

Three incidents make sense.

Four. . . I'm not down with four.

Four is wrong.

Four is a recipe for death—Regan only said that an hour ago.

Four I will not accept.

"For a guy who is five seconds from losing an eye, you ask a lot of questions." I'm forced to eat my rebuttal when Regan quickly adds on, "Although it shouldn't be any concern of yours, excluding you and your sneaky glances over a newspaper, I'm reasonably sure there have been four incidents total."

Before I can utter a syllable—or even a growl—a commotion at the side gains our attention. Isaac glides into the room. His face is awash with concern, his eyes wide.

"Jae called me when she saw your name on the admissions board. What happened? She heard rumors you knocked heads with some bozo in the elevator?"

I cough unexpectedly, regrettably shifting Isaac's attention from Regan to me. "Bozo. Nice to meet you," I greet, recognizing my cover has been blown.

I thrust out my hand, hoping my scruffy beard, bad need of a haircut, and the forty pounds of muscle I've put on since our last meeting will conceal my identity from him as well as it has fooled Regan.

A smirk crosses my lips when he accepts my gesture. I clearly have him deceived. Isaac's handshake is firm, tight, and as austere as his eyes. He's grateful I helped Regan seek medical attention, but annoyed he isn't the only alpha in the room. I had wondered a few weeks ago if he and Regan were more than friends. Now I know without a doubt their interactions only occur in one room— the boardroom.

Isaac is so desperate to be top dog, he'd never date a woman as fierce as Regan. He doesn't want a prudish wallflower, but he needs a woman willing to hand over the control. If I could look past my inane dislike of him, I could see a lot of similarities between us. He needs control. I have it. He wants to rule the world. I already do. He's successful. So am I—in my own way. All alphas have their own place in the world. Isaac's is in a jail cell. Mine is in Regan's bed.

What the fuck?

I snatch my hand away from Isaac's, panicked he heard my inner secrets. It wasn't his hand tightening around mine alerting me to his suspicion. It's the distrust in his eyes. He has the jealous, untrustworthy look down pat. He doesn't want Regan shouting his name, but that doesn't mean he'll let any random water her turf either. I understand. I interrogated my sisters' boyfriends all the time. It was so much fun watching them sweat, I even had the "talk" with boys not dating her.

Outside of work, I'd accept Isaac's challenge with a smile. Alas, I'm on the job. I shouldn't be conversing with him, much less without Theresa's permission. If she finds out we've been formally introduced, my head will be on the chopping block. This isn't a probability. It's a given.

I shift on my feet to face Regan. It only takes two seconds to gain her focus since her eyes were bouncing between Isaac and me as if watching a tennis match. Her pupils are massive, apparently as fascinated by Isaac's inflated chest as I am.

The confusion slashed across her gorgeous features vanishes when I say, "I'll be sure to jot down the correct apartment number before attempting another visit to my friend's home. Would hate to have more elevator incidents than necessary."

Isaac's stern gaze shifts to Regan when she mutters, "Where's the fun in that?"

Even an immense amount of egotism pumping through his veins doesn't impede Isaac from registering the disappointment in Regan's tone. He just lost a point in our game of tit for tat. I shouldn't be grinning like a newbie actor accepting an Oscar, but I am.

I nearly ask Regan for her number before I remember this isn't a game I can play. Although she hasn't done anything illegal in the time I've had her under surveillance, she still sits on the opposite side of the law. I am a lawman who follows the rules to a T. She's a lawyer who bends them at every possible opportunity at the request of her client. We would never work out. So instead, I dip my chin in farewell, pivot on my heels and bolt.

Any leverage I gained in our alpha male showdown is lost when Isaac's chuckle is the last thing I hear. He thinks he won our latest battle. I'm inclined to believe him.

CHAPTER NINE

"Seriously?"

Isaac's wide-with-suspicion eyes drift to mine. When I lift my brow, silently demanding he return his phone to his suit jacket, pain scuttles across my face. I have no clue why my body is registering pain. I shouldn't be feeling anything. I'm so doped up on sedatives, I mistook Alex's concern as something much greater.

He wasn't attentive because he felt the crazy current surging between us. He washed my wound as he was sickened with grief. The way he hightailed it out of here like his ass was on fire as soon as Isaac arrived was a clear indication of my ill-informed assumptions. He saw an out, and he ran for it.

My mood worsens when Isaac asks, "Name?"

He only mutters one word, but it's a harrowing reminder of his rigid security. Isaac is a protector. From the day he aided in my escape from Substanz, to last week when he ran a background check on a guy I planned to meet from Tinder, my safety has always been a top priority on his to do list.

At times, I thought his concern was due to the sister/brother comment he made years ago, but his interaction with Alex has weakened my hypothesis. He wasn't just parading his naturally engrained authoritativeness; he was marking his scent all over me.

Most of Isaac's behavior centered around two alpha males being in the same room, but a part—*a very minute part*—had nothing to do with business, and everything to do with me.

Call me cocky, but I'm confident in my assumption. I've never seen Isaac balk the way he did when Alex offered him his hand to shake. He seemed more interested in spitting at his feet than accepting his greeting. And then, not even two seconds after Alex fled, he yanked his cell phone out of his pocket. It isn't the standard run-of-the-mill cell you'd expect every twenty-seven-year-old businessman to have. It's an ancient phone — the one he only uses when he's causing trouble.

Isaac buckles down for a fight when I slip off the bed to get dressed. "Two seconds, Regan, and Hunter will know every aspect of Bozo's life."

"No." I bob down to gather my clothes neatly folded on the floor, ignoring the fury radiating from him. Although peeved my designer babies were left defenseless, I'd rather them be friendly with a sterile environment than be hacked to shreds.

"Regan?"

I pivot around to face Isaac, laying my clothes on the crumpled bedding on my way. "I don't want to know every aspect of his life."

"Only last weekend, you had Hunter run ten suitors through his system," he rebuts, visibly frustrated.

"That's different—"

"How?!" He sounds more annoyed at my sudden revoke of personal scrutiny than my reasoning behind it.

I take a moment to work out how to express my next words without sounding whiny. I shouldn't have bothered. I could only sound more whiny if I were a baby overdue for a bottle. "They were men I intended to use for visual stimulation. Bozo has no interest in warming my sheets."

"Huh?!"

I'm saved from hearing Isaac's laughter in an echo when the lack of walls in my bay sends it bellowing down the corridor instead.

"If I hadn't arrived when I did, not even a concussion would have stopped him."

He stops gleaming when I snarl, "Then why did you come rushing in, Kill-Joy-Tate? I'm a big girl. I can take care of myself. "

"Well, excuse me for caring, Ms. Vibe-Rator."

I snort, loving that his woeful mood didn't stop him from using my favorite nickname.

"Besides, I was under the assumption you 'didn't need a man to get you off.'" He air quotes one of my frequent sayings, forcing laughter to bubble in my chest.

Alex's naturally cocky demeanor must have done a real number on him. I've never seen a man as dominant and as in control as Isaac use air quotes before.

"I'm more than capable of getting the job done." I graze my teeth over my lower lip before issuing Isaac a flirty wink, ensuring his nightmares are well stocked the next two days. "But an occasional mix-up never hurts anyone. He could have been fun."

After working his jaw side to side, Isaac growls, "Even more reason to have Hunter look into him." His eyes stray in the direction Alex just left. "Something about him is off, Regan. I don't know what it is, but I'm not a fan."

"Then give yourself a pat on the back, Hercules. I doubt he'll line up for round two after your macho stance scared him away."

When Isaac's eyes snap to mine, full of narcissistic vanity, I drop mine to my clothing, praying it will hide the deceit blazing in them. Alex doesn't seem like the type of man to back away when challenged. If anything, it might increase his determination.

God, I hope so!

I wasn't deceitful when I said I spotted Alex in the restaurant Isaac and I regularly dine at. He's a hard man to miss. He didn't just have my eye; he had many other female patrons' and staff's as well. I don't have issues with low self-esteem, so usually, if a man like Alex captures my attention, I approach him without pause for thought. But there's something about Alex that stopped me. It doesn't make any sense considering we only met this afternoon, but I feel like I know him, even though we're strangers. I guess that's why I was so upfront with him? I don't see him as a stranger.

I've only had an instant connection like this once before in my life.

It didn't end well.

Mercifully, the pain medication making my head woozy blocks tears from welling in my eyes. Not a day passes without Luca entering my thoughts, but as the years move on, the tears have followed them. You can mourn someone without crying—it just takes years of practice.

The small wins keep coming when it dawns on me that Alex's undershirt caught most of the blood oozing from my wound before it could dribble onto my blouse. I would have hated tossing my favorite Oscar de la Renta feather-detailed blouse, but I would have had no other option. Whether on screen or in real life, I hate blood. Just the thought of my sister Raquel getting up close and personal with it makes me physically ill.

Raquel is well on her way to becoming a world-renowned surgeon. Just like me, she paid her dues at NY State before being accepted to medical school. Unlike me, she refuses Isaac's assistance in any form—money or contacts. In a way, I'm glad. I love working for Isaac. His empire broadened my skills years before I sat for the bar, but I'd rather he didn't need trauma surgeons at his beck and call.

If Isaac was aware of the secret I shared with Alex, he wouldn't only have a state-of-the-art hospital on standby; he'd have an entire sheriff's department tailing my every move. I'm not joking. That's how protective he is.

"Spin." I nudge my head to the curtain separating Isaac and me from the other dozen or so patients in the emergency department at Ravenshoe Private Hospital. Isaac and I have grown extremely friendly the past five years, but we're not so chummy I'll get naked in front of him.

When Isaac pivots with a playful grumble, I untether the cords pinching my neck. I don't know who dressed me, but my god, even with the gown being three sizes too large, I'm on the verge of being strangled.

The events between bumping heads with Alex and waking up in a hospital bed with half a dozen stitches above my brow are a little fuzzy. It was only after the nurse gave me an in-depth description of the man who refused to leave my side until he was carted out by security did I realize Alex had brought me to the hospital. She figuratively painted him with as many panty-wetting details as females do when describing Isaac, but the addition of blond hair and heart-thumping blue eyes gave away my suitor's true identity.

Considering he lied in the lead up to knocking me out, I should have had security escort him out of the building. But for some reason, I asked the nurse to fetch him instead of giving him his marching orders. I don't know why. He has an honest edge to him. . . well, when he's not visiting imaginary friends and faking the demure life of an accountant.

There's only one way a man as fit and bulky as Alex could be an accountant—he works for a steroids company.

I grimace. My pained expression isn't from my beloved blouse skimming over my stitches; it's recalling Ayden's declaration on steroid-using men. "It bulks up their muscles by stealing the nutrients from *much more* vital regions."

I doubt Alex has an issue with his manhood. You couldn't exude his choke-hazard confidence with a cocktail sausage for a cock. He's packing heat. Unfortunately, I'm not solely referring to his crotch.

I was barely lucid in the elevator, but I was cogent enough to recognize the heaviness digging into my rib. He was carrying a weapon. Knowing he was armed should freak me out, but the pain medication at this hospital is top notch. Worry is the last thing on my mind. It doesn't even enter the equation when I spot a pair of blood-splattered shoes peeking through the curtain of the bay next to mine.

If it weren't for my bent position, I would have never identified their owner. They are hard to forget since they were the last image I saw before a blistering of stars rendered me a blubbering idiot. Alex didn't charge out of here to disentangle an accounting nightmare. He took up a spying station in the bay next to mine.

I should call out his lurking ways. Shame him for the stalker he is. But instead, I tug my skirt up my thighs, throw on my shoes, then spin on my heels to face Isaac.

His earlier frustration vanishes when I say, "It's lucky you arrived when you did. My new friend was an *accountant*." I heave so loudly, half the residents of Ravenshoe hear me. "You know what I think about numbers men."

"The digits never stack up," Isaac and I express at the same time.

Nodding, I mock, "I like tigers in the sack, big heroic men like you. Not a pussy who thinks a five-second tumble in the sheets makes every woman shatter."

Isaac's eyes shoot my way. He's shocked by my underhanded compliment, but the surprise in his eyes is barely seen through his skepticism. On the rare occasion my battery-operated dates aren't cutting the mustard, I branch out to oxygen-operated ones. I don't have a type. A handsome man is a handsome man. But Isaac is well aware I have a fondness for blushers. It's cute seeing a man's cheeks colored by something other than anger.

Isaac should take a page out of my book. I've only seen his cheeks blush twice. Both times he was fuming mad. Thankfully, his anger wasn't directed at me, and I'd like to keep it that way. Even someone as confident as me would wither under his furious glare.

When Isaac arches a brow in suspicion, I grumble, "What?! Can't a girl mix up her prerogatives occasionally? We women are extremely versatile. You should try a change in palate. An entirely new world could fall at your feet if you altered your routine a little."

"New world or a new woman?" Isaac asks, hearing the innuendo in my tone.

I shrug, praying it will hide my smirk. "Whatever tickles your fancy."

I expect Isaac to recant that world domination is the only item on his agenda. Shockingly, he remains quiet. That's even more foreign than walking away from a man who spikes my heart rate as much as he does my apprehension.

CHAPTER TEN

"Did she say pussy or pansy?"

A gentleman with ghost-white hair and a face full of wrinkles notches his shoulder to his ear. He's been glowering at me since I darted into his bay unannounced ten minutes ago.

When I fled Regan's room, I had every intention of returning to my car to tail her home as I've done daily the past six weeks, but something changed my course. I want to say it was a solid hunch, but my reaction to being called a pussy or pansy or whatever the fuck derogatory word she called me, I'm reasonably confident I'm not donning a white doctor's coat and an angry snarl for the decency of the bureau.

I knew Isaac would pry into my private life before I began my placement at Ravenshoe. That's why I went to great lengths to ensure my information, along with the other three dozen officers on Isaac's case, was hidden from view. I'm not talking a standard concealment any half-assed hacker could unravel. I mean buried —*buried*. Even the government would have a hard time locating us.

So although I'd like to use personal protection as an excuse for my loitering, I can't. I wanted to hear what Regan had to say about me. Would she brush me off as some random she bumped heads with in the elevator? Or did the worry in my voice when probing her on her previous stalking cases compel her to decide we're long lost friends?

She doesn't seem like a liar, so I was skeptical the latter would occur, but I never anticipated she'd refuse to give my credentials to Isaac. I've watched Regan so intently the past six weeks, I can confidently declare she isn't a woman who jumps at barked commands. But Isaac is her employer. She's paid to follow his command. Yet, she kept my identity on the down low. I won't lie. My chest swelled with smugness. I may have even done a little jig on the spot.

Unfortunately, the air was let out of my tires only a few short minutes later. Hearing Regan admit she wants a tiger in the sack should have made my dick swell like it did my chest, but since she referenced a man I wouldn't piss on if he was on fire, it had the opposite effect. It riled me up with so much anger, the curtains quivered from my fury.

Isaac isn't a celestial being. He's a mockery to the very definition of an alpha male. He had a sniper lying in wait to take down federal agents. If that doesn't make him the scum coating the showers of the seedy motels scattered along Route 66, he's the dog shit every runner lands on at 5 AM when attempting to improve their fitness.

He's also the reason I'm leaving this hospital with a vast amount of resentment. If he hadn't shown up, I would have driven Regan home, wooed information out of her, then closed Isaac's case without the remotest tiptoe into Regan's personal life.

Now. . . now I'm back to the drawing board. This isn't the first time I've ditched one set of plans to unite with another. But it's the first time I've allowed personal opinions to enter the equation.

An agent is wired to follow commands, think impulsively, and get their man no matter what the cost. This is different. Regan isn't a man. She also isn't my target. I joined this team to take down Isaac Holt. Only now am I realizing he won't be the only one thrown under the bus when I snag my man. He'll take Regan down right along with him.

I can't stop the carnage. But I may be able to lessen the impact.

CHAPTER ELEVEN

A satin material brushes my forearm as a floral scent invades my senses. It's subtle yet captivating, conjuring up memories, both bitter and sweet. I take a step back before raising my eyes. Two months haven't diminished the effect she has on my body.

Regan is standing mere inches in front of me. Her reach for the elevator dashboard is the cause of her arm skimming mine. Her eyes are focused low, on nothing but the phone in her hand. She's ramped up her sexpot look today. Her sultry curves are barely concealed by her low-dipping dress and showcased by her sky-high heels.

Inconspicuously, I slant my head to the left before dropping my eyes to the screen of her phone. Unsurprisingly, she's returning a text message from Isaac. Although this is the first time I've seen her in person for months, I'm familiar with her daily routine.

Theresa didn't appreciate my request to transfer back to the original operation investigating Isaac, but with her superiors unhappy with the case's progress, her team dwindled from three dozen men to six, so she didn't have much choice.

The head of our department is growing restless. For some stupid reason, he believes Isaac doesn't have anything to answer for. With that in mind, he told Theresa last month she had six weeks to uncover incriminating evidence on Isaac or our investigation will be closed without prosecution.

The promise I made to Dane five years ago ensures I'll never let that happen. I worked my fingers to the bone scrolling through every shred of intel we've gathered on Isaac the past twelve months. Other than the occasional dabble in an underground fight ring, his business appears legit.

Unwilling to give up without a fight, I sought assistance to persuade our head of department against shutting down Isaac's case. It's both fortunate and unfortunate my grandfather's connections in the Bureau are solid. Fortunate—as it awarded us another three months to build a case on Isaac. Unfortunate—as it means my run in with Regan this time occurs with a date on my arm.

Josie, granddaughter of much-loved and revered Assistant Director Reginald Donavon, is beautiful, well-mannered, and highly educated. She's just missing the spitfire stubbornness Regan has in abundance. She doesn't ignite a spark inside me. She's demure. . . centered. . . *meh*.

Her well-to-do upbringing is even more noticeable when Regan murmurs, "Would you like me to forward you a copy of my message, Alex, or are you happy to continue reading it over my shoulder?"

Josie startles so much, the elevator car rattles in the aftermath of her balk. She's threatened by the snark in Regan's tone. The whiskey in my veins has me on the opposite side of the spectrum.

Challenge accepted, Ms. Myers.

"Depends. Are you sending anything risqué? Or just updating your Instagram followers on what you ate for dinner?" The flirtatiousness of my reply adds a heated edge to my words. I'm practically daring her to send me sexy pics.

Josie must have heard my statement as I had intended as her loud gasp nearly drowns out Regan's reply, "A lady never kisses and tells."

The sassiness in her tone curves my lips. I wish I could see her face. I'm certain it's as ravishing as the dangerous drop of her fits-like-a-glove dress.

I wait for the fine hairs on Regan's nape to finish bristling before replying, "I guess you're safe from prosecution then, aren't you, Ms. Myers?"

I mentally fist pump when my witty comment forces Regan to spin around. Any chances of me leaving this elevator alive are lost when my eyes drink in the front of her dress. It's even more risqué than the back. The dangerous spill of her cleavage has me longing to dress her in the hospital gown she donned two months ago.

Even then, it will only drop her sex appeal from a twenty out of ten to a nineteen. She's got the siren sexpot look down pat. Fuckable red lips, a skin-tight black dress, and heeled boots that would only look better digging into my ass cheeks.

Fuck—throw me in jail with the most dangerous convicts I've arrested thus far in my career, as I guarantee that would result in fewer injuries than I'll walk away with tonight. I'm not strong enough for this. No man is. I barely held it together when I switched her pricy garments for a dowdy hospital gown.

The emergency nurse assisting Regan was adamant she couldn't evaluate Regan's condition in the clothes she was wearing, so I either removed them or she would hack them with the jaws of life scissors she was clutching. I'm not overly familiar with fashion, but I knew Regan values the shimmery shirts and skin-tight skirts she owns, so I had no choice. I had to undress her.

I acted like the professional I am. Even the near swallow of my tongue when I discovered she was braless didn't jeopardize my gentleman act. My hands and eyes stayed forever locked on the safety zones. I didn't even sneak a peek of her breasts when they flattened against my pecs so I could tie the back of her gown. I was the perfect gentleman—even with my thoughts as sullied as a pervert with a criminal record a mile long.

I thought sprinting down a valley with my best mate on my back and the scope of a sniper on my head would be my hardest day. It had nothing on that afternoon in the hospital. When forced between life and death, you must always choose life. That day I didn't.

I've been miserable ever since.

After soaking in my new Vans, casual jeans, white tee, and blazer jacket, Regan returns her eyes to mine. Tension fires in the air. She's as appreciative of my casual look as I am of her sophisticated one.

"Are you saying I'm not a lady, *Mr. Rogers*?" She drawls out my name in a long, seductive purr, amplifying both the temperature in the cabin and Josie's unease.

Josie is so concerned I'm seconds from being slapped, she takes a step back, removing herself from the firing line. She should be concerned, but her worry is focused on the wrong person. Regan doesn't have me in her sights. She's going after Josie.

Little Miss Seduction doesn't like competition. That's why her lipstick has been freshly applied and her hair recently brushed.

She didn't breeze into my elevator on a whim. She staged her ruse as adeptly as I did our first elevator foray.

I shouldn't be thrilled by the concept, but I am.

"You sent the bottle of wine to our table." I'm not asking a question. I'm stating a fact.

Regan's shoulder touches her ear when she shrugs, but before a syllable can escape her lips, Josie says, "Oh golly gosh, you did?! That was so kind of you." Her voice is extra high and laced with sweetness. "I tried to bribe the waiter for the label, but he said it was from a private vineyard and not for sale. Do you know what vineyard it's from? The waiter hinted it was in the north of France but was unaware of the property's title."

Josie's niceties douse the fire in Regan's eyes. As I am sure many women have done to her, Regan judged Josie's slim frame, generous breasts, and traffic-stopping face as meaning she was snarky, cold, and a downright bitch. She couldn't be farther from that description if she tried.

Josie is the friendliest woman I've met. Regrettably, that weakens her appeal even more. I don't want a woman who will fight me at every turn, but I need one strong enough to stand at my side and fight alongside me, not cower in the corner the instant things get tough.

I'm on the road constantly. I miss Christmases, birthdays, and every other special occasion you can imagine. If you're relying on me to be your backbone, you're depending on the wrong man. Josie understands this. Her family has been a part of the Bureau for as long as mine. That's why our date is ending on amicable terms instead of me splaying her against the elevator and sampling her mouth as vigorously as I wish I could Regan's. She doesn't want me to be her backbone any more than I want to charge Regan with a crime.

The inappropriate thoughts screaming through my head double when I return my eyes to Regan. Her mouth is hanging open, her eyes brimming with uncertainty. She wanted Josie to come out swinging so she'd have an excuse to hit back even harder. Instead, she got an ally, not the enemy she was hoping for.

"Ah. . . the wine is from a friend's vineyard in the south of France. His production is for private use only. He doesn't need the money nor the praise. He's well stocked with both."

Regan's reply pisses me off. Don't ask me why. I'm just stating things as I see them.

"Oh poop. I'd love to gift a bottle to my grandfather for Christmas. He adds to his extensive collection every year. A privately labeled bottle would make a wonderful addition. Are you sure your friend can't spare a bottle or two?" Josie begs, her tone as polite as her beseeching eyes.

Regan shifts her eyes to me, wordlessly pleading for me to throw her a lifeline. I could, but then she'd never learn the consequences of her actions. I offered her salvation years ago; she threw it back in my face by siding with another man.

After glaring at me in silent warning my lack of assistance won't go unpunished, Regan directs her focus back to Josie. "If you pass me your phone, I'll give you my number. I can't make any guarantees, but I'll see what I can do."

Josie nods before rummaging through her purse. Her hunt for her phone lasts mere seconds, but it's long enough for the energy bristling between Regan and me to morph from warm to catastrophically hot.

Not all Regan's liveliness is sexual, though. She's more mad than turned on. Me, on the other hand, I'm far from angry.

Josie squeals like a school girl when Regan hands her back her phone with her details saved in the contacts. "Thank you so much. My goodness—you have no idea how excited he'll be."

Regan freezes like a statue when Josie throws her arms around her shoulders to give her a quick hug. "I'll be in touch later this week. Tell your friend money is not an issue. I know people in high places." A frisky wink accompanies her comment.

Regan laughs as if she thinks Josie is sweet. In reality, she's mortified. I understand her awkwardness. I've not once witnessed Regan with any female friends in the months the Bureau has had Isaac under surveillance. This is as foreign to her as my desire to hand in my credentials two months ago.

I didn't want to leave my position, but the way I handled things with Regan that afternoon was unprofessional. If any of the men I had under me in my last position acted as I did, I would have torn them to shreds.

Obviously, I didn't learn a thing from my last expedition into the unknown. My stupidity is even more noticeable when I ask, "Did you dine alone tonight, Rae?"

"Yes," Regan grinds out. "Do you have a problem with women dining alone?"

"Not at all." You can hear my smile in my words. I love her sassiness. It warms both my belly and my heart. "I was just going to have a quiet word with your date about personal security. It's late. He should have escorted you to your car."

I allow my eyes to voice the last half of my statement: *even more so with what you told me the last time we talked.*

Much to Theresa's dismay, I looked into Regan's claims she

was being improperly watched. My search was thorough, but I didn't unearth any concrete evidence. Theresa brushed off my concern as if Regan is unaware of the attention she gains when she enters the room. I'm doubtful appreciative glances were the cause of Regan's claims. You can't be as attractive as Regan and not be used to handling admirers. She knows she's beautiful, and the fact she isn't ashamed about it makes her even more attractive. I love her confidence. It's one of her most stellar attributes.

Although Theresa demanded I drop my investigation into Regan's stalker case within hours of starting it, she has no say on what I do in my downtime. Regan's case is still open—but it isn't being run by the FBI. It's personal, which means it won't close until a suspect is arrested.

Regan's annoyed huff returns my focus to her. She has her hip cocked and her brow bowed. There's the stubborn, determined woman I've dreamt about every night the past two months. Whether she's running away from me or toward me, she's forever featured in my dreams.

Unappreciative of the smirk crossing my lips, Regan snarks, "Didn't our last foray teach you anything? I can take care of myself, Mister Fancy Pants."

Josie's eyes fall to my jeans before they return to their bounce routine they were undertaking before Regan dropped my nickname.

"Do you like my jeans? Another JC Penney creation." I barely hold in the rest of my reply: *they'd look even better on your bedroom floor*.

Regan's eyes roll skywards. "Not particularly. But I guess if that's all an *accountant* can afford, they'll have to do." She growls my false field of expertise. "Your shoes, though. . ." A gasp of disdain finalizes her lie.

The giggle Josie is unable to stifle hums in my ear. She's loving Regan's feistiness even more than she adored the pricy bottle of wine she gifted us.

"The jeans are my fault," Josie admits when the heat firing between Regan and me becomes too great to ignore. "I told Alex to dress casually. We were supposed to meet Mark at a bar. When he cancelled last minute, our plans changed."

"Mark?" Regan queries, her inquisitive as excessive as mine. *Who the hell is Mark?*

"Yeah, Mark. My husband," Josie replies casually before her hand darts out to tap Regan's arm. "Oh my, did you think we were on a date?" She thrusts her hand between herself and me.

When Regan nods, Josie laughs as if the thought of dating me is hysterical. I don't know whether to thank her for not blowing my cover or scold her for making the idea of dating me sound so appalling.

The latter is less likely when Regan asks, "You're married and not interested in Alex whatsoever?"

The elation in her tone has a massive bout of egotism joining our party. She sounds as if she just discovered the dweeb who took her virginity doesn't count, as half-penetration is excluded from all sexual partner quizzes.

My wish to scold Josie returns stronger than ever when Regan asks, "Then why are you associating with him? He doesn't seem like the best company. He's an *accountant,* after all."

There she goes again with another underhanded snark at my supposed career choice. I feel like I'm being hung out to dry when Josie shrugs in halfhearted agreement. "He does save us thousands in taxes every year, so the least I can do is take him out for a meal every once and a while."

Regan's face pales as mine flames with anger. Anyone would swear it was Josie's arm that got twisted to agree to this date—not mine.

A bucket of cold water is thrown over my flaming cheeks when Regan mumbles, "Hold on. He's your accountant?" She snarks out the word "accountant" as if it's part of a fresh batch of vomit.

When Josie nods without pause, Regan takes a stumbling step back. "Do you own a steroids company?" Although her comment was only meant for her ears, she grumbled it loud enough for both Josie and me to hear.

Josie slaps Regan's forearm, her laugh like a hyena. It bellows around the elevator, adding to the debilitating tension firing in the air. Regan is gobsmacked by Josie's admission. She isn't the only one. Josie's acting skills are so top shelf, I'm beginning to wonder if I've slipped into a time warp.

"But you. . . your hip. There was. . ." Regan stops talking to glare at the spot where I usually carry my service weapon. She won't find it. Since I'm off the clock, my gun is off my hip.

The elevator dings, announcing it has finally arrived at the lobby. Rotating restaurants at the top of a skyscraper sound like an ideal night. . . until you're stuck in the elevator with a woman as captivating as Regan. I feel like I've aged a decade in ten minutes.

"Where did you two say you met?" Josie asks as she steps into the lobby.

"We didn't," Regan and I answer in sync.

Regan is so caught up sorting through her confusion, it takes me placing my hand on the curve of her back for her to exit the elevator. If I thought the temperature in the elevator car was roasting, now it's ten times worse. Her dress is practically backless, meaning I had no other option but place my hand on her bare skin. This scenario couldn't get any more dangerous. The slightest whiff of her floral scent already has me acting reckless, let alone the heat of her skin under mine.

I'm dragged from my inappropriate thoughts when Josie shouts, "Hold on one dang minute. It isn't. . . She can't be. . . Oh Alex, you little devil. How did I not put two and two together earlier? Is this Regan from Hector? The one you bumped heads with instead of measuring our new kitchen cabinets as you had promised?"

Josie shifts on her feet to face Regan, who is peering at her with as much bewilderment as me. Excluding Theresa, I never told a soul about my altercation with Regan. I filed an incident report, handed it to my superior to be signed off on, then tried my best to forget about it. As far as I am aware, our run-in is not public knowledge.

Josie fills our silence by saying, "Alex is an accountant, but his hands. . .O. M. G. . .their skills will set your pulse racing." She says her comment as carnally as it sounds, not pussyfooting around her assumption I want my hands on Regan. It's a fact, but I'd rather it not be common knowledge. "The cabinets in our apartment are to die for. The tenants are in heaven."

"You have an apartment on Hector?" Regan asks Josie. When Josie smiles and nods, Regan adds on, "And Alex was planning to measure the cabinets the day we bumped heads?"

"Uh-huh. Did you see the toolbelt he swears when doing carpentry? Rawr."

I glare at Josie. She may as well strap on a dildo and take me for a ride. She just fucked me over. The tiger roar was too much.

Skilled hands—yeah, Regan could have accepted that. Helping out friends—yep, what nice guy doesn't? But wearing a toolbelt underneath a suit—un-fucking-likely. A moron with half a brain knows this, so there's no way a woman as smart as Regan will fall for Josie's on-the-spot ruse.

I'm forced to eat my words when Regan mumbles, "Ah. . . and here I was the whole time thinking he was happy to see me."

I want to say, *"Don't worry, it wasn't just my gun digging into your ass that afternoon."* Instead, I settle on, "I arrived at Hector with the intention of helping out a friend, left with the threat of eye dismemberment."

Regan splays her hands across her cocked hip. I really wish she wouldn't. It amplifies the perfect swells of her curves. I don't know why I believed I'd ever be strong enough to look past my attraction to her. I should have manned up and requested a transfer to another unit the instant she breezed back into my life, as distance is the only way I am guaranteed not to lose my job when it comes to this woman.

Taking my silence as annoyance, Regan mumbles, "Cut me some slack, Alex. You crowded the elevator panel like a twenty-one-year old's first time at a strip club. Then you said apartment 34."

"You said apartment 34?" Josie intercepts, her voice high with shock.

"Yeah. So?" I reply, acting like it's no big deal.

Josie's eyeroll is nowhere near as sophisticated as Regan's. "Everyone knows the apartments on Hector don't have any number fours. It's bad Fengshui."

I would respond to Regan's pompous glare if I could take my eyes off Josie. *Who the fuck is this woman?* She started our date as a demure wallflower who spoke when spoken to and ended every reply with a question. She leaves as fierce and impenetrable as Regan.

Josie gives me a look. It's a look that reveals more than words ever could. Just like my family, her family has been in the Bureau for years. Unlike my family, it isn't just the male members doing their bit for society. She's one of us.

No. Fucking. Way.

Hearing my silent denial, Josie winks before faintly nodding, as if to say, *Yes. Fucking. Way.*

Is that why our plans altered? The one lie Josie didn't deliver tonight was our change of location. We had every intention of dining at a burger and wings joint a few miles out of town. It was only after Josie took an unexpected call did she request a switch up.

When suspicion consumes me, I take a step back. Does she know Regan is on the FBI's radar? If so, why is she pushing us together? She can't be acting on Theresa's "do anything and everything to get my man" stance, or she would have initiated contact hours ago. But what other reason would she have to change our plans from a twenty dollar a plate meal to one that made my eyes water while scanning the menu?

I answer my own question when a man with jet black hair and blue eyes pops out of the elevator next to ours. He darts across the marbled foyer, his brisk steps shadowed by a large, Maui looking man.

"Mark, hi," Josie presses a phone against her ear, "you're waiting outside?"

I'm trained to notice the lack of illumination from her phone screen when she pivots to face the door the blue-eyed man just darted through. Regan isn't as clued in as me. She floats back a few paces, giving Josie privacy she doesn't deserve.

"I'll be right there. Just give me a sec to say goodbye to my friends." She pulls her cell away from her ear and slides it into her clutch purse. Rookie mistake. All good agents know you push the end button to make your call look legitimate.

"Mark is waiting outside for me. Little twit locked himself out of our apartment. It was lovely seeing you again." Her words come out in a flurry, her eagerness to leave uncontained.

"Play nice with this one, Alex. I like her spunk. If you don't snap her up, the Bureau might," she mutters in my ear when she leans in to press a kiss to my cheek.

Her comment annoys me more than it pleases me, but I'm left void of a retort when her focus returns to Regan. "It was a pleasure meeting you, Regan. No matter what this klutz does tonight, I still want that bottle of wine."

Regan smiles, then nods. She's uncomfortable with Josie's overfriendliness, but it's growing on her. "I'll have a bottle or two delivered to you later this week."

Josie is so eager to hunt down her target, she nods before practically sprinting out of the lobby. She's lost in a sea of foot traffic within seconds of dashing through the revolving glass door.

Confident her ruse has no chance of being broken, my eyes drift to Regan. She has an odd expression on her face. It doesn't reflect joy or humility. In all honesty, she looks a little constipated.

Noticing I've spotted her odd expression, Regan straightens her spine. "So you're not just an accountant who dabbles in cabinetry on your days off; you go on dates with married woman while wearing holey jeans and shoes only teenage boys should wear."

I quirk my lips before doing a halfhearted nod. Unamused by my blasé reply, Regan rolls her eyes before pushing off her feet.

For some stupid reason, I follow after her. "Admit it: you would have hammered my outfit whether I was wearing dress shoes or flip flops."

"Flip flops would have gotten you tossed out of the restaurant, saving Josie the embarrassment of being seen with you looking like. . . *that*."

"Hey!" It's lucky her voice is laced with cheekiness, or my ego would have been insulted. "Josie likes my casual look." *So do you; you're just too afraid to admit it.* "She said I reminded her of Nate from *Gossip Girl*."

"That wasn't a compliment," Regan advises with a giggle.

My strides cease. "It wasn't? Why?"

I'm not acting daft; I seriously want to know. Wasn't Nate one of the rich guys? If so, shouldn't that instantly make him top shit?

"Nate was a pathological liar who had an inability to love," Regan explains.

"*Gossip Girl* fan?" I ask, shocked by her quick-witted reply.

She shakes her head. "No. I've never watched an episode. I'm just good at studying people for who they truly are." She stops walking to rake her eyes down my body. "Hmm. Now that I think about it, Josie's assessment was fairly accurate."

She friskily winks before continuing for the door.

CHAPTER TWELVE

My snappy remark stumps Alex for barely a second. His frozen state doesn't last long enough to weaken the energy bristling between us the past ten minutes, but it gives me a moment of reprieve.

I'm so shocked, my mouth is bone dry from the number of times it was left hanging open in the elevator. Alex can't be an accountant. Nothing against them, I love my accountant, Jerry. He claims my excessively priced dresses and shoes as a tax write-off since it's my job to look presentable, but the portion of his stomach that sticks out the bottom of his polo shirt is hairier than his head. He drinks orange juice from the carton and talks when his mouth is full. He's a grommet.

Alex is not.

Seeing him tonight undid all the hard work I've done the past two months. You have no idea how impossible it was for me to decline Isaac's numerous offers to run a background search on Alex when I failed to find him. I may have even ridden the elevator at my apartment building at the same time every day the past two months just in hopes of seeing him again.

I'm not desperate!

Well, I am, just not in the way you're thinking.

I want to know why he spied on me. I get Isaac's persona can be overwhelming, and he may have regretted his abrupt departure, but he could have manned up and entered the room as stealthily as he did the first time. He didn't have to hide behind the curtain like a weasel.

His lack of assertiveness was why I sent the bottle of wine to his table instead of behaving like the pathetic ass I was in the elevator.

Josie was nice—*bat shit crazy*—but nice nonetheless. I should have never lumped her in the same pile of shit I wanted to rain down on Alex. I don't know why annoyance was the first thing I felt when I saw him again. He's a stranger who aided me after he hurt me. That makes us even. He doesn't owe me anything, and I owe him sweet fuck all—right?

Right. Then why did I want to gouge out Josie's eyes every time she laughed at Alex's corny jokes?

Tequila.

I should have listened to my mother. No good comes from a final shot of tequila. If I had stopped drinking when I said I would, my every step wouldn't be shadowed by a man I'm dying to see nude. *Can you be charged with indecent exposure if your clothes are removed involuntarily?*

My head emerges from naughty clouds when a gruff voice says, "Let me."

Not waiting for a response, Alex snatches my coat from the doorman's grasp, then jerks his chin up, requesting for me to spin around. He barely touches me when he drapes my coat over my almost bare shoulders, but the spark of electricity shooting through me makes it seem so much more. The zap is so strong, my heart jump a few beats.

"How far down are you parked?" Alex asks as his eyes scan the populated street.

When I fail to answer him, he returns his eyes to mine. "Did you use the valet?"

"No," I say with a shake. "I walked."

"You walked?!" My ears ring from his furious roar. "In that?!"

His eyes drop to my scarcely concealed cleavage. Before I can laugh at his absurd reaction to my favorite LBD, he yanks me forward by the lapels of my coat before he does up the buttons. He grumbles several times under his breath, but I can't hear a word he's speaking. I've once again been rendered stupid by costly cologne and the scent of a hot, virile man.

"I need to breathe," I garble when Alex fastens the top button of my jacket. "No one uses all the buttons on a trench coat. They are there for symmetry—not comfort."

"Not now, they ain't," he fires back before curling his hand over mine and marching for the exit doors.

I try to put up a protest, but a man as strong and sturdy as him is too much of a challenge. So, instead, I use words. "What are you doing?"

He ignores me. It should piss me off more than it excites me, but for some reason, it doesn't. I have a fondness for blushers, but taming a wild, beast of a man is a challenge every hot-headed woman loves. He wasn't on a date, much less carrying a weapon the last time we met, so I'm free to explore the brutishness pumping out of him.

See—you should always put down the last shot of tequila. It makes you stupid.

Alex hails a taxi before dropping his eyes to mine. They don't have to wander too far. With the heels on my boots lifting me the extra four to five inches he has on me, we stand at a similar height.

"In." He nudges his head to the taxi idling next to me.

After undoing the top three buttons of my jacket, I snarl, "Ladies first."

Anger blisters across his face, but shockingly, he holds in his retaliation before sliding into the back seat of the taxi. *Mojo killer!* Peeved at his deficient backbone, I clamber in after him.

We only travel a few feet before the reason I decided to walk smacks into Alex. The traffic in Ravenshoe on Fridays is the worst of the worst. We've barely crawled an inch.

"Are you ready to call defeat yet?" I ask a short time later.

Alex mutters a curse word under his breath before digging his wallet out of his pocket. After throwing a handful of bills at the driver, he requests for him to pull over.

I laugh when we scramble onto the sidewalk. We're literally half a block from the restaurant. After yanking me to his chest to ensure I'm not knocked over by a bicyclist zooming down the sidewalk, Alex scans the street. "Which way is your apartment building?"

"Ah. . . I think it's that way."

I twist my neck to the left, truly unsure. My uncertainty can't be helped. Alex's body is extremely firm, even firmer than his head that cracks open skulls with nothing more than a measly bump. He works out. That's not an assumption. It's a fact. You can't have a body like his without putting in an effort. My six mile run every morning ensures I can't be mistaken.

When Alex curls his arm around my shoulders to guide me in the direction I nudged, I raise my eyes to his. "I don't recall requesting a chaperone home?"

"I don't recall needing permission to be a gentleman," he snaps back.

My abrupt chuckle startles a couple standing next to us. After a whispered apology, I return my focus to Alex. "You're being a gentleman?"

As we sidestep a homeless man begging for change, Alex makes an affirmative noise with his lips. His hum switches to a groan when I break away from his stride, spin around, then make a dash for it. I watch his reflection in the shop window. I swear he looks five seconds from throwing me over his shoulder and stomping to my building like a caveman. The only thing stopping him is the realization that I'm not fleeing. I'm merely bobbing down to hand the homeless man a twenty dollar bill.

"You shouldn't give them money," Alex cautions when I return to his side.

"Why? Because he'll spend it on booze and cigarettes?" My voice is full of attitude. . . until the homeless man proves Alex right. My jaw quivers when he throws off his blanket and races into the closest liquor store.

"Save it as a life lesson." Alex grips my elbow, impeding my mad stomp to the ass-peddler. I worked hard for that money. Perhaps not as hard as some people, but I still earned it. It wasn't handed to me.

After a few more steps, Alex suggests, "If you truly want to help the homeless, donate to shelters. Whether it's an hour of your time or a monetary amount, they'll put your generosity to good use."

The knowledge in his tone slicks my skin with sweat. It also keeps my mouth shut for the next several blocks.

"I swear to god this place is a minefield. The town planner should be shot," Alex grumbles when we pass the same pizza shop for a third time in a row.

I could put him out of his misery, but watching him sweat as he "takes charge" is too enticing. Once he finishes throwing around his authoritativeness, I'll advise him my apartment building is half a block up. Until then, he can keep sweating.

"That's cheating," I mumble when he seeks directions from a cab driver grabbing a slice of pizza.

They only interact for a few seconds, but it's long enough for me to realize my ruse has been unraveled. Alex's jaw is ticking more now than when a group of men on a bachelor party asked if I could be their stripper. They already had one in tow but were more than eager for another. I swear, Alex nearly burst a blood vessel in his hand from how fast he clenched his fists.

When Alex's eyes drift from my apartment building to me, I push off my feet and make a dash for it. I weave through standstill traffic without any fear for my life. Alex is on my heels thirty seconds later.

"You play dirty." His growl ruffles the fine hairs on my neck more effectively than the air-conditioning when I take off my coat. Add the full-blast AC to a three-mile trek through a human jungle, and you have a sweaty disaster. I can't remember the last time I've been this sweaty...

My inner monologue trails off when disappointment takes its

place. I had no problems flicking the bean until a pompous, egotistical asshole walked into my life. Now, I can't achieve half the thrill. You'd think Alex's panty-wetting face would be sufficient to get me off, but no, for some frustrating reason, my body doesn't want to play pretend. It wants the real deal.

Ugh! An accountant! Seriously, you could do so much better, I scold myself before entering the waiting elevator car.

I whip around so fast, I give myself whiplash when a pair of teenage shoes scuffle across the silver tracks of the elevator car.

"What are you doing?" I ask Alex, my voice brimming with snarkiness.

I'm not angry at Alex. I'm peeved at my lack of libido. Whether it's done by my own accord or with the assistance of a handsome suitor, I'm a sexually promiscuous person. The drought I've been crawling through the past two months hasn't just made my vagina depressed, it's made me an irrational, aggravated bitch.

If Alex enters this elevator, he better be packing heat, because concerns about being shot down by a man carrying an actual gun may be the only way I'll handle him and his schmexy scent at the same time.

Alex's head flops to the side like a little puppy when it's in trouble. "I'm making sure you get home safely. Elevators are magnets for creeps. Who knows what you'll be subjected to between here and your penthouse?" He smirks, acting smug.

His smile is wiped straight of his face when I ask, "Who said I'm going to my penthouse?" Pretending his balk didn't create an earthquake in Japan, I add on, "Don't act shocked. No woman on the planet goes to this much effort to eat *and* sleep alone." My overemphasis of certain words ensures he can't mistake what I'm referencing.

"Then I'll make sure you get to *the* apartment you're visiting." Alex's words fly out of his mouth like daggers as jagged as his final step into the elevator.

"Perhaps you can follow me to *his* door? You know, to protect me from the boogeyman hiding in the shadows." The snark in my tone shocks me. Clearly, extreme horniness is more detrimental to my sanity than tequila shots. I've never been so unhinged.

It doesn't help that Alex's attitude is fed by my arrogance. "Uh-huh. That's precisely what I'll do. I might even stay outside *his* door until you're done. Boogeymen don't disappear when the sun rises, Rae. They just find a new shadow to hide in."

He twists his body to face the elevator panel, hiding his flaming-with-anger face from my view. He shouldn't bother. I can feel the tension radiating off him. It makes his scent more masculine and pulse-quickening delicious.

"Floor?" he growls a few seconds later.

Incapable of backing down when challenged, I nearly mutter off a random number. I would if I weren't concerned every man on that floor would be placed on Alex's hit list if I did. I don't give a shit if he crosses his heart and hopes to die, there's no way he's an accountant. He's too alpha to sit in an office all day crunching numbers. He craves adrenaline as much as I do. That's why the heady scent of lust bouncing between us is so strong.

"Floor, Regan," Alex demands again. His deep and dangerous voice increases the sticky situation between my legs.

Not wanting him to discover I'm a woeful liar, I lean across him to hit the penthouse button. My hand isn't even halfway across his broad shoulders when he snatches my wrist, twirls me around, then pins me to the wall with his impressively firm body.

Kill me now. I'm a goner.

"There are only three men in this building who could come close to bedding a woman like you. One is married; the other is away on a business trip; so that only leaves one lone soldier—the owner of this building. Is that who you're visiting tonight, Regan? Are you going to pay your rent in a lump sum payment?"

He doesn't look at me while speaking, not even from the corner of his eye. He just glances past my shoulder, acting as if it's perfectly acceptable to pin a stranger to a wall while interrogating them with an eye-opening amount of knowledge.

I know the three men to whom he's referring. At one stage or another in the past five years, they've been added and removed from my list of suitors.

"It's the owner of this building, isn't it? That's why you were texting him on your way out. You were giving him time to prep for your visit."

To a normal person, the possessiveness in his tone would be classed as borderline psychotic. Unfortunately for all involved, my fucked up head isn't settling on the same theory. My body is thrumming with anticipation, loving the ownership beaming out of him.

There's only one way our exchange could get more panty-wetting: if I were given the devotion of his eyes. I want to see if they're clouded with dominance or narrowed with anger. I can hear his heart thrashing against his ribs, smell the manliness pumping from every orifice of his body, and feel the thickness a pair of jeans and a winter coat can't hide, but I want his eyes on mine—badly.

"Answer me, Regan. Who are you visiting?"

I moan before I can stop myself. His growl of my name was

better than any fantasy I've had the past two months. It was thick and hot and utterly devastating.

My throaty groan grants me my final wish. I'm given Alex's eyes. They are as devastatingly beautiful as I anticipated. He appears both angry and confused, torn between wanting to possess every inch of me and walking away. His fight or flight instincts have kicked in full force.

I save him from making a bad decision by slinging my arms around his neck and sealing my mouth over his. Worry I haven't just lost my self-pleasing mojo smacks into me when he doesn't respond to my boldness in the way I'm hoping. He seems willing yet alarmed by my tongue piercing his stern lips.

It's fortunate persuasion is one of my finer points.

It takes several strokes of my tongue to calm the tension in Alex's jaw, but when it does, mayhem ensues. His fingers weave through my hair as he returns my kiss with so much passion, I feel as if I am being claimed. He takes advantage of all the strong points on his face to dominate our exchange. His teeth sink into my lip before his tongue glides along the area throbbing with aroused pain. His Viking beard tickles my chin and neck when he drags his nose down my cheek to coat my face with his delicious scent, and the strokes of his tongue are purposeful and sensual.

His kiss leaves my mind filled with only thoughts of him. I can't escape the madness—I'm trapped by his smell, taste, and warmth.

When the elevator comes to a stop on my floor, we stumble down the hallway, all legs and arms, neither willing to surrender our mouths from the other. The crash of our bodies on my apartment door is loud enough to wake the residents of my building. My moans will take care of the ones we missed.

After splaying my back against my door, Alex buries his hand deeper into my hair before taking our kiss to another level. Wetness pools between my legs when he teases my mouth with precise strokes of his tongue and sweet, controlled movements of his lips. His kiss is anything but innocent, but he doesn't seem to care—*finally.*

He holds all the reins in our exchange, and I'm happy to hand them over. I don't usually encourage a change of guard in the bedroom, but only a fool would feign disinterest in exploring his sexual prowess. Furthermore, we're kissing, not fucking, so until then, I can let him take charge.

My nerve endings zing with pleasure when Alex rocks his hips forward. Layers of clothes can't hide the thickness throbbing behind his zipper, begging to be released. He's long and hard. His body's response to our kiss isn't surprising. It isn't chaste. It's steamy and hot, a perfect opener for what's about to occur.

As Alex's tongue strokes mine, I blindly hunt for my keys in my clutch purse. I find them two seconds later, but it isn't quick enough for Alex. His hand has already slithered under my dress to cup my engorged breast. He twists my nipple, causing goosebumps of arousal to pepper my skin. He's barely touching me, but a violent storm brews low in my core. This is the sensation I've been missing the past two months: the chaos that arrives with both devastation and relief.

"Not yet," I throatily purr when his fingers sweep away the material clinging to my hardened bud, nearly exposing my naked breasts to his avid eyes. "There are motion-activated cameras in every hallway of Hector."

Agitation spikes through me when Alex's eyes lift to mine. I hear the million thoughts streaming through his head without a word escaping from his mouth—just as much as I can feel them. He's panicked, yet confident. Ready, yet hesitant. Blinded by lust, yet still holding back.

I don't know how he does it. From the instant his scrumptious taste engulfed my taste buds, I've been in a dream-like state. I'm not drunk. . . unless fumes of lust are classified as a drug? If so, sign me up for rehab.

My heart rate triples when Alex scans the corridor for the security camera I mentioned. The tightness our kiss removed from his jaw returns stronger than ever when he locates its dome.

He bites out a string of profanities. I wish that was the worst of the tragedy. Unfortunately, it isn't. The removal of my legs from his waist is the biggest blow I've endured this year.

Actually, scrap that. Make it the past five years.

I don't know whether I should be humiliated or pleased by his rejection. If a simple grind up against a door under a watchful eye is too far out of his comfort zone, how will he ever handle a woman like me?

In less than a split second, the magic is over, our spell undone. I've never seen such an array of emotions cross someone's face as I am seeing now. *Confusion. Shock. Anger.* And perhaps even a little bit of resentment.

The final realization helps me regain the reins I lost while trapped by lust. This is the very reason I usually keep them firmly in my grasp. It's the only way I'm guaranteed to be free of burden.

With a shimmy of my shoulders, I return my eyes to Alex's. The heat burning my veins simmers when I spot one thing in his eyes I never thought I'd see. *Sorrow.*

"It's okay," I assure him when he attempts to speak but can't.

"You don't understand, Rae." His words are barely whispers. "This isn't. . . I can't—"

"Wait to get out of here. I get it."

If I had any chance of fooling you with a declaration that my tone was confident, I'd tell you it was swimming in it. It's a pity my libido isn't the only thing that packed up and left town a few months ago. My ego went right along with it.

My back splays against my door when Alex takes a step closer to me. His kiss-swollen lips, mussed hair, and dilated eyes are a brutal reminder of what I'm being denied. "That's not it at all, Rae. It's just. . ."

I save him the hassle of rummaging up a better excuse by dipping under his arm, jabbing my key into the lock and entering my penthouse apartment.

The brutal slam of my door drowns out anything he says next.

CHAPTER THIRTEEN

I stand outside of Regan's door for the next ten minutes. I don't say anything. I can't. There isn't anything I can do to change the monumental fuck up I just made, so why bother? I have no excuse for the jealousy card I played except that this is foreign to me — all of it.

That possessive, narcissistic asshole I portrayed in the elevator isn't me. There's just something about Regan that brings out my chauvinistic side. Just the thought of her with Isaac. . . *Ugh!* My blood boils just thinking about it.

I told myself she was stirring me, that she wanted me to react to her taunts, but no matter how many times common sense screamed at me that I was a better man, I didn't hear a fucking word he spoke.

I wanted to piss a circle around Regan to mark my territory. I wanted to fuck her so hard, my name would ring in Isaac's ears for years to come, but one confession unraveled it all.

Isaac lives in this building. His apartment is the one sitting opposite Regan's, so you can be assured any surveillance equipment in this hallway was infiltrated by the FBI the instant Isaac was placed on their radar.

That means they have our kiss on camera. If that isn't bad enough, they may even have glimpses of Regan's bare breast. It's probably only a bit of cleavage, but that alone has my legs pumping as fast as my heart.

I charge down the corridor before throwing open the emergency exit door next to the elevator bank. The shoes Regan despised batter the stairs as hard as my heart smashes against my ribs. I take the stairs two at a time, my focus on one thing and one thing only—protecting Regan.

By the time I make it onto the sidewalk outside Regan's building, only half a lung is in operation, but a new record-setting pace has been achieved. As my lungs work through their oxygen deprivation, I scan the congested street. In a town as bustling as Ravenshoe, even the Bureau has issues finding parking spots.

I find what I'm looking for half a block down. The faded pizza sign on a dark blue van makes it appear authentic, but the lack of movement on a Friday night assures me it's the vehicle I'm seeking.

When I throw open the unlocked door of the van a few seconds later, a man I'd guess to be early to mid-twenties startles. He has the same blond hair as me, a similar wonky smile, but his shoulders are two sizes smaller than mine and his personality a whole lot more timid.

"Move," I instruct, shoving him away from the bank of monitors he's seated in front of.

It takes me flashing him my ID before he does as instructed. If my endeavor to remove Regan from the FBI's surveillance mainframe weren't my utmost priority, I'd commend his commitment to the job. Not many tech agents come out of the gates firing. Most wilt away within the first six months on the job. The fact he didn't flinch when given a direct order has me curious about how long he's been on the job, and why he requested to be a technician instead of an agent.

When he eyes me with suspicion, I add to my ruse, "We got word our target is piggy-backing off our surveillance. I need to check the servers to ensure they're clear."

I'm talking nonsense. I'm a field agent for a reason. This technical mumbo jumbo isn't my field of expertise. Fortunately for me, I only need to know one button to fulfill my goal: the delete button.

"That can't be right. I coded this program myself. It's unhackable," the young technician assures, his voice more confident than his facial expression.

"Is that so?"

When he nods, I add on, "Then what's this? Why is our target visiting her now?"

I point to a monitor on my left that shows Isaac knocking on Regan's apartment door—the same door I pinned her to with my cock as I assaulted her mouth with my tongue.

Our kiss—*fuck*. How can you describe something you've never experienced before? I've kissed plenty of women, but I've never had an all-encompassing, *I'll never seek release without it entering my thoughts* kiss before.

The fact I'm thinking this way after nothing but a kiss proves the power Regan has over me. I don't just want to break the rules for her. I want to rewrite them.

I'm snapped from my dangerous thoughts when the technician mumbles, "He could be borrowing a cup of sugar?"

He laughs, apparently amused. I'm glad he can find humor in our situation. I am anything but amused. I left Regan in a . . . *vulnerable* state. The last thing I want is Isaac relieving her of her predicament.

"Listen. . ." I read the technician's name off his ID badge, ". . .Brandon. I've been running this operative from the ground the past four months. Isaac doesn't borrow sugar. I kissed a member of his team to see if he would react. He's reacting."

"Your kiss was staged?"

My chest puffs high from the shock in Brandon's tone. He either thinks I'm a brilliant actor or full of shit. Praying it's the former, I continue to pull the wool over his eyes, "Yes. You've met our head of unit, right?"

He nods before his hand darts up to tug at the collar of his polo shirt. It's not hot. The temperature inside the van is sitting at a pleasant 74°F. He's merely responding how every rookie agent does when they meet the very definition of a ball crusher.

"So you're well aware Theresa demands her agents to go above and beyond the norm, right?"

Looking a little ill, Brandon nods again.

"That's why I kissed Rae. I was following orders."

"Rae?" Brandon double-checks, somewhat confused.

I curse under my breath before stammering out, "Rae, Regan. What's one blonde to another?" I backhand his chest, acting like an Grade A moron. "We should call them all 'babe' to save the awkwardness in the morning when you can't remember their names." I laugh, ending my chauvinist routine worthy of an Oscar nomination.

In the corner of my eye, I spot Isaac walking away from Regan's unopened apartment door. When he enters an empty elevator car a few seconds later, a sense of relief washes through me. Not enough I forget my original campaign, but enough to unclench my jaw.

"Pass me a pen. We should be jotting this down so we can forward it to Theresa for analysis." I'm referring to Isaac's movements—not my kiss with Regan. I gesture to a stack of pens on Brandon's far right, purposely knocking his mug of coffee onto the box responsible for backing up surveillance images.

"Ah, fuck. Jesus. What did I do?" I grab the wad of napkins under his half-eaten donut to soak up the mess sprayed across his keyboard while he frantically strives to save the mainframe from fritzing.

Confident he's distracted, I remove any traces of my exchange with Regan from the startup system before it's transferred to the mainframe.

When it's all said and done, I feel no less guilty. I expected a weight to lift off my chest the instant I removed Regan from Theresa's vindictive strike. All I get is more worry.

This is wrong. I am a federal agent. I don't destroy evidence. I gather it to charge criminals and protect the innocent.

I guess I could use that as the reason why I've allowed Regan to misalign my moral compass twice in my career. She's an innocent caught up in a game she doesn't belong in.

Even with a shattered kneecap, I followed the Substanz case with an eagle eye. What Regan said that night was true. There was no evidence whatsoever that she was part of the illegal brothel operating as a side business from Substanz. She was purely a dancer—a good one.

Who's to say that isn't the case this time around as well? Perhaps she's just Isaac's business lawyer. The corrupt are known for surrounding themselves with honesty. It's how they fly under the radar so long. No one scans their own backyards for criminals.

When I slump into my chair, perplexed, a note scribbled on Isaac's movement sheet captures my attention.

Electrician arrived at the apartment across from target at 9:16 PM. Departure time:

No departure time has been noted. I drop my eyes to my watch, noticing it's a few minutes short of 11 PM.

"Why didn't you jot down a departure time for the service-man? Although we no longer have agents allocated to Isaac's team, we still track their movements like we do Isaac's. Every bread-crumb must be noted."

Brandon dumps coffee-soiled papers into a bin with a grumble before twisting around to face me. His eyes are narrowed, and his lips are hard-lined. He's peeved. Rightly so. One swipe of my hand ruined hours of surveillance while adding more work to his already tight schedule. Lucky for all involved, Isaac's routine rarely alters. A quick copy and paste of yesterday stats will cover my "mishap."

After dropping his eyes to the note I am referring to, Brandon returns them to me. "He hasn't left yet."

My brow cocks, certain I heard him wrong.

I didn't.

"It must have been a private callout—he entered the apart-ment unattended. Usually, the front desk has someone escort them."

He rifles through a pile of handwritten notes, oblivious to my bubbling anger. I don't know why I am angry, but with no other plausible explanation for my skyrocketing blood pressure and reddening cheeks, I'll assume it's anger.

"I requested the guest registry the instant he entered the apartment. I have it here somewhere." Just as I am about to rip the papers out of Brandon's hands to search them myself, he murmurs, "Here it is."

Paper shredding booms over his whiny voice when I snatch the document from his grasp. My jaw ticks as I scan the extensive guest registry. Unease invades my gut when I reach 9 PM. There are only four names jotted down between then and now. None of them are for an electrical company.

"Are you sure it was an electrician you saw?" I ask Brandon, my voice picking up with unconcealed suspicion. It has the same cocky edge it held when I interrogated Regan about her supposed after dinner date.

Brandon's throat works hard to swallow. "Yeah. I'm fairly sure—"

"Fairly sure? Or one hundred percent sure?" My tone advises I will not accept a pansy-ass reply. We don't run on assumptions here. We work with facts—stern, unapologetic facts.

"I'm confident." His voice doesn't relay this. "He had an electrician logo on the back of his overalls."

Leaning over my body, he taps on the keyboard three times. It brings up the image responsible for my panic. At precisely 9:16 PM a man approximately five foot eight with light sandy hair and a dark cap glides down the corridor separating Regan's apartment from Isaac's. As Brandon advised, there's an electric company logo emblazoned on the back of his overalls.

Although he's carrying a large metal toolbox, the veins in his hand aren't showing the exertion you'd expect if it were brimming with tools. Come to think of it, his hands are dainty and smooth—unlike any tradesmen I've seen.

"Run his company through the system. We can track his movements from there," I suggest to Brandon, hoping his knowledge of the FBI database is more extensive than mine.

It doesn't even take Brandon thirty seconds to run the electrician's details through our system. It isn't because he's brilliant at what he does. It's because the search comes up empty. There's no company of that name in the world database, much less the state of Florida.

I swallow away a bitter taste in the back of my throat. "Are you sure you didn't miss his exit?"

You can hear desperation in my voice. Regan entered her apartment twenty minutes ago. Isaac knocked and didn't get an answer. That hasn't happened once the past four months I've been tailing them. This can only mean one thing: Regan is being stalked as she presumed months ago.

When Brandon remains quiet, I growl, "Did you take a break? A piss? Fall asleep? At any time tonight were you away from these monitors?"

When Brandon shakes his head at each of my suggestions, I leap to my feet. "Where's your service weapon?" I throw open compartments surrounding his computer station before half my sentence leaves my mouth. I need to get to Regan, and I need to get to her now.

Brandon shocks me by removing his gun from a holster on his waist. Standard technicians don't carry their guns like normal agents. Some don't even have government-assigned weapons. Realizing now isn't the time to discuss semantics, I check that Brandon's weapon is loaded before hightailing it out of his van.

"What do you want me to do?!" Brandon shouts, slowing my steps down the still-bustling sidewalk.

A few of my fancy-dressed sidewalk companions balk when I reply, "Maintain surveillance. If you hear gunfire, call in back up."

I should be advising him to summon back up now, but since I don't want Regan to discover my secret life with a circus act in tow, I'll go in alone. I'm armed and confused—a lethal combination in itself. The electrician better hope Brandon failed to notice his departure, or he's in for one hell of a fright.

I thought fleeing Regan's apartment building would be the only record I'd smash tonight. My return is just as dramatic. I'm sprinting down the corridor of Regan's floor with forty seconds still under my belt.

"Rae!?" I bang on the gleaming white door of Regan's apartment. "I know you're pissed, and I'm more than happy to take an ear bashing, but you need to open the door first."

Whoever said "silence is a good answer" is a moron. I'd give anything to hear Regan's voice right now. I'd even hand in my badge.

I press my ear against her door, praying she's just being stubborn.

I can't hear a fucking thing.

"Rae?! If you don't open the door, I'll kick it down." My low tone indicates the honesty in my threat.

Silence—I get nothing but heart-clenching silence.

Recalling the cautionary countdown Regan did on me months ago, I growl, "Five... Four... Three ..."

I don't make it to two. I'm too fucking impatient.

After taking a step back, I rear up my leg and kick at the lock on her door. The thick white material is sturdy, but it has nothing on my determination. It pops open nicely under my boot, the safety latch coming away just as easily.

"Rae." I enter her apartment with my gun held high and my heart rate out of control.

It marginally settles when I fail to spot any ruckus upon entry. Usually, if you are attacked unaware, it happens during entry. Regan's keys and purse are resting on an antique table on my right, and her shoes are kicked off halfway down the elongated foyer.

Earthy tones of blue bombard me when I enter her massive living room. Regan's apartment spans one half of the top floor of Hector. I love space, but it comes at a cost. An impressive eyesore is a bitch to keep clean, much less sweep for a suspected intruder.

Confident the triple-sized living area is empty, I direct my focus to the left. Although I've never been inside Regan's apartment, her floorplan appears to be an exact replica of Isaac's—it's just mirror-reversed.

"Rae?" A faint hum jingles through my ears. I'm shocked I can hear anything with how hard my pulse is thrumming through my body. I feel like I'm trapped underwater, submerged by worry.

When another groan filters through my ears, I quicken my pace. It was a moan laced with painful frustration.

After sweeping a guest bedroom on my right, I continue down the hall. I know which room is Regan's as it has a light beaming through a partially cracked open door.

"Rae?" I call out again, praying she's alone, but petrified of scaring her. "Are you in here?"

The door creaks when I push it open. No signs of human life are seen or heard. Her bedroom is a similar palette to her living room, although I don't have time to admire it. A tormented scream shreds my eardrums. It's closely followed by a loud bang.

I charge for the door the noise bellowed through, my steps as hurried as my heart rate. Although her bathroom door could be unlocked, it suffers the same fate as Regan's front door. It buckles under the force of my foot, its elegant design wiped in an instant.

With my finger curled around the trigger of Brandon's gun, I merge deeper into the steam-filled space. The fact Regan neglected to voice anger at the demolition of her door has me worried. That isn't something she'd take sitting down. She'd be up in my face, demanding immediate repair.

I understand why she's not complaining when an image breaks through the fog surrounding me. Regan isn't being held captive by a gun-toting swindler with a death wish. She's taking a bath. The earbuds lodged in her ears have music pumping through her veins as rapidly as her bubble-covered skin has blood pumping to my cock.

Although the image of her unharmed cools my turbines, it doesn't completely quell my worry. The steam vaping from the scorching hot water adds a whole new dimension to my unease.

Forgetting Regan has noise-cancelling instruments wedged in her ears, I demand, "Rae, get out of the bath."

When she remains in place, humming a tune, I tug an earphone out of her ear before repeating my request. Wish for my own noise-cancelling headphones engulfs me when Regan screams blue murder. She darts out of the tub, the slippery oils coating her skin not hampering her efforts in the slightest.

Though she's issuing me every death threat I've been given the past six years in under a minute, I snag a fluffy towel off the towel rack and hand it to her. Usually, it would be the fight of my life to keep my eyes off her naked frame, but since I can't remove my eyes from the death threat messily scrawled across her large vanity mirror, the fight isn't as torturous.

"What the hell?" Regan murmurs, finally spotting the cause of my concern. "Who did that?" She tugs her towel close to her body as if it will protect her more than my gun.

I start my interrogation like always, "Did you notice anything out of place when you arrived home tonight? Missing articles of clothing? The TV turned on when it should be off?"

Regan shakes her head, her eyes unable to leave the threat guaranteeing brutal mutilation of her body. I step into the path of her vision, blocking the horrifying words from her view. When I'm given the devotion of her wide-with-terror eyes, I ask, "Has anything like this happened before?"

She shakes her head once more, its juddering as violent as the shake of her hands.

"It's okay," I assure her, my tone calm even though I'm feeling anything but. "I won't let anything happen to you."

She accepts my pledge more quickly than I expected. It's probably more because of the fear enveloping her than blind faith.

I stop removing my cellphone from my pocket when Regan garbles my name. My eyes jackknife to hers, stunned by the sheer terror radiating in her voice when she asks, "Did you arrive with company?"

Before I can respond, a flurry of black captures my attention. Someone is darting away from the door I just kicked in.

"Stay here," I demand of Regan before taking off after a shadow. They were so quick, I didn't register any details of their face, much less what they're wearing.

When I enter Regan's living room, I head to the right, the groan of someone crashing into a firm surface directing my steps. As expected, the assailant is hightailing it down the corridor of Regan's apartment building. He's wearing the same overalls

Brandon mentioned during surveillance, but the straps have been undone, exposing a spotlessly clean wife beater shirt.

"Stop or I'll shoot," I warn, lining up my target from the doorway of Regan's apartment.

He tests my patience by continuing down the hall. He shouldn't. This is the first time I've mixed business with pleasure, and I don't see it ending well. He was conspiring to hurt Rae. If his threat is anything to go by—badly!

"Fuck!" I curse when he throws open a laundry chute halfway down the hall and dives inside. Because of his svelte frame, he fits through the trap door with ease.

I nearly fire off a shot, but years of experience tell me my effort will be too late. While charging for the emergency stairwell, I raise my hand to my ear. Because I'm so accustomed to being on the job, it takes me several long seconds to recall why I don't have access to my usual equipment. My feet stomp faster when I realize I don't have the ability to radio in assistance.

Just as I throw open the fire exit door next to the elevator bank, Brandon barrels into the corridor. He's wheezing and out of breath. "Assailant. On. Camera. Saw. Him. Re-enter." He breathes deeply through each word, showcasing why he's a technician instead of a field agent. He's extremely unfit.

"Where do the laundry chutes exit?" The hammering of my heart echoes in my tone. It's not racing a million miles an hour because I am weak like Brandon; it's the fear enveloping me responsible for its frantic beat.

Brandon attempts to speak through his pain. "B. . bas—"

"Basement," I fill in, hurrying him along.

When he nods, I demand, "Send a crew to the basement

before calling in forensics. I doubt he left any evidence, but we won't know if we don't check."

Brandon peers at me as if I asked him how long his cock is.

"The basement, Brandon. Send men to the basement," I repeat as if he's stupid.

"We don't have any men," he advises, "much less ones I can boss around."

I wish he were lying. I wasn't being deceitful when I said Theresa's crew was sliced to a few men earlier this month.

"By the time either of us get to the basement, he'll be long gone." Brandon's eyes drop to the ground, unsure how to voice his next set of words. I can understand his worry when he stammers out, "I also don't think it's wise to bring Theresa in on this. She'll arrive with a truckload of questions—ones I'm certain you don't want to answer."

Although he's being honest, his words aren't easy for me to stomach. I want the person responsible for the pain that tore at my chest when I spotted Regan's death threat held accountable for his actions. I want to pound him as mercilessly as my heart is smashing into my ribs. He wants to hurt Regan, so you can be assured I *will* hurt him.

"Then what do you suggest I do, Brandon?" I articulate his name with a sneer, annoyed just at the prospect of seeking his advice. I don't ask for advice, and definitely not from a man beneath me.

Shockingly, Brandon doesn't balk at my threatening tone. His cheeks flush, but I'm certain that's more from his marathon stair climb than my angry snarl.

"Do what you've been doing the past four months."

I growl. This time he balks.

His throat works hard to swallow several times in a row before he mutters, "I mean run your own investigation. Theresa is bad news. You don't want her or her crew on this."

His reply stumps me. That isn't something a standard technician would say. He's more deeply involved in the Bureau than a standard techy. I just can't fathom how?

Before half a notion can filter through my brain, a sweet voice interrupts it. Regan is calling my name. It isn't the way I want to hear it shouted. She sounds scared.

Wanting to end one fight before taking up another, I instruct Brandon, "Remove the last ten minutes from the surveillance log and call in a disturbance. If Theresa believes the incident of the electrician's failure to leave requires further investigation, let her men come in."

"And if she wants to leave it alone?" Brandon asks, intuiting my thoughts.

"Then I'll handle it."

He nods, preferring our second solution.

I hand him back his gun, suddenly wishing I was armed twenty-four-seven. He takes it before pivoting on his heels and stalking away. While waiting for the elevator to arrive to Regan's floor, he calls in a disturbance.

I wait for him to be given further instructions before shouting his name. When he turns around to face me, I say, "Although this investigation is taking a slight turn, I expect to see your report on my desk first thing Tuesday morning."

He looks at me strangely, as if to say, *you have a desk?*

"Theresa may do things dodgy around here, but not all of us are like her," I explain, hoping he'll see sense through the madness. "We're agents before we are anything."

My last sentence doesn't come out as strong as my first, probably because it was laced with dishonesty. I don't know what I would have done if I had caught Regan's assailant tonight. A dark, wet basement seems rather enticing right now, all the more so when Brandon's exit coincides with Regan's entrance.

Her towel has been replaced with a silky black negligee she's thrown on in a hurry. The uneven hemline isn't the only evidence of her quick dressing. The fact her negligee is inside out is another indication.

After scanning the corridor to ensure we are alone, Regan locks her eyes with mine. Her brows tack together as she clenches her fists into tiny balls. She's not scared like I anticipated earlier. She's downright fuming mad.

CHAPTER FOURTEEN

Alex

"An accountant, my ass," Regan grumbles under her breath as her eyes drop to where my gun was holstered the afternoon she recognized I was carrying a weapon.

Anger curtails my windpipe when her eyes return to my face and I see the apprehension behind them. She's afraid I can't protect her, worried I'll let her attacker make true on his threat. With or without my gun, she has no cause for fret. I'll protect her until my dying breath.

Before I can assure her of that, she sneers, "Is this a set up? Did you arrange this so you could gallop in like some kind of savior on a white horse?"

What the fuck? Shouldn't she be hostile with the man who snuck into her apartment with the intent to harm her, not the one who stopped it from happening?

"This wasn't my doing," I fire back, shadowing her to her apartment door.

My words don't come out as strong when she attempts to slam

her door in my face. Thankfully, the wood is too warped to shut without extreme force.

"That was me," I admit somewhat cockily. "I came back to apologize for the way I behaved. I heard moaning and groaning. When you failed to answer my numerous calls, I found my own way in."

"Because all accountants carry guns, break down doors, and harass women until they can't get themselves off!" She freezes, stunned she vocalized her last confession.

"I'd strap napalm to my chest before I let anything happen to you, Rae."

Hearing the honesty in my words, Regan's angry stance weakens.

I take a step closer to her. "You're scared. That's okay—it's perfectly natural in these types of situations to release your adrenaline in a negative way."

"I'm not scared," she assures, her low tone hindering her objective. "I'm annoyed. Frustrated." Our eyes meet before she says, "Sick of being lied to. Tell the truth, Alex. Are you an accountant?"

My eyes stray to the flashing contraption hanging in the corner of her hallway. The vein thrumming in Regan's neck pulsates when she follows my gaze. Realizing this isn't a conversation she wants recorded by her boss's surveillance camera, she reluctantly invites me into her apartment with a wave of her trembling hand.

Within seconds of us entering the foyer, I cup her jaw in my hands. The violent quiver of her lips relaxes from my gesture. She's putting on a brave front, but she's petrified. I understand. The threat was one of the most intense I've seen. It didn't just threaten mutilation; it mentioned numerous body-degrading things.

After three gentle strokes of her white cheeks, I shake my head to her earlier question.

She releases a sharp breath. "You're not an accountant?" She sounds disappointed, as if she'd grown accustomed to the idea that I'm just a standard, regular guy.

"No," I reply with a twist of my lips. "I'm similar to an investigator."

I wish I could tell her the truth, but since I can't, this must do.

"An investigator?" When I nod, she adds on, "Like a PI?"

I grimace. Those guys are the worst of the worst. "Kinda." Although it's only one word, it kills me to say it.

I joined the agency because I wanted to bang my chest and proudly declare I am an agent at the Federal Bureau of Investigation. I thought the title would make women swoon like the stay-at-home moms did any time my dad arrived to pick me up from school. When you're six, you have no idea that popularity isn't solely gained by a job title. It takes a shit ton more effort than that. Fortunately for both the Bureau and me, I fell in love with the job more than the praise.

Although I'm not seeing it with the same esteem right now.

My eyes drop to Regan when she questions, "Have you investigated incidents like this before?"

"Uh-huh. That's why you'll do precisely what I tell you to do at the exact time I tell you to do it."

My heart rate breaks into a can-can when anger flashes through Regan's eyes, proving my attempt to goad her paid off. I much prefer her temperamentally unhinged than on the verge of crying like she was mere seconds ago.

With a stomp of her foot showing years of study didn't tarnish her diva attitude, she shouts, "Like hell I am!" She breaks away from me, her strides as wobbly as the vehement snarl of her top lip.

I shadow her to a fancy crystal bar at the side of her living room. "We either do this the hard way or the easy way, Regan. I'll get pleasure from them both."

She slams down the tumbler of whiskey she was in the process of pouring to glue her eyes to mine. "No man but my daddy tells me what to do, so why the hell would I listen to you?"

"Because you know I'll keep you safe. That I'll never let anything bad happen to you," I reply without pause for thought.

The little vein in her neck that's been working overtime since I walked in on her bathing stops fluttering when I take a step closer to her. I can see in her eyes she wants to deny my statement, but the honesty of my pledge is too potent to deny. I will protect her. I will keep her safe. And I will do it all without having her beneath me.

When Regan remains quiet, I strengthen my campaign. "You either let me investigate this case, or we call in the authorities."

From how her face pales, anyone would swear I just told her I'm her brother. She'd rather prostitute herself out than have police enter her premises. I don't know which notion pisses me off more.

After swallowing down three fingers of whiskey as if it isn't scorching her throat, Regan utters, "I'm not agreeing to anything until you spell out your terms."

I shake my head when she dips the whiskey my way, word-lessly asking if I'd like a drink. Although I am not officially on the job, I don't drink when I'm on a case.

While Regan downs another hefty serving of whiskey, I scan

her apartment. It doesn't take long to note her lack of security. Except for the camera in the hallway, there isn't a single safety measure in place.

"You need better security measures implemented in your home." I sound pissed. Justly so. I am pissed—peeved as fuck. Regan is a beautiful, highly successful woman. She's a prime target for neurotic, insolent men with too much time of their hands. "You don't need cameras like the ones in the hall, but something more than a lock that can be kicked in without effort."

Regan grumbles something under her breath, but with a whiskey glass attached to her mouth, I miss what she says. Before she can swallow her fourth double shot in less than a minute, I swipe the glass out of her hand and place it on the circular table she's standing beside. She attempts to protest, but pressing my finger to her lips stops her.

I wait for lust to overtake the panic in her eyes before saying, "I want you to come stay with me at my apartment."

"Nope. No. Nada. Uh-huh. No," Regan replies, imitating Tracy Morgan's character in *Cop Out.* "That's not happening. I'd rather be mutilated than go anywhere with you."

I ignore yet another rejection. "Then once better security has been installed, we can return here."

"*We?* What do you mean *we!* There's no *we! You* walked out of here, leaving *me* hanging. I couldn't even. . ." She paces on the spot, seemingly lost on how to voice the rest of her reply.

"You couldn't even. . .?" I push along, unashamed. The best thing I can do for her in her panicked state is keep her talking. The faster she releases the tension in her stomach, the faster she'll help me identify the person responsible for her anxiety. It will be a win-win for both of us.

My plan goes to shit when Regan locks her furious green eyes with mine. Her flaring nostrils and gritted teeth reveal she isn't panicked—she's frustrated.

The reason behind her frustration comes to light when she sneers, "Even with how badly you left me hanging, I couldn't get myself off! Why do you think you heard 'moans and groans'?!" She air quotes my earlier reference. "They weren't happy ones! They were made in frustration!" She steps closer to me, aligning her thrusting chest with mine. "You don't need to rush in and protect me, Mr. Fancy Pants. I haven't come in over two months. I'm as dangerous as I can get, so you'd do best not to cross me."

I've got nothing. No words. No reply. Just a raging fucking hard on that's in the process of busting the zipper in my jeans. Thank fuck I wore jeans tonight as the flimsy fly in my suit wouldn't have withstood the pressure.

Recognizing I'm five seconds from relieving Regan from her predicament, I mutter, "You need to pack quickly. The last bus arrives in twenty minutes."

Disgust crosses Regan's features. I don't know if the mention of public transport is the reason for her greening gills or the fact I failed to acknowledge her inability to climax since I arrived in her life.

Upon spotting a tempestuous storm brewing in Regan's eyes, I yank my cellphone out of my pocket. "Fine. If you don't want to do things my way, I'll call in Ravenshoe PD. At least you're wearing black; the ink stains on your fingers won't be obvious."

The facts included in my admission cause Regan to balk. "Why would I be fingerprinted?"

Although she is asking a question, I don't need to answer her. I can tell when she reached her own conclusion as she growled a curse word under her breath.

"You play dirty," she sneers before pushing off her feet.

"You have no idea," I mumble as I follow her through her palatial apartment.

Once she reaches her bedroom, she yanks down a bag before setting to work on packing her belongings. She hasn't given in. The constant murmur of checking into a hotel assures me of this. There's no way in hell she's staying at a hotel, but since she's packing of her own free will, I have no reason to advise her of this. Not yet.

I stop grinning at the number of F-bombs she drops while shoving designer clothes into her bag when she enters her bathroom. Although not as clear as it was earlier, the evidence of the crime committed here tonight is still shocking. She didn't just have her privacy invaded; her life was targeted.

"Come on," I say, curling my arm around her shoulders to guide her out of the bathroom. "I've got spare toothbrushes at my place. Anything else you need we can get in the morning."

I gather her bag off her monstrous bed and a coat from her closet before heading for her front door.

Regan remains mute the entire time, only shaking her head when I ask, "Do you want to drop by reception on the way out to request a new door?"

I manage to close the door, but with the wood swelling under my boot, it's a tight fit. I doubt it can be reopened without a crowbar and a whole lot of muscle.

My swollen chest stops inflating when Regan advises, "I have a friend in construction. I'll ask him to drop by tomorrow and replace it."

I don't know what compels me, but I can't help but ask, "Does he happen to own this building?"

Relief swallows me whole when Regan shakes her head. "I'd rather my landlord remain unaware of my adventurous night." Put off by my surprised expression, she quickly adds on, "He might raise my rent if he thinks I'm destroying the place."

After a quick nod to hide my suspicion, I chaperone her to the elevator bank at the end of the hallway. We ride the elevator in silence, my thoughts elsewhere. Regan's confession was one development I never anticipated. I thought she'd run to Isaac at the first sign of trouble. Instead, she's hiding from him.

I shouldn't get pleasure from this, but I do.

"I thought you said we were catching the bus?" Regan murmurs when I flag down a taxi outside of her building.

"I thought you said you were staying in a hotel?" I reply with an arrogant smirk.

With a roll of her eyes, Regan clambers into the taxi idling at the curb. In a true show of defiance, she slams the door shut, then advises the taxi driver to leave without me.

It takes me threatening the driver with a lifetime of parking tickets before he finally relents. Lucky—I wasn't joking.

"You shouldn't have given in. He's *only* a PI," Regan advises the driver when I slide into the seat next to her.

With her words hindered by both alcohol and laughter, it's a struggle for me to understand what she says, but her sneer when she mentioned my fake title was as bad as the time she believed I was an accountant. Both were laced with disgust.

While our taxi makes the ten-mile trip to my apartment, I seek Brandon's details in the FBI database. I don't have to be discreet.

Regan is too busy glancing out the window, lost in thought, to pay me any attention.

I find Brandon's information relatively quickly. As suspected, he's so fresh out of the academy, he's still wearing diapers. He was recruited to Theresa's division only four days ago.

Preferring old school conversations over evidence-encrypted text messages, I dial Brandon's number then raise my phone to my ear.

He answers two seconds later. His greeting isn't one fellow agents generally give. "How did you get my number?"

I smile, pleased by the evidence his tone just unlocked. Brandon is as methodical as me when it comes to his job. Otherwise, how did he know it was me calling?

"I have my ways."

A groan is the only reply Brandon gives.

"Listen, I need you to gather evidence from Regan's apartment. Fingerprints, photos of the scene, and anything else you might think is useful. . ."

My words trail off when Brandon asks, "Such as a bright pink vibrator sitting discarded on the bathroom floor?"

I pull my cell away from my ear, clear any congestion inside with a quick wiggle of my finger, then reattach my phone. "What did you say?"

"A bright pink vibr—"

I cough, drowning out the remainder of his sentence. "I heard what you said. You don't need to repeat it."

Brandon chuckles, amused by the pain in my tone. I'm glad he finds our conversation entertaining. The only reaction I'm gaining from it's suspicion.

"Why are you already at Regan's apartment?"

The mention of her name for the second time in under a minute gains Regan's attention. I smile to assure her everything is fine before twisting my torso away from her.

"I saw you leave, figured you wouldn't have had time to adequately assess the scene," Brandon answers.

Although he's right, it doesn't weaken my suspicion. I don't like others up in my business, and Brandon is so far up there, I feel like the evidence he just unearthed is being used on me as his intrusive instrument of choice.

"Vibrators don't get logged into evidence—"

"They do if they pertain to the crime," Brandon corrects.

"In some cases, that can be true. But in this case, it's *not* required," I grind out through clenched teeth.

Brandon's life hangs precariously in the wind when he laughs. "I know, I was just messing with you."

His hearty chuckle is pushed aside for a noisy swallow when I snarl, "Do it again and see how it ends for you." Even knowing he's helping me hasn't lessened my jealousy in the slightest. This isn't a standard case for me. This is as personal as it gets.

My focus shifts from Brandon to the taxi driver when he pulls into the entrance of a hotel on Westward Way. "What are you doing?"

Regan's swift exit from the backseat answers my question on his behalf. I call out for her, but she's swallowed by a sea of foot traffic not even two steps later.

"I'll call you back," I advise Brandon before thrusting my FBI identification onto the glass panel separating the driver and me. "If you so much as budge an inch from where you are parked, my threat won't be a threat."

His eyes meet mine in the rearview mirror before his head

bobs up and down. Confident he'll follow my order, I take off after Regan. Since she's lugging a bag full of clothes and a stomach full of whiskey, it doesn't take me long to close the gap between us. She's standing at the check-in counter of the hotel, her foot tapping in sync with the clerk attempting to check her in.

The alcohol in her system must be affecting her smarts. Every man, woman and child knows the first thing a manic stalker does is search for their target in the hotels and motels bordering their town. That's why they scare you out of your home, to drive you out of your comfort zone.

Regan's eyes rocket to mine when I snatch the hotel card from the receptionist's hand and dump it back on her side of the counter. We fight like a couple on the verge of divorce when her bag is the next thing seized. She already wants me dead for forcing her out of her apartment without all the girly necessities she believes she can't live without. Now she wants to kill me with her bare hands for stripping her beloved clothing from her grasp.

Realizing she'd rather live with me than without her shimmery slips and tight skirts, I wretch her beloved bag from her grip and hightail it to our taxi.

Just as I anticipated, Regan is on my heels two seconds later. "This is against the law. I could have you prosecuted!"

After throwing open the taxi door, I fling her bag inside. When she dives in after it, her flaring coat awards the men eyeing her a rare peek at her bare backside.

I scan the men's faces into my memory bank before sliding into the taxi after Regan. The tightness of my jaw and narrowed eyes is all the driver needs to see to understand my demands. He locks the doors in a jiffy before continuing our trip.

Regan jingles the locks for the next three miles. When they

fail to unlatch, she resorts to pleading with the driver. When he suddenly develops an inability to understand English, she snatches my cellphone out of my hand and slides her finger across the screen. "What moron doesn't have a lock code on their phone?"

Since her question isn't rhetorical, I don't answer her. She dials a number known by heart before pushing my phone close to her ear. I could shut down her attempts to flee more diligently, but I'm hoping a little bit of leniency will reveal I have no intentions of keeping her against her will. I merely want to keep her safe.

My efforts appear to go unnoticed when Regan stammers, "Isaac, it's Regan. I. . .ah. . ." She sighs softly before adding on, "I left my cellphone on the entranceway table. I know how upset you get when you can't reach me, so I just wanted to let you know if you need me you'll need to contact me via this number."

She shifts her eyes to mine, wordlessly asking if my number is private. When I shake my head, she says, "It should be displayed on your screen. I don't know how long I'll be out of town. Probably just a day or two. Don't panic. Hunter ran a full background search before I agreed to meet with him."

Even though I know she's lying, jealousy blackens my veins. I hate the idea of her with anyone, much less the fact Isaac keeps tabs on who she's dating.

"If I don't talk to you before, I'll see you on Monday, okay?"

She waits as if she expects him to answer. It's a clever ploy of deception I didn't think her hazy brain could create in her inebriated state. If I hadn't heard the familiar beep of a voicemail kicking in at the start of their call, I would have assumed their conversation was two-sided.

After a few more seconds, she says, "Bye," hangs up, then wipes Isaac's number from my recently called list. With a shit-eating grin spread across her beautiful face, she hands my phone back to me.

"Just a lawyer, eh?" I ask, sliding my cell into my pocket. Deleting Isaac's number from my phone won't stop me from finding it, but for now, he's the least of my problems.

Well, for the most part.

"Who's Isaac?"

"Who's Brandon? I thought PI's went it alone?" Regan retorts, proving she's more clued in on underhanded surveillance than I first gave her credit for.

"He's a colleague of mine," I answer truthfully, hoping it will open a line of communication between us. "I only met him tonight. He seems alright, but I'll hold my verdict until I know him a little longer." I lick my dry lips. "Your turn."

Confident I am telling the truth, she says, "Isaac is also a colleague of mine. I've known him for a few years. He's a little overprotective, especially when it comes to bozos overtaking his protective detail."

I smile, my acting skills top notch. "Ah, he's the guy from the hospital? Your knight in shining armor?"

Regan nods, believing my pathetic attempt to act coy. Her eyes fall to her thighs when I ask, "If he's a friend of yours, why didn't you tell him what happened tonight?"

"As I said, Isaac is a little overprotective."

I return her eyes to mine via her chin. I try to ignore the extra flutter her neck gets when I cup her jaw, but my acting skills have been so overused tonight, I have no talents left.

"What happened tonight isn't normal, Rae. There's no shame speaking up about it."

"I know," she agrees with a halfhearted nod. "It's just not

something I want vocalized."

"That you have a stalker—?"

"That I have an extensive collection of sex toys," she interrupts, gaining the attention of the cabbie.

His attention is so rapt on Regan, he veers into oncoming traffic before an overcorrection hurls us toward a railing. Once he has us back on the right side of the road, he apologizes profusely. It's lucky his eyes are brimming with remorse, or I'd arrest him with a lot more than just reckless driving to his list of convictions.

Regan waves her hand to the driver, using him as an example when she explains, "I was joking, but clearly some men love the idea of a woman pleasing herself." She huffs before continuing, "Others can't stand the thought. They get paranoid they're being rendered obsolete."

Although shocked at the change of direction in our conversation, I know where it stems from. She's using her appeal to sidestep my interrogation. It's a pity for her I've interrogated the best evasion artists in the country during my years at the Bureau.

"Some men are intimidated by a knowledgeable woman. But not this little black duck." I give her a saucy wink. "Only men not worthy of the challenge would find it concerning." I seek her gaze. When I get it—wide-with-lust eyes and all—I murmur, "However, this isn't about your sexual capabilities. It's about your safety. That should always come first, Regan."

And just like that, our conversation is back on track.

"My safety comes before anything," Regan assures me, her drunken slur not detracting from her sincerity. "That's why I tried to check into a hotel. You've lied to me more times than you've been honest, and you dissed me within minutes of kissing me, yet all I want to do is shred off your clothes and jump aboard for a ride.

That's not something a sane woman does. You make me unhinged, Alex, and quite frankly, I don't like it."

Jesus. Fucking. Christ. They don't prepare you for this in the academy. No red-blooded man could be trained for this. Regan is dynamite. She's beautiful, smart, and brave. But she's also bad for business. I am an agent. I'm investigating her boss. This cannot happen.

Her breathing shallows when I scoot closer to her. It stops altogether when I ask, "What if I promise to keep my hands to myself. Will you follow my plan then?"

Regan sighs a long and disappointing moan. Some good comes of it. The whiskey fanning my face ensures me I'm doing the right thing.

"I'll take that as a yes—?"

"I'll take that as your solemn vow that you're gay?" Regan bites back, stunning me with her quick-wittedness. "Goddammit, my gaydar is usually rock-solid."

Even aware she's goading me for the hundredth time tonight, I can't harness my ego. "Did our kiss not assure you I'm straight? You couldn't *feel* the effect it had on me?"

I'm two seconds away from being charged with indecent exposure when Regan screws up her nose and gags, as if turned off at the prospect of another grind up against her front door.

"Mercifully, I'm saved from prosecution when she faintly mumbles, "I felt it. Why do you think I want to see it?"

My ability to reply is lost when the taxi pulls to the front of my building. When I attempt to hand him some bills from my wallet, he gestures for me not to bother. "The entertainment more than covered the fare."

"I bet he wouldn't say that if you had whipped your cock out like you wanted to," Regan murmurs into my ear, the alcohol heating her veins making her forget the serious reason we're here.

Not wanting any resident of Ravenshoe to owe me a favor, I squeeze a bundle of bills through the partition separating the driver and me. He grumbles something under his breath but pockets my money all the same.

"It's a little shady for a PI," Regan insults when I join her on the sidewalk of my building. The slur of her words proves my assumption that she's tiptoed from tipsy to drunk during our travels. "I guess it makes sense. If you live amongst the riffraff, they won't be as suspicious about your loitering eye."

Her fake snotty tone forces a smile to crack my mouth. "It's definitely not up to your standards, but it has a bed, toilet, and hot water. What more do you need than that?"

The creak of a security gate drowns out Regan's reply. She remains as quiet as a church mouse when we make our way up the cracked concrete stairwell of my building. Thankfully, the department adhered to my request for a mid-floor dwelling, as Regan sounds two seconds from passing out. For a woman who runs every morning as if she's outrunning the boogeyman, she's a little unfit. We've barely scaled four flights of stairs.

I realize my assumptions are way off the mark when Regan mumbles, "Have they heard of security lighting? This place is really dark."

After switching her bag from my left to my right hand, I curl my other hand over hers, halving its shake. "Just one floor to go, then we're in the open."

She nods but remains silent. Her pulse stops thrumming through our conjoined hands when we reach my floor. I had an outdoor security light fitted the day I arrived in Ravenshoe. It flicks on the instant our feet hit the landing.

"Is this you?" she asks when we stop at my door, but her tone relays she already knows my answer.

I nod anyway.

She takes in the two doors next to mine. "How many other tenants are on this floor?"

"It's just me right now. Ms. Emerson moved out a couple of weeks ago, and Carly's away visiting her parents."

Regan's eyes snap to mine. "Why doesn't Carly get a fancy salutation?" Jealousy energizes her tone.

I smirk, loving her possessiveness but hating it at the same time. I'd give anything for our situation to be different, for her to work for anyone but Isaac, but I learned a long time ago that wishes are never granted to men like me. I have to work for everything I have—including relationships.

"Carly is twenty-four. Ms. Emerson is sixty-five," I explain when anger stretches from Regan's stomach to her face from my delay.

She spreads her hands across her cocked hip, making my night even more torturous. "Your point being?"

My smirk morphs into a genuine smile. She's extra cute when she's green with envy. "My momma taught me to respect my elders, that's all," I force out through the annoyance clutching my throat. *She's not cute. She's not yours. She's an assignment— nothing more.*

"Oh." Her lips twitch, but not another syllable leaves her mouth.

It's for the best. The only solution I could think of to tame her sass was sealing my mouth over hers. That's not a sensible thing for a man in my predicament to do—*again*. I broke god knows how many rules kissing her, but the backlash I could endure if anyone discovers I brought a target to a government building would be mammoth.

I could have protected Regan at any hotel of her choosing, but the apartments stacked above and below mine are swarming with agents—old and new. She's safer here than she'll be anywhere. For that reason, and that reason alone, she will stay here. I'd rather lose my position than put her life in jeopardy. I can't explain it any more simply than that.

Regan's hands fall from her hips when my front door pops open with a creak. The floor plan of my apartment is modest, but it's clean and nicely furnished.

I enter and flip on a light. One bulb lights up my entire property. "My bedroom is through the hall; the bathroom is opposite it."

"*The* bathroom, as in you only have one?" Regan gingerly shadows me into the manly space.

When I nod, she groans, making it apparent tonight won't just be hard on me.

"The kitchen is to your left, the living room to the right. That's pretty much it."

Regan stops so abruptly, I crash into her. "What about the guest room? Where's that?" Her eyes scan the dimly lit space as if she's willing an additional bedroom to magically appear.

When several blinks fail to summon one, I notify her, "There's only one room."

Her eyes rocket to mine, but the lust quickly dims when she hears my reply. "I'll take the couch."

Her cheeks redden as a growl rumbles in her chest cavity. "Three strikes and you're out of the game!"

I don't have a chance to question her cryptic reply before she snatches her bag from my hand and hotfoots it to the only hallway in my apartment. I can tell the exact moment she discovers my bedroom. It isn't because she slams the door with the same dramatic edge as when I forfeited our game of tonsil hockey. It's the lack of door slamming that gives away her location. Because the hinges on my bedroom door were broken, I removed it two months ago with the intention of replacing it. The hinges are now brand new, but I never got around to putting the door back on.

"If I discover the toilet seat up, I'll murder you in your sleep," Regan shouts in warning before violently shutting the only door in my apartment. It's attached to the microscopic bathroom that's been lacking fresh towels since I moved in months ago.

I gulp loudly. I thought my biggest battle tonight would be getting Regan to my apartment. Only now am I realizing keeping her here will be the real challenge.

CHAPTER FIFTEEN

I don't know why I'm showering. My skin is so clean, it's gleaming like I'm vying for a part in *Twilight*.

It's a pity soap can't clean my insides just as well.

The whiskey heating my veins has me feeling fearless, but the shake of my hands started long before alcohol scorched my throat. When I walked into my apartment this evening, the same odd feeling I got at Substanz years ago bombarded me. Instead of validating my intuition, I brushed it off as a consequence of my botched attempt at seducing Alex. I thought my lack of mojo had me misreading the facts but I should have known better. My intuition has never led me astray. Not with Luca. Not with Alex. And not now with the deranged person who wants to cut off private regions of my body and send them to hell where I supposedly belong.

Angry women I am used to. No matter how many times I pledge that taken men are not on my radar, they never believe me. I'm not out to steal your husbands, ladies. Even a faint discoloration on the ring finger has me running for the hills. So if your man is out trawling for a date, project your issues onto him instead of the poor, unsuspecting victim he wants to buy a drink. I didn't ask for him to sit next to me, just like I didn't ask for you to call me every derogatory name under the sun. We women should stick together when it comes to lying pieces of shit who pretend they're single the instant they leave home, not drag each other down. We are sisters, so how about we start acting like it?

Although I've dealt with my fair share of ill-informed women. I am fairly sure tonight's incident isn't a revenge-seeking wife. It had a personal edge to it, like the assailant knows me better than half the people in my inner circle.

What gives it away?

The fact they called me Rae. No one calls me Rae anymore—not even my dad. The instant he discovered it was my "stripper" name, he went back to calling me Regan. Even though I assured him multiple times that cabaret dancing isn't stripping, he claimed the amount of cleavage on display made it seem as though it was.

So that only leaves one person who calls me Rae: Alex. You'd think that would make him suspect number one. But for some reason, he isn't on my hit list. Although stupid to admit considering I hardly know him, I trust him. He reminds me a lot of Isaac. He's protective, stern, and has a heart bigger than Texas. *He also doesn't want to touch me with a six-foot pole.*

Whining at my inner monologue, I remove the suds from my body before stepping out of the shower. The knocks keep coming when I realize I forgot to bring a towel in with me. I could use my satin slip to dry myself, but then what will I sleep in? It's freezing in here.

"Alex!" I shout, hoping there's a magic way he can bring me a towel without seeing me naked—*again!*

My hands dart up to cover my breasts when Alex answers not even two seconds later. His voice is so clear, I swear he's just outside the bathroom door.

My suspicion is proven spot on when I notice a shadow under the door. He either bolted to the door the instant I called his name, or he's been standing behind it the entire time I've been showering. Recalling his snooping ways in the hospital months ago, I'll go with the latter.

"Did you need something?" Alex asks, shocked by my delay.

"Uh." I scan his bathroom one more time to make sure I haven't missed seeing a towel. "I need a towel."

"Uh-huh. Do you want me to bring it in?" Hope rings in his tone. . . *or is it wit?*

Wanting to test a theory, I reply, "No! I'm naked. Just leave it by the door."

Alex groans. "Okay. Party pooper."

His shadow doesn't budge an inch—not even for a second—before he says, "It's by the door, waiting for you."

"Thanks." I grimace, having no idea what to make of this. I wait for Alex's shadow to disappear. It's a long and cold minute.

"Alex?"

"Yes, Regan." He answers me in the same manner he did when I shouted his name. It's virile and hot, and it makes me squirm.

Hating the lust-crazed idiot I'm becoming, I snarl, "I can see your shadow under the door, you nincompoop!"

The need for a towel is lost when Alex replies, "I know." His voice is laced with self-assuredness.

People see confidence as a bad thing. I do not. Games, on the other hand, they piss me off something major. I don't play games. . . unless I'm the one instigating them.

After throwing my satin slip over my bone-dry body, I toss open the bathroom door with just as much force. Alex is standing on the other side, looking as smug as a lion in mating season. He keeps his eyes locked on my face, but I know he doesn't need to lower them to take in the whole picture. The snarl of his top lip is all the indication I need to know he is disappointed about my covered frame.

His eyes return to my face when I bark, "I don't play games, Alex. Haven't since I was a child."

I barge past him and storm into his room, only to remember halfway there his room has no door for me to hide behind. Peeved, I spin back around. Except for the cozy living room on my right, there's nowhere for me to go, and Alex knows it. His smile is stretched ear to ear, his chest puffed high.

"Is this why you brought me here? To add to my torment?" He physically shunts from my snappy tone, but it doesn't stop me saying, "I've been fucked around multiple times tonight, so unless you intend to fuck me for real, leave me the hell alone!"

"Hey, come on, this wasn't my intention," he replies when he spots stupid moisture looming in my eyes. "I thought a little playfulness would loosen the tension between us, not make it worse."

"Well, you were shit wrong!" I push out through the lump in my throat.

I hate dramatics; I'm just too scared by tonight's events to reel in my feelings. The hate in the note scrawled across my vanity mirror scares the shit out of me. A madman was in my house. If Alex hadn't showed up when he did, who knows what would have happened.

"Obviously, I have a lot to learn when it comes to comical acts," Alex remarks, stepping closer to me.

"Clearly." I'm shocked at his submissiveness. He took the reins so well tonight, I would have never guessed he'd hand them over just as quickly.

While he bridges the distance between us, my eyes drift to the wall, hating the sympathy brimming in his. "What's going on, Rae? You were in that shower so long, I was growing worried you had escaped via the exhaust fan vent."

A smile cracks my lips. His question was laced with worry, but there was pure panic in his last statement. He truly believes I'd crawl through a vent to elude him. Apparently it isn't just his comedic schtick needing some work—my flirting skills also need some. I'm not running from him. I'm struggling not to chase him.

"I tried to escape." I rub my cheeks with my hand to ensure no tears have fallen. They haven't—thank god. "The hole wasn't big enough for me to squeeze through."

Alex shakes his head, barely concealing his smirk. I flinch for the quickest second when he raises a towel to my shoulders to dry the water puddled there. Although the heavy decline of his Adam's apple discloses he noticed my cowardly response, he acts oblivious.

Once my shoulders are as dry as my throat, he switches his dedication to my hair. While he pampers me as no man ever has, I take in another slow breath. I study him carefully, confident he will not only protect me—he could utterly destroy me. Before him, I didn't care if my actions were seen as slutty. I was who I was. Nobody was going to change me. But as I stare into Alex's endless dark gaze, my thoughts turn dangerous. I want more—*I deserve more*. He just doesn't seem willing to give me what I want.

My eyes stop dancing between Alex's when he asks, "A penny for your thoughts?" His old saying leads to the first genuine smile on my face all night. That's an adage my great grannie always said. She was the light of my life before she lost her battle with cancer two years ago.

I answer Alex's suggestion in the same manner I always did to my gran, "My thoughts are worth more than a penny, so I'm inclined to counterbid."

His oceanic eyes drift around his clean but bland apartment. "Look around, Rae. I've got nothing but pennies to offer." His saying seems more directed at the thoughts I kept in my head than the ones I vocalized. When he returns his eyes to mine, he adds on, "Unless all you're after is an ear? I've got two of them."

For the first time tonight his voice sounds genuinely sincere. "Is this on the clock, or. . .?" I leave my question open for him to answer how he sees fit.

I can see myself talking to him as a friend. I have a lot of male friends—way more than female—but if our chat is part of the secret life he doesn't want to disclose, his offer will be a no-go for me. If I want someone to rush in and save me, I'll call Isaac. I don't want that. I want someone willing to help me sort through my confusion, not eradicate it on my behalf.

Although Alex's to and fro routine frustrates me, the fact he knew I was in a low place without asking what crawled up my ass proves he could be the man for the job. He just needs to decide if he's man enough to accept the challenge.

He proves it without a doubt when he pledges, "I'll never be on the clock with you, Rae. *Ever.*"

His reply seems more detrimental to him than me. I don't know why?

His interrogation starts before I've had time to prep for it. "Do you have an inkling on your stalker's identity?"

Disappointment darts through his eyes when I shake my head. "No, but I'm reasonably sure he's from my past."

"What makes you say that?" He continues drying my hair as if it's a perfectly normal thing for him to do. It's a smooth move on his behalf. His subtle nurturing is relaxing me so I can address his questions.

"Did you recognize him? If you saw him, a sketch artist could compose an outline of his face. You'll be amazed by the details unearthed when someone is asked to describe someone. Husbands recall things they failed to notice in day to day life when they depict their wives."

"All I saw was a blur." The defeat in Alex's eyes is pushed aside for hope when I quickly add on, "But the message left on the vanity mirror is more revealing than his face." I swallow several times, hoping it will help me ease out my next set of words. "He addressed me as Rae. No one calls me Rae anymore."

"Except me," Alex fills in the words I couldn't produce.

When I nod, he asks, "Are you suspicious of my intentions?"

The caution in his tone makes my lips furl. "No. Not at all. Even Superman couldn't take up residence in my bathroom in the short period of time between our kiss and you breaking down my door. Although, I'm a little skeptical about a few things."

I can see he's dying to ask me what I'm doubtful about, but he doesn't want to push me. That has me opening up to him more easily than usual. "Why did you come back?"

I realize an hour long shower didn't eradicate my tipsy state when Alex's tongue delves out to replenish his lips. I'm in the process of the first deep and meaningful conversation I've had since Luca's death, and all I'm thinking about is how I can get another taste of Alex's mouth. *What the hell is wrong with me?*

My eyes lift from Alex's mouth to his eyes when he says, "As I said earlier, I wanted to apologize—"

"Bullshit," I shout, calling him out as the liar he is, while also praying he'll mistake the conflicting emotions in my eyes as anger. "If you wanted to apologize, you would have done it over the phone. That's how all liars cover their asses."

When I push off my feet to head into his room, he shadows me. "We're not done with our conversation, Rae."

"Yes, we are. I'm too tired to handle *this* right now." The way I emphasize "this" assures him I'm not referring to my home invader. "You should have just kissed me and left."

"And let him hurt you? No!" The brutal shake of Alex's head makes me dizzy.

I throw down the duvet on his bed with force. "What do you think you're doing, Alex?"

He takes a step back, shocked by the devastation in my tone. He isn't the only one. I'm not needy. I don't cling to men and beg for their scraps. I'm fierce. I'm independent. *I'm so fucking drunk on this man, he's more damaging to my senses than the whiskey I guzzled to forget his brutal rejection.*

After folding down the covers to match my side of the bed, Alex discloses, "I'm trying to keep you safe."

Honesty rings in his tone, but it doesn't stop me from saying, "By treating me like I have an STD. I'm clean, you know. You can't catch a disease from a dildo."

When he fails to respond to my taunt as I hoped, I stomp my foot down as if I am a child. "Why won't you touch me?!"

"Because I can't!" Alex shouts, his voice so loud I hear it twice when it bounces off the stark walls of his room. "I'm not a normal man, Regan. I have responsibilities, an oath to serve—"

"Believe me, I know you're not normal," I interrupt, hearing only what I want to hear. "Normal men don't knock back the chance to bed a woman like me." I freeze when a notion I haven't considered before smacks into me. "You're not married, are you?"

While cursing under my breath, I scan his room for evidence of matrimony. I can't believe I was so caught up studying his super long eyelashes and devastatingly handsome face, I didn't adequately evaluate his relationship status as I do every other man I've "dated." I guess my lapse in procedure can be excused. We're not dating. We're not anything, really.

The color stops draining from my cheeks when Alex wiggles his ring finger in the air. There isn't the slightest discoloration to be seen.

I wait for relief to engulf me.

It never comes.

I'm more confused now than I've ever been. If he's not married, why is he holding back? I can see he is struggling as much as me, and his naughty thoughts aren't being encouraged by alcohol either. I'm certain the heady scent of lust doesn't solely belong to me.

"Do you have a girlfriend?"

Anger fades from Alex's face before he shakes his head.

"A semi-casual hookup?"

He continues shaking his head. "No, Rae. It's nothing like that."

I twist my lips to hide the sly grin I shouldn't have before questioning, "What about a boyfriend?"

Alex glares at me, making me sticky enough for another shower. "I'm not gay."

I know he isn't; I'm just perplexed by why he looks at me as if he wants to devour me and curse the day he met me at the same time.

Realizing a woozy head won't get me close to unraveling a man as complex as Alex, I slip between the sheets on his bed. I don't know why I thought whiskey would be the answer to my confusion. I'm a cosmopolitan girl for a reason. Hard liquor causes a direct hit to my senses, making me more unhinged than usual.

"Is this bed even a double?" I grumble when my feet dangle off the mattress. I'm tall for a girl, but I'm still a few inches shorter than Alex. "How can you sleep in here? Your knees must be around your ears." An alcohol-inspired giggle rolls up my chest. "Oh. Now it makes sense. Why let a woman please you when you can do it yourself?"

My faint giggle turns into full-blown laughter when Alex hooks my ankle to yank me to his side of the bed. He leans over me, bringing him and his six-feet-plus glorious body parallel with my suddenly aching frame. If he weren't holding his weight off me with his elbows, vital parts of our bodies would fit together perfectly.

When our eyes lock, something changes between us. His gaze is hot enough to burn Satan and cold enough to freeze water. I don't know how it's possible for him to have conflicting responses, but there's no doubt he's torn.

I stare at him, doing my best to plead my case without words. My pleas will stop altogether if he'd just answer one of them—the most important one. The one thrumming between my legs.

My endeavor to seduce Alex without words is lost when he

mutters, "Quit your whining. You're not a baby. This is a bed. You sleep in it. That's it."

"Sleeping isn't the only thing you can do in a be—"

He cuts off my sentence by pressing his finger to my lips. The zap of his touch could light the country for a week. "Sleep is the only thing you can do in my bed."

If I could cross my arms over my chest, I would. Instead, I glare at him. *Asshole!*

He smirks as if he heard my inner monologue. Good. If his finger wasn't glued to my mouth, I'd throw a few more choice words into the mix.

Believing he has me subdued, he returns to a standing position. He's discreet, but I don't miss his quick glance at my bare thighs. If I were a lady in waiting, I'd yank my negligee to a respectable level. Pity for all involved, I'm anything but modest.

Even more so when Alex murmurs, "Sleep, then in the morning, you can make me breakfast." An arrogant wink finalizes his stone age statement.

"I'm not making you shit." I sound like a spoiled princess. Rightfully so. I am one. My daddy treats Raquel and me as if we are royalty, so why shouldn't every other man in our realm?

Alex continues speaking as if I never spoke, "Then, once you've cleaned up, we'll go through the evidence Brandon gathered—together. If we put that big brain of yours to use, you might stop listening to its evil counterpart."

I shouldn't smile, but I do. Usually, it's the guys who are accused of thinking with the head between their legs instead of the big one on their shoulders. This is the first time I've been accused of it. I like it.

When Alex gives me one final glance before heading for the

door, the thrust of my lungs doubles. He's not being a bigoted pig because he's a narrowminded idiot stuck in the fifties. He knows there are only two options when it comes to tackling someone as defiant as me. He either fights me into submission or fucks me into it.

Before I can advise him I'd much prefer the latter, he mutters, "Goodnight, Rae." His voice is mired with disappointment.

Not waiting for me to return his farewell, he exits his room without so much of a backward glance. I would go after him, but my limbs are weighed down by confusion. All I can do is stare at the tiny strip of flooring separating us. It's only a few feet in width, but it feels bigger than the ocean.

CHAPTER SIXTEEN

"Who did you say it was for?"

I scrub at my tired eyes while Brandon replies, "I used Isaac's case file number on all correspondence. Technically, I'm not being insubordinate."

An approving murmur vibrates my lips. That's smart. Regan is part of Isaac's team, so forensics wouldn't be suspicious about a set of gloves collected from Isaac's apartment being logged into his evidence chain.

"How long until we get a match?" I stretch to loosen the massive knot in my back. I haven't slept on a couch since my college days, so my back is on a long list of body parts feeling the effects of my restless night.

I want to blame a lumpy sofa for all my restlessness, but it only accounts for one-tenth of the shit I've been dealing with the last eight hours. Leaving Regan untouched last night. . . frankly, I didn't think I had it in me. My chest tightens just at the thought of the sleepy smile she gave me in the seconds leading up to my departure. She knows I'm holding back; she just has no clue why. I could come clean and save us both a whole heap of heartache, but considering I'm more scared of losing her than keeping her safe, that option didn't linger in my mind for long.

Brandon breaks my train of thought by disclosing, "We may not get a match. I handled the gloves carefully, but you know how finicky latex is. With the amount of powder coating the fingers, any evidence may be too degraded to process." His tone is as disappointing as the sigh parting my lips. "No useable hair follicles were found in the hat."

It pains me to say, but I somehow manage it, "That's not surprising. Good perps don't leave a contaminated crime scene."

Brandon murmurs, agreeing with me. While raking my fingers through my hair, which is still in bad need of a cut, I drop my eyes to the evidence Brandon had couriered to my apartment over an hour ago. Regan's stalker is as smart as the woman he's harassing. Her apartment was spotless, even more than usual since he drenched every surface he touched with bleach. He even wore the disposable socks and overalls our forensic guys don while combing a crime scene. Unfortunately, they disintegrated in Regan's fireplace before Brandon could salvage them.

"What about surveillance? Are the security personnel at her building being cooperative?"

Brandon makes a *pfft* sound. "They say access can't be granted without authority from the owner. He's supposedly on a business trip until next month."

The slam of a van door drowns out my huff. "Lucky I don't need his permission. I've got all the data I need right in front of me." A keyboard stroke bellows down the line before Brandon asks, "Who do you want the unencrypted data sent again?"

"Dane Lieberman." I spell out Dane's surname to ensure it goes to the right person. "He's not officially in our agency anymore, but he has a way with computers. He'll find an entrance no matter how tight their doors are shut."

A tense stretch of silence crosses between us. It's so long, I'm wary our call has been disconnected. If it weren't for Brandon's heavy breathing from his gallop down the stairwell of Regan's apartment, I'd check our connection.

Brandon's silence comes to an end when he asks, "He's not a rogue agent, is he?"

A rumbling of laughter bubbles up my chest, more a pained laugh than one of happiness. It's similar to my laugh when I convinced myself over a dozen times last night that Regan didn't want me to reenter my room to answer the questions I left wide open. She wanted me to return for the same reason I wished I could have. It's distressing how quickly she has slithered under my skin. Five years ago, I excused my stupidity based on my age and rookie status. I can't use that excuse now.

Annoyed by both Brandon's insinuation and the shitstorm I've thrown myself into, I snarl, "Dane is as far from a rogue agent as you can get."

"Then why is he unofficial? There are only two ways agents leave: they're either dead or on charges. Which category does he belong to?" The authoritativeness in Brandon's tone shocks me. He's too demure to pull off such a tone.

"Your pulse doesn't need to flatline for this job to kill you, Brandon." I say his name with the same sternness he used when addressing me, but mine is more convincing of my anger. "Dane paid his dues in ways you'll *never* understand, so I suggest the next time you consider insinuating he's a corrupt, rogue scum, you stop and take a hard fucking look at yourself because Dane has more patriotism in his pinkie finger than you have in your entire body."

Regan's entrance doesn't prevent me from continuing my speech. If anything, her presence adds gasoline to the fire brewing in my gut. "A hero is a man who walks into the gunfire—not the one directing him from behind a safety barrier."

Stealing Brandon's chance to reply, I disconnect our call. Unlike last night, Regan barely blinks at my temper when I peg my phone across the living room. It shatters on impact, scattering warped plastic and glass onto the carpet the Bureau had installed two weeks before I moved in.

I drag my hand across the scruff hiding my jawline while sucking in deep breaths. It takes several slow inhalations before I garner the strength to raise my eyes to Regan. Thankfully, she isn't scared by my display of violence. She's turned on by it.

That's not something I can handle right now, not with Dane in the forefront of my mind. I've told myself many times the past five years that Regan isn't responsible for Dane's injuries, but I'm having a hard time swallowing that argument this morning. If I hadn't gone after Regan, Dane wouldn't have backed me up. If he didn't always have my back, he wouldn't have been shot. That makes Regan just as much to blame for Dane's life-altering injuries as I am. We both played a part in that fateful day.

"Tell me everything you know. I need to know it all, Regan."

When Regan shakes her head, either denying my request or advising she's unsure of my demand, I growl, "The perp is approximately twenty-six to twenty-eight years old. He has golden hair, similar to mine. From his slim build and lack of strength, he would have been the dweeb at school, someone people like you and your hotshot friends would have picked on—"

"Hey!"

I continue talking as if she didn't interrupt me. "Stalkers don't turn violent for no reason. You must have done something to him, pissed him off in some way. This could be as simple as denying an advance or circulating a dick pic he sent you, but it has to be something. He didn't target you for no reason, but if you continually play the victim, we'll never understand why he wants to harm you, possibly even kill you. . ."

I stop talking when an apple smacks into my chest. The hit is so brutal, my chest protests by making me cough up half a lung. My brain has barely registered the first blow when I'm struck again. This time, it's an orange.

"Don't you dare put this on me!" Regan snarls before tossing a pear, banana, and a thankfully ripe dragon fruit across the room. "I'm playing the victim because I *AM* the victim! I didn't ask him to stalk me, and I sure as hell didn't ask you to rush in and save me!"

Out of both fruit and words, she charges for the front door. Her anger is so white-hot, she doesn't register she's wearing only a satin slip and has bare feet. I guess she doesn't need to be concerned about being harassed on the street. Her glare is sufficient to have any man running scared. Me included. Except, I'm not running away from her; I'm running to her.

Before she can escape my apartment, I slam the door shut and crowd her against it. She has the ability to take me down in under a second. I've witnessed her complete the necessary maneuver multiple times during the self-defense classes she takes twice a week at a local gym, but since she knows I have no intention of hurting her, she keeps her elbows tucked into her sides and forehead braced on the door. If I couldn't see the tears threatening to spill down her cheeks, I have no doubt she'd put up more resistance.

"You saw what I saw, Rae. You read what he wants to do to you. If you don't open up to me, he *will* hurt you." The honesty in my tone can't be concealed. I've seen cases like this many times in my career. It rarely ends well for the victim. "I swear to you, you know who he is. You've just got it locked away as a bad memory or don't want to recall it because it will riddle you with guilt, but I guarantee you, during some stage of your life, you have met the man responsible for what happened last night. It could have been last week, or it could have been years ago, but you know him. You've just got to dig deep to unearth his identity."

When she remains quiet, I push back from the door, giving her enough room to slip away from me. With memories of Dane's injuries holding my empathy bone hostage, I went in too hard. I shouldn't have pushed her, I'm just. . . *scared*. You have no idea how hard that is for me to admit. I didn't sleep a wink last night because all I could see was Regan's stalker's threat being played out. I've seen some fucked up things in my time, but this was by far the worst. Her stalker doesn't just want to disfigure her, he wants to mutilate both her body and spirit. And in a way, I just played into his hand by placing the blame on Regan's shoulders instead of the man truly responsible.

"You're right. This isn't your fault. I should have never made out it was, but I stand by what I said about you knowing who this is. Everything before that was bullshit. You're not to blame—"

"Yes, I am," Regan interrupts, her voice strong enough to break through the tension teeming between us. "I am to blame, just not in the way you're thinking."

Her knees clash when she pivots around to face me. She's on the verge of tears, making my guilt bone-crushing.

"I don't circulate dick pics, nor am I nasty to admirers. I merely keep my distance. Some men are okay with that. Others. . ." she peers straight into my eyes, ensuring I know I am in the "others" category, ". . .have a hard time with it. They don't understand why I don't demand they call me in the morning, or they introduce me to their parents. They want me to care about them when I don't. I don't sugarcoat anything, Alex. If I want you, I'll tell you. If I don't, you'll know that just as quickly. If this is the reason I am being stalked, then you can drop your investigation. I'm not changing who I am because one man's ego got bitch-slapped. I've done that once in my life. It didn't end well. I'm not doing it again."

Pretending her last comment didn't pique my curiosity, I say, "I can't drop this case, Rae. I won't let him get away with this."

"Why, because you're a PI, and investigating people is in your job description?" The sneer of my job title tells me she doesn't believe I'm a private investigator, but for some reason, she's not calling me out as a liar. This time, anyway.

I shake my head. "This has nothing to do with my job description and everything to do with you."

The fire in her eyes reveals I answered as she hoped, but that isn't why I said what I did. I am being straight up honest.

"You have the right to turn down whoever you want without worrying about the repercussions. The idea of you with anyone agitates the shit out of me, but if you want to walk out of my life right now and head straight into the arms of another man, there's sweet fuck all I can do about it. That's your right."

"You'll let me leave if I want to?" She sounds as pained to ask her question as I felt hearing it.

I swivel my tongue around my mouth, easing the dryness inside before answering, "If that's what you want, I'll let you go. But I'm not dropping this case." My eyes dance between hers, which are greener than usual. "Is that what you want, Rae? Do you want to leave?"

She deliberates for barely a second—*it seems like a shit load longer*—before gingerly shaking her head. I try to rein in my delight; my attempts are borderline. She may need protecting from me more than anybody, but I'll never let anyone harm her—*not even me.*

"Can I show you something?" My voice is less angsty than earlier, more understanding.

When Regan nods, I direct her back to my living room. Her unease makes the usual three strides from the door to my couch double the length. She's not accustomed to giving in without a fight, although I'm not really sure she's giving up. Her defenses are still up, primed and ready to pounce if necessary.

After clearing the fruit platter Regan unknowingly served me for breakfast, I gesture for her to sit. Although I pigheadedly requested she make me breakfast, I never expected she actually would.

Regan dips her chin, scarcely concealing her grin. I stare at her, stunned. She heard my thoughts without even looking at me. *Who the fuck is this woman?*

Shrugging off my desire to drill her for more information, I gather the evidence Brandon amassed overnight. From the number of photos in the file, his investigation was extremely thorough for a rookie technician.

"Can you look through these and tell me if anything is out of place? It could be a missing item or something added." Regan's eyes dart up to mine during my last confession. She seems more creeped out about being left a parting gift than having her possessions stolen. "It could be the most unexpected item, so you need to be diligent. . ."

My words trail off when Regan advises, "A photo frame is missing from my mantel." She points to a group of photos nestled above the open fireplace in her bedroom. "They rearranged the frames to make the gap inconspicuous, but there's a photo missing."

"Are you sure it isn't in another location?" When she shakes her head with certainty, I suggest, "Scan the rest of the photos just to make sure."

She huffs, somewhat frustrated by my lack of trust. I trust her; I just know how discombobulated your brain becomes when you're panicked. That's why I acted so poorly this morning.

"It's not in any of these photos," Regan advises a short time later, placing the paperwork on the coffee table. "It's not a picture that can be easily missed. Luca stood out in a crowd. He never faded into the background."

The possessiveness in her tone annoys me, but since she's talking in past tense, it isn't as notable. The man she's referencing isn't my competition—not right now, anyway.

After scanning my spotlessly clean apartment, Regan returns her gaze to me. "Did I pack my purse? I have a duplicate of the photo in my purse."

The pain in her eyes intensifies when I shake my head. "My priority was getting you out of harm's way, so I didn't grab your phone or purse."

Ignoring the jealousy in my tone that she carries another man's photo with her everywhere she goes, she asks, "Can I borrow your phone then. . .?" Her question falls short when she recalls me demolishing my phone against the brick wall. "What about a laptop? Surely you have one of those?"

My backside lifts an inch off my couch before I remember there's no way she can use my laptop. It isn't just brimming with information on her employer and his scheming ways; there are numerous images of her splashed across the monitor—ones not used for investigative purposes.

"Ah. I don't own a laptop." I curse a million times inside my head for my weak tone before adding on, "Well, I do, but it's at the shop. I got a virus last week. Destroyed the mainframe or some shit like that."

Regan's glare pins me in place—she knows I am lying. Regrettably, her stare doesn't have the same paralyzing effect on her legs. She charges across the room at the speed of a bullet. Her pace is so fast, she'd barely create a blip on the radar.

When I follow after her, I'm once again torn between being a man and an agent. With her satin slip discarded on the floor, she's standing before me in nothing but a scant pair of panties and an impenetrable ability to destroy me. Her body is downright faultless. Smooth long legs, curvy hips, tiny waist, and breasts Hugh Hefner would have liquidated the Playboy mansion for to feature in his magazine. She's perfect—nothing less than pure fucking perfection.

I stop staring at the swell of her bountiful bosoms when she asks, "How many blocks away is the internet café we drove past last night?"

She tugs a tight pair of designer jeans up her thighs while she waits for me to answer. I stare at her, unmoving and unspeaking. She can't seriously expect me to carry a conversation while her tits are out, staring at me, begging to be consumed.

I'm drawn from my inappropriate thoughts when Regan drags a satin shirt over her head. You'd think being denied the opportunity to gawk at her naked breasts would snap my focus back to the task at hand. It doesn't. Her nipples are budded against the satin material of her shirt, and the fit is so snug, if it weren't for its purple coloring, I could pretend she's still naked.

Regan clicks her fingers in front of my face. She appears stunned by my braindead response. I don't know why. I'm neither an agent or a man in her presence. I'm a bumbling idiot.

"What would you prefer?" When I stare at her, fucking lost, she fills in, "The internet café or my apartment? Which is the safer option?"

"Neither." I'm not talking with my cock. I'm being straight up honest. Her stalker isn't a standard run-of-the-mill crazy. He's dangerous. So, until he's apprehended, I'd rather she stay right here, preferably with a similar amount of clothing she was wearing thirty seconds ago. Perhaps even a little less. Her panties were tiny, but they still hid a treasure trove of goodness.

Regan's rolls her eyes. "We're doing one or the other, Alex, so pick quickly, or I'll choose for you."

Ignoring my beet-red cheeks warning of my growing anger, she heads back for the living room. She doesn't stop like I expect. She crosses straight through it, her focus on my outdated kitchen. The black knee-high "fuck me" boots she put on sometime during my coronary attack click the tiled floor as she seeks something apparently hidden in the bare bones of my kitchen cupboards.

When she discovers nothing but tubs of frosting and the occasional condiment, she pivots around to face me. I can tell she's curious about my apparent obsession with calorie-laden foods, but with her focus on other matters, she reins in her need to know everything. *Barely.*

"Where are the pennies you referenced last night? I've got no purse or phone, which means I have no way to fund my campaign, leaving the task to you, my campaign manager."

Before I can voice an objection, she spots my wallet sitting on the dining nook separating the living room from the kitchen. I push off my feet, beating her to my wallet by half a heartbeat. I'm not worried she'll fleece the handful of bills not depleted by our taxi ride last night. I don't want her seeing my ID. Not yet.

Regan's top lip forms a snarl when I slip my wallet into my back pocket. Hoping to evade an interrogation on my sudden back-flip on a trip to a cafe, I caution, "You should reconsider your shoes. The café is at least three blocks from here."

Although I declared minutes ago that she's safer here, with her standing mere inches from my working and unlocked laptop, a morning adventure sounds mighty enticing right now.

"Puh-leeze. I can walk miles in these babies." Even with enough room between us to park a train, Regan's chest somehow scrapes mine when she scoots past me. "It's only when they're digging in some random guy's ass do issues arrive."

With a growl, I follow her giggling frame out of my apartment, striving with all my might not to react with the same idiocy I used last night. Let me tell you, it's a fucking hard feat.

CHAPTER SEVENTEEN

I turn away from Alex when I feel tears pricking my eyes. I haven't scrolled Luca's Facebook page in nearly two years. I thought as the years moved on, so would the number of posts added to his wall each day. I was wrong. His page is as up-to-date today as it was the day his life perished nearly eight years ago. I shouldn't be surprised. He was loved by many, even though he was only truly known by one: me.

After eradicating the nerves from my face with a few sharp breaths, I divert my focus back to the computer monitor. The image I am looking for is concealed by many, but just as I told Alex earlier, Luca could never fade into the background.

I locate the photo I am looking for in under a second. It's imprinted in my mind as indelibly as Luca engraved his name on my heart.

"This is the photo missing from my apartment," I advise Alex, pointing to a picture of Luca wearing a bright orange jumpsuit with a bunch of leaves woven through his dark locks. "Someone called him a fruitcake at a school dance. He apparently missed the cake part of his statement. Determined to stop bullying, he wore an orange suit for a week. If it wasn't for his mother demanding to wash it, who knows how long his protest would have gone on for."

"How many times was his head flushed in the toilet that week?" Alex asks, somewhat amused, somewhat apprehensive.

"None," I reply with a smile, wordlessly assuring him the sheen in my eyes isn't from bad memories. "Everyone loved Luca, just as he loved everyone." My smile fades at the end of my sentence.

Nodding, Alex jots something down on the notepad he borrowed from a waitress after she took our order. If she had it her way, I'm confident Alex's request for a straight black coffee with three sugars wouldn't be the only dish she'd serve him today. She's cute, but her clumsy, *look at me, you're so pretty I'm falling over my feet* routine is lost on Alex.

I heard his back molars grind together after her second "accidental" drop of dishware had her bosoms scraping his thigh, and I'm fairly sure he was two seconds from combusting when his request for a refill had more than a coffee pot thrust in his face. The waitress wants to believe my presence is the sole reason Alex has rejected her numerous flirtations, but I know that isn't the case. Alex wants a woman who challenges him. That's why I didn't bolt the instant he gave me permission to leave.

Bickering with him has been the most entertaining thing I've done the past five years. Working for Isaac is great. My extensive knowledge on business acquisitions and keeping his assets away from the prying eyes of the IRS in a legal manner has kept my bank account well nourished, but nothing can replicate the high of bantering with someone as equally stubborn as you. It's the reason

Luca and I immediately clicked. We were similar, yet so very unique. It's just unfortunate his baggage was a lot more complicated than mine.

I stop glaring at the waitress's impromptu grind of a stool when Alex asks, "Do you recognize anyone besides Luca in this photo?"

I drop my eyes to the photo. "To be honest, until now, I didn't notice anyone milling around in the background. I've only ever saw Luca."

Alex grinds his teeth for the second time in under twenty minutes. His jealousy is utterly ridiculous. Luca is dead—he can't come back from that—but even if he could, they would never be in competition. Jealousy cost Luca his life. I won't let that happen again.

Pretending I can't feel my heart whacking my chest, I appraise the photo more diligently. There are over a dozen people snapping Luca's picture during his protest against bullying. They're all smiling at him. . . all except one.

"Who's that?" Alex asks, spotting Danielle's slumped lips as rapidly as me. "How tall is Luca? She seems around the same height as him."

I shake my head. "The angles in the photo are off since Luca is standing at the top of the quadrant. Danielle was so much shorter than him, everyone always joked she'd need a chair to kiss him." My breaths shorten as fading memories trap me. "She brought a foldable stepladder to prom."

Recalling what Alex said earlier, I lock my eyes with his. "I *never* picked on her, but I didn't stop the ridicule either. The last time I saw her, she barged past me, clearly distraught."

Alex reaches out to touch me, but something stops him. "I doubt she's your stalker, Rae," he advises, lowering his eyes and hands back to the computer we're commanding. "The assailant is approximately five-eight. You said she's short."

I shake my head so sternly, tears nearly tumble down my cheeks. "No. I said she was shorter than Luca. He was six-foot-four. That's nearly eight inches difference. It could be her."

When Alex's lips twist, revealing he needs convincing, I take up the campaign. "You said the assailant had feminine hands. That he was on the small side—svelte or slim or whatever the fuck you said. Why can't it be her?! Not all stalkers are men."

"Rae. . ." He clasps his hand over mine, gaining the attention of both the waitress and me. "Why would Danielle threaten you now? Stalkers don't wait decades to put their notions into play. They act impulsively, often before fully evaluating their plan of attack—"

"Not when they're clinically insane!" My words instantly stop Alex's crusade to calm me down. They also gain the attention of every customer in the café.

After a few deep breaths, I explain myself better, "Danielle had. . . *issues*. Instead of handling Luca's rejections with dignity, she often lashed out violently. Luca took it in stride. I wasn't as willing to let things slide." Alex listens intently, not once interrupting me. I don't know him well enough yet to decipher if that's a good or bad thing. "After an incident that involved my car being spray-painted, I sought help from a third party."

"You contacted the police?" Alex asks, hopeful.

"No," I reply, my tone as appalled as it was last night when he suggested the same thing. I have no qualms with law enforcement officers, but after the incident at Substanz, they aren't the first people I call when in trouble. "I spoke to the pastor at Danielle's church."

Alex's brows stitch, seemingly unaware of the consequences of bringing someone's faith into question.

I use his silence to my advantage. "He divulged private information—stuff I wasn't to mention to anyone."

"Things you told Luca?" Alex asks, finally clueing in.

I nod.

"And Danielle discovered you were his source?"

My nod turns into a shake. "That's when things took a dangerous turn. Luca wouldn't tell Danielle anything. It shifted her obsession from manic jealousy to . . . *this*." I wiggle my finger at the photo we are discussing.

Alex jots down a few more notes. "How long after the photo was taken did Danielle arrive at prom with a stepladder in tow?"

It sounds even more ridiculous coming from an outside source, but I still answer, "Around six months."

Alex purses his lips. "So something must have happened between this photo and prom to switch her focus back to lust so quickly?" Because he's more summarizing than asking a question, I don't answer him. "We just need to discover what it was."

"So you believe me? You think Danielle is responsible for the incident last night?"

"I didn't say that." Standing from his chair, he gathers the half dozen pages of notes he scribbled down the past hour. "But we'll never find out here. We need to gather more evidence."

My wide eyes dance between his. "Evidence? From where?"

My heart launches into my throat when he nudges his head to the photos scattered across the computer monitor. They all featured Luca and me at our favorite hangout spot when we were seventeen: the football field of our local high school.

"You're certifiably mad. We can't go to Texas!" I shout when the truth smacks into me.

"Why not? It's Saturday. I'm not expected anywhere until Tuesday, and you told Isaac you'll be unreachable for a few days. Why can't we go to Texas?"

He waves his hand in the air to summon the waitress. She's at his side two seconds later, stealing my chance to reply. When he rummages through his wallet to find the correct change to pay our bill, I delve my hand into his faded leather pouch, snag every one of his bills in a firm grip, then thrust them into the idiotic brunette's chest. She doesn't deserve the massive tip I just awarded her, but if it gets her on her merry way and my conversation with Alex back on track, she can have every damn bill I can conjure.

Unfortunately, a big tip isn't what the waitress has her sights set on. She wants something big—it just doesn't hold monetary value.

"Buzz off." I shove her away with an aggressive push.

Alex watches her disappointing retreat before returning his slit eyes to mine. "Do you know you can be arrested just for placing your hands on her?"

Hating that he's taking her side, I snarl, "Do you know I could sue her for emotional distress? I may never get a full night's sleep again after watching her inappropriate barstool hump." My stupidity is even more apparent since I barely slept a wink last night. "Come to think of it, I'll aid the barstool in prosecuting her for sexual assault! He didn't ask to have her skanky cooch ground against him!"

I take a step back when Alex unexpectedly twangs my pouty lip. "Fuck you're sexy when you're jealous."

He grunts when my fist lands in his stomach. "I'm not jealous! I'm . . ." *I've got nothing — not a single fucking thing.*

Loving my inability to deny his claim, Alex smiles a cocky grin, forcing me to snarl, "You're a moronic asshole who has no chance in hell of taking me to Texas!"

After snagging my jacket from the back of my chair, I spin on my heels then leave. I make it two steps down the cracked sidewalk of the cafe before I remember I have no transportation. The blisters on my feet are the size of Mount Everest, and I am without my cellphone and purse. Fortunately, my firepit stubbornness forces me to continue my expedition—one slow step at a time.

Ignoring Alex's repeated offer to give me a piggyback ride as he had earlier this morning, I gingerly take a step forward, closely followed by another and then another.

After ten dozen painstakingly slow strides, Alex says, "You do realize you're walking in the wrong direction, right? My apartment is that way." I can't see him, but I can imagine him hooking his thumb behind his shoulder.

Incapable of backing down without a fight, I respond, "Who said I was going to your apartment?"

"The closest pay phone is over a mile away. My apartment is half a mile, maybe a little less. Figured you'd prefer the latter."

I growl at the humor in his tone. It isn't a husky little pussy cat roar. It's a tigress about to maim the carcass it slayed.

"Who said I'm seeking a pay phone? Perhaps I am on the hunt for a gullible idiot with more than a few pennies to his name," I seethe through clenched teeth. "I'm sure he'll drive me home without a single dime being mentioned. There are plenty of ways for a girl to make payment without handing over her hard-earned money."

The last half of my childish remark comes out with a squeal from Alex curling his arm around my waist and hoisting me off the ground. He tosses me over his shoulder without breaking a sweat before stomping in the direction of his apartment.

While pounding his back with my fists, I scream blue murder, begging for a random passerby to save me from the madman holding me captive.

I'm sickened to admit, no one comes to my rescue.

"I'm going to have you arrested for kidnapping!"

"Oh goodie," Alex replies, his tone more snarky than happy. "While you're at it, make sure they draw up the charges as a federal offense, as this crime is about to cross state borders."

"We are *not* going to Texas!"

CHAPTER EIGHTEEN

"We're going to Texas."

How in the world Alex got me to agree to this, I truly don't know. It was somewhere between him pinning me to his bed and throwing me in a cold shower. *Or perhaps it was a combination of them both?* He only stopped me clawing at him by holding me hostage on his bed with his body, and he couldn't calm me down with a cold shower without entering the stall with me, minus his shirt, of course.

That must be the issue? My stupid ass libido found her voice again, but instead of focusing on a man deserving of her time, she wants the dumb ass standing in front of her.

Apparently, Alex's chivalrous remark on me being free to leave when I wish only counts when jealousy isn't at play. I shouldn't goad him like I do, but what can I say, it's fun. Alex is a handsome man, but when he's angry—walking on the blistering sun! That's the only way I can describe it. He's *THAT* hot.

Although I wish he weren't right now. He has two first-class flight attendants' panties in a twist as easily as he did when he had his ticket upgraded from economy to first class. I booked our flights in different sections for a bit of breathing space, but all it took was a couple of words and a smile, and Alex's hundred dollar ticket was exchanged for one that costs nearly a thousand dollars.

When I demanded the check-in clerk amend my ticket price to match Alex's, she glared at my fancy platinum credit card before her eyes drifted to the address on my license. I argued that the credit card and penthouse apartment on the wealthiest street in Ravenshoe are perks of my job, but she wasn't having any of it. If I wanted to travel first class, I had to pay for the privilege.

I should have switched Alex's ticket with mine. There are plenty of men in first-class with us, but there's no way I could match the attention he's receiving. First the waitress, then the check-in clerk, now two pretty bimbos whose legs stretch for miles and smiles just as big.

James, the head attendant for our section, is downright gorgeous, but even if my gaydar were utterly awry, I'd still know he has a fascination with handsome blond-haired, blue-eyed men. How? He's been fussing over Alex as much as the female attendants.

The man gliding down the aisle, on the other hand, sign me up. I can understand the stewardess's offer for a free upgrade. He's so handsome, I'd let him ride me for free. A five o'clock shadow darkens his jaw, which makes his devastatingly handsome face even more dangerous. He has dark eyes, either green or brown, I can't tell from this distance, and his body is lean yet appealing enough to set my pulse racing.

When he takes the seat opposite me, his head casually slants my way. The friendly smile he offers me gains him the devotion of every female within a one-mile radius. Not because Alex has competition, but because they lose Alex's attention.

The instant Alex spotted the direction of the stranger's welcoming gaze, he left the first-class bar for the first time since the seatbelt sign was switched off nearly thirty minutes ago.

The slight flutter in my pulse due to the handsome stranger's face triples when Alex stops in front of me. Just the vast span of his sexy thighs wipes the stranger from my thoughts, but in case they didn't, he bobs down to align our eyes.

Handsome stranger? What stranger? Is all my brain computes when I'm awarded the utter devotion of Alex's oceanic eyes. A hint of familiarity clears some fog in my envy-laden brain when his squinted gaze burns into mine. I've often wondered if our friendliness was an effect of the crazy sexual current firing between us, but now I'm not so sure. There's more at stake here than just sexual hunger. It's something deeper and more compelling. I just can't for the life of me work out what it is.

"Scoot over," Alex requests, nudging his head to the plush cubical that's been vacant the past thirty minutes.

Pheromones pump out of him when I shake my head, denying his request. "I'm fine here."

After his eyes drift to the suit-clad gentleman sitting across from us, watching our exchange with attentive eyes, Alex returns them to me. "You wanted the window seat; I'm giving you the window seat. Scoot over." His volume rises with each syllable he speaks. It's laced with jealousy and utterly delicious for my dented ego to devour.

Thankful for the chance to even the playing field, I push Alex to the side as I did the waitress earlier today. "Shove off; I've got business to take care of," I purr with my hankering eyes locked on the hottie across from me.

I'm lying, but Alex doesn't know that. If I wanted to play with the gentleman in seat 4C, we'd already be swapping spit in the sandpit, but he isn't the man I want to share germs with. It's the man glaring at me, unappreciative of my quick return in the marathon tit-for-tat game we've been playing the past two months.

Alex should be grateful a majority of my focus this weekend has centered around discovering the identity of the person invading my privacy, because if it didn't, I might have moved on from our game of cat and mouse by now. I don't play well with others. That's why I've gone it alone so long. People get burned when I let my emotions enter the mix. *Some even die.*

Imprisoned by painful memories, I move to Alex's seat like he requested. I need a breather before I say or do something I'll regret. The adrenaline Alex's attention comes with far exceeds the worry of being harmed by my stalker, but the other emotions it arrived with aren't as welcoming. I'm a confident, classy lady. . . who feels like she's on a Slip'n Slide with no end in sight. It's fun while you're riding it, but no matter how enjoyable the ride is, you'll forever be on the bottom rung once it's over.

Since he was anticipating more of a challenge, Alex remains quiet as he fills the seat my ass has kept warm since we left the tarmac. When he places an untouched glass of gin on the side table between us, I seize it, swallow it, then signal for another.

Spotting James's agreeing nod to my request, Alex shakes his head, retracting my order. I shoot him a vicious glare. "I need a drink—"

"You need to talk. Vent. Scream. You do *not* need alcohol to do either of those things," Alex interrupts, his voice a cross between stern and remorseful. He doesn't like pushing me out of my comfort zone any less than he hates his inability to rein in his jealousy when it comes to me. Both are as frustrating as hell to him.

"Bottling up your emotions never works, Rae. The longer you hold them in, the bigger the explosion will be once they come undone."

I let the gin speak on my behalf: "Maybe they'll never grow big enough to explode?"

Alex doesn't say a word; he just stares straight at me, expressing a million thoughts without a single syllable escaping his lips.

His understanding has me whispering words I swore I'd never utter, "I can't tell anyone; I promised to keep his secret forever."

"There are no secrets that won't be revealed with time." When I stiffen, physically erecting my defense wall, Alex quickly adds on, "But that doesn't mean you have to be the person responsible for revealing them. You can tell me as much or as little as you want. I'm not grading your honesty, Regan. I'm being your friend."

The first half of his statement makes my heart flutter. The second half causes my stomach to heave. He's the second man in my life to place me in the "friends zone." I want to say it impacts me the second time as much as the first, but nothing will knock me as hard Luca rejecting me.

"I loved Luca," I whisper, staring at my fingers twisted in the hem of my shirt. "But he never loved me the same way." My words choke a little when I confess, "Instead of accepting what he could give me, I wanted more."

I smile through the tears attempting to roll down my face. "For years, we appeared to have the perfect relationship. He was the beloved sports star and all-around mentor of our high school, and I was the wild child he wrangled into the wholesome country girl I was born to be. It truly seemed as if we were destined for greatness."

"Until it came tumbling down?" Alex questions, reminding me I am not just reminiscing; I'm admitting to sins I should have confessed to years ago.

I nod. "Things went downhill rather quickly when we left for college. Our relationship was easy in high school. There were only a handful of students in our class. Most were in long-term relationships, and those who weren't didn't have any interest in neither Luca or me. Excluding Danielle, we never had any issues."

Alex sits on the very edge of his chair, bringing our knees within touching distance. "College doesn't just bring temptation into play; it comes with an assortment of crazy shit. Some grow. Others wilt."

His comment makes me smile. "Luca prospered. He was the happiest I had ever seen him." It's the fight of my life to express my next set of words without a cracking voice. "At the time, I thought I was the one responsible for the goofy grin on his face. It was only when I walked into his dorm room the night of his accident did I realize his happiness had nothing to do with me, and everything to do with the person he was wrapped up in."

I swipe a stupid rogue tear slipping down my cheek before shifting my eyes to the window so Alex won't see my tears. "If I had just accepted his decision, we wouldn't have fought, and he wouldn't have made the decision he made that night. I'm the reason he's dead. I was so enraged with jealousy, I broke a promise I swore to keep for eternity. I revealed his secret to the world."

Alex's warm breaths fan my nape when he assures, "What happened wasn't your fault, Rae—"

"Yes, it was. I am the reason he's dead. I made him choose. I told him he had to pick." My eyes glisten with tears as secrets I've kept for years involuntarily spill from my lips. "I wanted him to pick me, and to everyone around us, that was what he did. As far as anyone was concerned, he forever put me first. Only I know that wasn't true. He didn't pick either of us that night. He chose to perpetuate the lie he had been living for years." *He continued pretending he was straight.*

I grow worried I said my last confession out loud when Alex's interweaves our fingers. I'm not looking at him, but I can tell he wants to say more. He just can't force his tongue to fire words out of his mouth. I have no doubt his mind is racing a million miles an hour as he struggles to click the pieces together. He'll be working on the puzzle for years to come. I'm still struggling to understand all the jagged edges, and I'm a prime piece of the picture.

I was in love with a man who could never love me back. If that didn't already make me an idiot, I left Luca's frat party thinking I had won. What can I say? I was naïve and stupid.

The truth rained down on me not even ten minutes later.

Within minutes of us leaving campus, Luca's cellphone blew up. Guests at the party had recorded our fight, spreading rumors of his sexual proclivities through our school like wildfire. Luca wasn't just fielding calls from his friends and teammates, though, he also had Coach Gulliver seeking confirmation on his "homosexual ways."

It was in that instant it dawned on me why Luca asked me to pledge what I did on his sixteenth birthday. The college we both attended was small, but the mindset of the locals was even smaller than that. No matter how much he contributed to the community, it was all forgotten because of stupid words screamed in anger.

I don't know the exact moment Luca made the decision he did the night of our accident, but I am reasonably sure it was somewhere between the numerous messages demanding he rat me out as the two-bit liar I supposedly was and his father's twentieth unanswered call.

Our hometown has been stuck in a time warp since the seventies, but at the time, it appeared as if Luca's secret had reached his parents' ears.

Luca was devastated—beyond my ability to comfort him.

If he had just answered his father's call, he would have realized they were none the wiser to his secret. His dad was merely calling him to update him on his grandma's condition after her second hip replacement.

To this day, his parents are still unaware of his sexual orientation.

And if I have it my way, that's how it will stay.

CHAPTER NINETEEN

James loiters at the end of the aisle, unsure whether he should adhere to Regan's request for another gin and tonic or abide by my stern warning for him to keep away. Considering Regan's chest is currently open and exposed for the world to see, I signal for him to approach.

He does, albeit hesitantly. After shoving a double shot of bitter liquor into my hands, he skedaddles away. His desire to flee isn't shocking. I hate the pained expression on Regan's face, and I'm the man responsible for it.

When I urged her to open up to me, I never anticipated the confession I got. I've been on edge from the minute she announced the missing photo from her mantel was a man. I didn't care who Luca was, or how influential he had been in her life; I hated him with every essence of my being.

The way her eyes lit up when she talked about him filled me with an immense amount of jealousy. That's why I've been such an asshat since we left the internet café. I was so focused on removing Luca from her memories, I didn't register her grief when she spoke of him. I thought he was an old flame—a competitor. I'm a moron.

Hoping to make matters right, I hand Regan the glass James gave me. She smiles in thanks before taking a delicate sip. I want to continue our conversation, but I don't know if she's truly up to it. I've pushed her so far out of her comfort zone the past twenty-four hours, she's most likely having a hard time recognizing herself. I love Regan's stubborn, beautiful, determined personality, so anything I can do to stop her from changing, I will.

I'll even talk with her about another man. "How did you and Luca meet?"

Regan's lips arch against her glass as her glistening eyes stray to mine. They are nowhere near as troubled as they were minutes ago. "Did you know alpacas are flame-resistant?" She asks her question as a six-year-old would to her peers during show and tell.

I've heard rumors that alpacas have fire-retardant coats, but that doesn't stop me from faking ignorance.

When I shake my head, Regan informs me, "Luca wanted to test the theory on my pet alpaca."

"You have a pet alpaca?" Now my interests are genuine. Regan exhibits glam to the nth degree. Imagining her with a farm animal as a pet is an entertaining thought.

"Had. She went to alpaca heaven a few years ago," Regan explains.

When I give her a look, she slaps my arm. "She died of natural causes."

"Uh-huh, sure she did."

She slaps me again, her giggle attracting the attention of everyone surrounding us. James smiles with glee, happy Regan's back to her usual self. The female flight attendants aren't as over-joyed as him. They prefer us bickering over bantering.

I like when we do both.

"Did I tell you about my brother's cunning ability to lick his elbow. . .?"

By the time we land at an airstrip just north of Texas, Regan and I have spilled a lifetime of secrets. I even shared with her the time I peed my pants in the first grade, and my brother covered it up by telling everyone I sat in a puddle. I don't know how he got away with it. The wet patch was in the front of my shorts, not the back.

Regan laughed hysterically when I told her the infamous nick-name Dane made up for me, and her cheeks turned beet red when I revealed my mom forces me to FaceTime with my cat once a week. I have no idea why she got flustered over that. From her wide eyes and inflamed cheeks, you'd swear I was confessing to more risqué activities. . .

My thoughts trail as reality dawns. Stopping halfway down the gangway, I lock my eyes with Regan. "I called Maxx a pretty pussy, didn't I?"

She doesn't answer me. She doesn't need to. The leering grin stretching across her face tells me everything I need to know.

"How many times did I say it?"

"More than enough to keep my fantasies well stocked for the next few weeks," Regan replies with a sassy wink.

While recalling the number of times she squirmed, blushed, and chewed on her lower lip during my confession, I guide her toward the exit I was told our driver would be waiting at.

Upon spotting my name sprawled on a white chauffeur's board for a local hotel, Regan stops walking. "Ah. We're not staying at a hotel." She locks her massively dilated eyes with mine. Our flirty interactions the past two and a half hours have unjumbled the confusion in her eyes, leaving nothing but painstakingly gorgeous green irises. "If my parents discover I was in Texas and didn't visit, I'll be shunned from family gatherings for eternity."

"It's just a night—"

"They wouldn't care if it was a ten-minute layover. When you're in town, you visit. No questions asked." She scans the gathering of people milling around the departure bay waiting for loved ones. "I'm shocked Daddy didn't sense my arrival. He has a weird intuition with his children. When his ears twitch, it's either going to snow, or one of his babies is coming home."

Before I can laugh, a deep barreling voice booms into my ears. "I knew it! My ears don't twitch for no reason!"

My hand darts down for the gun I'm not carrying when Regan is hoisted from the ground by a giant man with dirty jeans and a smile more blinding than the low-hanging sun. He holds Regan so close to his body, I'm confident she's moments from being crushed to death. I should be rushing in to save her from the man with biceps as big as my head, but the only response I can conjure when Regan squeals her father's name is a long, penetrating glare.

The giant standing in front of me isn't close to what I pictured when Regan shared stories about her father. I was anticipating a meek, knee-slapping farmer with pencil thin legs and a crooked smile. My assumptions were so far from the bullseye, my throws didn't even nick the board. Her father is tall and wide, and glaring at me like I'm two inches of foam on his recently poured beer.

"Sir," I greet with a dip of my chin.

When I hold out my hand in offering, he places Regan back on her feet. He doesn't accept my greeting, though; he merely bounces his eyes between Regan and me as though he's assessing if I am a random Neanderthal cozying in on family time, or I'm with Regan.

I drop my hand to my side when his eye does a weird twitching thing. Years of studying body language ensures I can't mistake his annoyance. Mr. Myers is not a fan of mine. He knows my intentions with his daughter aren't noble, and he has no qualms wordlessly notifying me of his knowledge.

My neck cranks to the side when a familiar giggle rings through my ears. It's the same laughter I've heard numerous times the past two hours. When Regan's amused gaze meets mine, I nudge my head to her father, demanding an introduction. She cocks her hip as her arms fold in front of her chest. She's not being straight-up rude; she just loves my uneasiness too much to alleviate it.

I give her a look warning of my impending retribution before returning my eyes to her father. With his daughter failing to jump in with an introduction, the task is left to me.

"Alex," I introduce, once again holding out my hand. "I'm a friend of Regan's."

"Hmm-mmm. *Friend.* Right." Any buzz still thrumming through my veins from our trip dissipates from the irritation in his tone.

When he lowers his eyes to Regan, she stops grinning at my uncomfortable swallow. "Is he your *friend*, baby girl?" His tone reveals precisely what he intends to do to me if Regan says no. I'm mincemeat.

Regan stews on her answer long enough a bead of sweat forms

on my nape. It dribbles down my back when she eventually stammers out, "He came to support me at Luca's memorial."

Now, I'm not the only one sweating. Regan's dad looks just as uncomfortable as me. His reaction makes it clear that this weekend is the first time Regan has attended Luca's memorial. But if it didn't, his next question leaves no doubt. "You're attending this year?"

Regan halfheartedly nods before bumping her hip against mine. If she wants a hero to jump in and save her, she's looking at the wrong man. I have no clue what to say to ease the pain in her eyes, except perhaps, "It's time for Regan to move on. Luca would want that more than anyone."

It dawns on me who Regan gets her knockout smile from when her dad grins as if all his Christmases came at once. I'm glad he got comfort from my reply, but Regan appears on the complete opposite end of the spectrum. The hurt in her eyes has returned stronger than ever, and once again, I am the man responsible for it.

"I'm proud of you, baby girl," her dad assures, hating how pale her cheeks have gotten as much as me. "Your momma and I have wanted you to move on for years. We knew you'd eventually come around, because everything happens at its own pace."

When he tucks her under his arm, she nuzzles her face into his broad chest. I'm left standing in the middle of a busy departure gate when he pivots on his heels and walks away, carting an unsuspecting Regan along with him.

Unsure if their gathering is a private party for two, I stay rooted in my spot. I want to comfort Regan in the same manner her father is, but to do that, I'd have to step over a father who is consoling his daughter. That would never be achieved without violence. And since there's only one time I've taken down a man double my size without a weapon—when I arrested Dwain at Substanz—I'm not eager to put those tactics into play.

If Regan discovers I can take down a man the size of her father, my cover would be jeopardized. Although I'd give anything to take away her pain, I can't let that happen. If she doesn't trust me, every inch of mud we've dragged each other through the past twenty-four hours will be for nothing. I'm standing in Texas for one reason and one reason only: to keep Regan safe. That comes before anything—even my position.

I'm saved from doing something desperate when Regan's father shouts, "Fetch the bags, city boy, and be at my truck within five minutes, or hitchhike your ass home."

His words barely leave his mouth as they disappear through dark tinted doors. Thankfully, Regan agreed to travel with only carryon luggage, meaning there are no additional bags for me to gather. I'm on their heels in under thirty seconds, and in even a shorter amount of time, squished between a cage of baby chickens and a goat as we make the fifty-mile trek to Regan's family home.

CHAPTER TWENTY

I twist my neck back to face Alex when he asks, "Do the goats always ride in the cab of the truck?" His eyes dart between mine and my dad's glaring at him in the rearview mirror as he adds on, "I get the chickens—they're just babies—but this goat appears full grown."

Before I can assure him he isn't going crazy, my dad butts in, "That's Clancy—Regan's pet goat. When Regan's home, Clancy goes wherever Regan goes." He mumbles a few more words under his breath but they're quiet enough neither Alex or I can hear them. "Pet him. He's real friendly."

Missing the brisk shake of my head advising him against it, Alex does as instructed. He pays for his trust not even two seconds later. Clancy's bite isn't firm enough to draw blood, but I'm reasonably sure Alex's hand will bear the imprint of his teeth for the next three to four days.

I pat Alex's knee, enticing his eyes to mine. "He's a bit of a chewer—"

"That's not true," my dad interrupts, hating that I'm soothing the sting to Alex's ego. "He just doesn't like *strangers* moseying in on his turf." He overemphasizes the word "strangers," ensuring Alex can't miss that Clancy isn't the only animal in this truck harboring some disdain. "We don't do well with city folk around here."

Alex braces his chin on his chest to hide his smirk when I roll my eyes at my dad's pompous attitude. I've always loved that my dad is so big and brawny, he didn't just scare boys my age into being gentleman, he also petrified their fathers, but it doesn't have the same effect on me today. Alex doesn't want to hurt me. He wants to save me. Both notions are as frightening as the other.

When I return my eyes front and center to wordlessly warn my dad to quit the larks, a scrap of paper at my feet captures my attention. It's a receipt with flight details scribbled on the back.

After gathering the receipt in my hand, I shift my eyes to my dad. "Who told you I was coming? It was Maisy, wasn't it? Or Beatrice?"

Heat surfaces on my cheeks as I run through the short list of women over seventy in our home town. They and their belittling ways are the reason Luca could never be who he truly wanted to be. He was too concerned about maintaining an image than pursuing happiness. That's why his depression was so hard to overcome. It fed off their negativity until it combusted in the most horrific way.

"Answer me, Dad! Which one of the know-it-all old biddies yapped in your ear this time?"

My dad keeps his eyes on the road, knowing he can't look at me and lie. "No one. It was my ears. You know how they twitch when you girls. . ." His words trail off when I yank on his steering wheel, bringing his beloved truck to the very edge of the asphalt. "Rae! Have you gone tooting mad?! You could get us killed!"

Although I love the return of the nickname he hasn't called me since I was twenty-two, the anger in his tone holds back my joy.

"You lied!" I shout, tossing the crumbled up receipt into his chest. "Those are the *exact* details of our flight today!"

His lips wobble, but not a word escapes them.

Recalling the strict rules my momma raised me with, I shout, "Out!" I nudge my head to his door, giving him his marching orders. "You lie, you walk. That's what momma always says."

"Rae—"

"Out! What's good for one is good for all," I quote, using his words against him. "Liars don't prosper. They also don't get a free ride, so out you go!"

Alex remains as quiet as a church mouse when my dad throws open his door before clambering onto the roadside. He barely squeaks a peep when I slide into my dad's spot, slam my foot on the gas pedal, and leave my dad in a pile of dust.

He doesn't say a word until my dad is nothing but a speck of dirt in the low-hanging sun. "Rae. . ." He articulates my name more sincerely than my dad did. "You can't leave him. We still have over thirty miles to travel."

Our eyes meet in the rearview mirror. "So? That will give him plenty of time to cool down."

"A cold shower is a much better solution for calming down an out-of-control Myers." He aims for his tone to come out cheeky, but all I hear is sexual innuendo. He's amused, but not enough to smile. It's a pity for him I don't need to see his grin to know it's there.

I lower my speed to a less dangerous pace when Alex climbs

into the passenger seat. I am as mad as hell, but I don't want him getting hurt.

The anger blistering my veins simmers when a manly scent engulfs me. Even hours after his last shower, Alex smells clean and fresh. . . and a little bit like Clancy. It doesn't dampen his appeal in the slightest. It suits him. He should wear country more often.

"Did you just sniff me?" Alex asks, sliding into the empty space next to me.

"No!" I immediately retort, lying through my teeth.

My bones jump out of my skin when Alex shouts, "Out!" He yanks on the steering wheel as abruptly as I did a mile ago. "What's good for one is good for all."

"But I wasn't lying," I lie.

Alex waits for me to pull over before arching a brow. He doesn't speak. He doesn't need to. I can read the shit-eating pompousness beaming out of him.

Incapable of ignoring his stern glare for a second longer, my voice wavers, "It was barely a whiff; it doesn't count!"

"You lied; get on your bike." He leans across me to yank on the rusty door handle. When the driver's side door pops open, he nudges me in the shoulder. "You better get a wiggle on; you've only got an hour of sunlight left."

I slam the door shut. "I am not walking. There could be coyotes and rattlesnakes, or god knows what else hiding in the bushes waiting to pounce on me!"

"And honesty?" Alex asks with a twist of his lips. "There could also be that."

I grunt like a wild animal, unappreciative of his underhanded swipe at my integrity. "Who are you to preach?! You've done nothing but lie to me since the day we met!"

He says nothing—of course! A liar doesn't defend himself with lies. He keeps quiet.

Enraged with anger at his continued deceit, I throw open the door I just shut, then slip out of the truck. I barely make it three steps away from the hood when Alex is on my tail.

"When have I lied to you?" his voice roars through both my chest and the deadly quiet afternoon.

I whip around to face him so fast I give myself whiplash. "Oh, I don't know, how about the accountant speech you gave me at the hospital?! Or what about the whole toolbelt incident instead of admitting you were carrying a gun—"

"That was Josie, not me."

I continue talking as if he never spoke, "—Or the fact that you continuously deny me when I know you want me?! How many more examples do you want, Alex? A hundred? I can give you a hundred just from the number of times you've looked at me the past twenty-four hours." He remains quiet, perplexed and blind-sided by my honesty. "A lie doesn't need to be vocalized to be heard. You just have to think it."

"What do you see when you look at me, Regan? A man who can't stop thinking about you? That you're on my mind from when the sun rises to when it goes down, no matter what's happening in my day? That you are the most beautiful woman I've ever fucking seen?! They aren't lies. Nothing I've said or shown you are lies! They are omissions of the truth."

"They're still lies!"

"No, they're not," he denies, stepping closer to me. "A lie is something you do when you are deceiving someone. An omission of truth is sometimes the only option you have when you're trying to protect someone you care about. I don't want to lie to you, Rae, but I sure as fuck don't want to lose you either."

I clutch my chest, trying to lessen its leaps from his words. I thought it was just me. The crackling. The fire. I thought it was all my imagination. But he just proved it isn't. He's as deeply invested as me. Just as confused, but definitely devoted.

Even with a hundred theories running through my head, I can't help but ask, "Who are you, Alex? Really."

If I were to believe the hunch I've been running with since the night we bumped heads in the elevator, he's either an undercover cop or a spy. I honestly don't know which scenario I despise the most.

He licks his cracked lips. "I can't tell you that."

"Can't or don't want to?"

"Can't," he answers without pause. "Yet," he quickly adds on when he spots disappointment in my eyes. "But I will. One day."

"Just not today?"

He smirks, hoping his heart-fluttering smile will have me feeling no pain when he confirms, "Not today. But soon. I promise you, Rae. When the time is right, you'll know everything."

Trusting the honesty beaming out of him, I ask a question I've wanted answered since we met. "Why do you call me Rae? There are only two times I've been called Rae. By my daddy when I was a child, and by the clients at. . ."

I didn't think this through. From what I've heard via the grapevine, Substanz is still in operation. Jayce is no longer at the helm, but the cabaret dancers and cigar-smoking clientele are still in abundance. Although I doubt Alex would judge me on my past, I like the way he looks at me. I don't want to ruin that for anything.

I raise my eyes to Alex's. His quirked brow reveals he didn't miss my fade-to-black comment. "I take it this is what you meant by an omission of the truth?"

With a smile, he nods. "It isn't that you don't want to be honest, just sometimes you can't be. It's like when my sister asked if her butt looked big in her prom dress, even if it was the size of a submarine, I'd never say it was. An omission of the truth isn't about harm; it's about keeping the other person from getting hurt."

His words impact me more than I can explain. For the past eight years, I've felt like I've been living one big fat lie. Now it doesn't feel so bad. I'm not lying to the people I love. I'm stopping them from getting hurt. Those are two entirely different things. So as much as Alex's inability to be honest frustrates me, until I come clean on the lapses I've had the past decade, I can't preach morality.

"Rae. . ."

I slant my head to the side, confused as to why Alex's voice mixed with my father's. For the first time in months, my muddled mind gets a moment of reprieve. I didn't imagine two influential voices mixing together. I heard them as one, delivered with the same amount of sorrow. My father's for lying, and Alex's for his ability to read me like no man ever has.

After thanking a local for the lift, my father closes the gap between us with long, brisk strides. Alex also moves closer. His steps are more imposing than my father's. I should pull away when he lifts his hand to my face, but with his eyes finally free of betrayal, I can't. I want his touch. I want his hands on me. Even more so since I've just realized we're standing mere feet from a parcel of land I will never forget.

I was so caught up bickering with Alex, I didn't recognize the landscape we were driving past, but with my dad's savior whipping past us with his headlights on, the truth is viciously crashing into me. I forgot to turn off at Smith Street, meaning I've driven right into the eye of the storm. We are mere feet from the site of Luca's accident.

"What's going on, Sweetie? Why did you stop here?" my father asks, catching up to us.

He yanks on Alex's shoulder so rigidly, his thumb slips from my mouth. The concern in both Alex and my father's eyes doubles when they scan my ashen cheeks and moisture-filled eyes.

"I. . . uh . . I forgot to turn off," I reply, my voice as low as my heart rate.

Stunned by the sheer terror in my reply, Alex follows the direction of my gaze. Nearly eight years have passed since I visited this site, but the gap in time hasn't hindered my observation skills in the slightest. Even if it had, the late afternoon sun illuminating the cross on the tree that claimed Luca's life quickly floods me with memories.

Although the sun rays bouncing off the white paint appear angelic, the absolute horror tearing at my chest is anything but. I forgot him. It may have only been for a minute, but I still forgot. That's unforgivable.

Upon spotting a rogue tear careening down my cheek, my dad murmurs, "Oh, baby girl." His cracking voice adds to my devastation. "We'll head back to Smith Street; go home via Duke's place. Come on."

Faster than I can blink, he helps me into his truck via the hanging open driver's side door. I bite on the inside of my cheek to stifle a sob when Alex reenters the cab from the opposite side of my father. Instead of sitting where he did earlier, he takes my spot in the passenger seat, squishing me between him and my father's slumped shoulder.

The tension is so high, nothing but the erratic thump of three hearts is heard. After my father executes a U-turn, we quickly slip away from an area responsible for tearing my heart in two, but it comes too late. Nothing can impede the train wreck of memories hammering me: the horrifying words Luca and I screamed at each other as he dangerously careened down the narrow road we are traveling on, the smell when I awoke after twenty minutes of unconsciousness, his low-hanging head. They crash into me like a violent wave, ensuring my eyes have no choice but to release the flood inundating them.

"Don't," Alex murmurs when I protest him seizing my wrist to pull me into his lap. "You either let me hold you, or I'm gonna cut down that damn tree with my bare hands."

My dad's tightened jaw slackens from Alex's comment. He has threatened to destroy a certain tree many times the past eight years.

Although I feel utterly ridiculous grieving one man while nuzzling into the chest of another, I can't help but accept Alex's comfort. He peers down at me without a single pang of doubt in his eyes. His comfort comes with no strings attached. I won't owe him a single dime if I accept what he's offering. He's with me because he wants to be, not because he feels obligated.

That was all I ever asked from Luca.

Only now am I realizing it was the one thing he never gave me.

CHAPTER TWENTY-ONE

"I've got her."

Regan's dad, Hayden, glares at me. "She's my daughter, which means she's my responsibility."

Before I can give him the old, "You can pick your friends, but you can't pick your parents line," a pretty blonde I'd guess to be early to mid-fifties joins our intense standoff. Even though a willow tree shadows half her face, I can confidently declare she's Regan's mother. She's just as beautiful and seemingly just as confident.

"Supper is now over; dessert is up next. If you two aren't inside within the next ten minutes, I'm feeding your share of the pie to the dogs."

After her eyes drift between me sitting in the passenger seat of her husband's truck with a sleeping Regan in my arms, and Regan's dad standing guard at my door, she pivots away with a laugh, leaving me stranded with a man who believes I'm incapable of carrying his daughter up a flight of stairs.

Once the creak of an old screen door screeches through the uncomfortable silence, Hayden's slit eyes lock back with mine. "God dang it, boy, if you make me miss out on Sally's homemade pie, I'll suck out your gizzards with a bucket milker."

I don't know if he's putting on a country accent because we're surrounded by his family dairy farm, or because his patience is running thin. Either way, I'm not giving in. Regan trusts me enough she fell asleep on my chest. I'm not giving that up for anything.

"I swear to you, I won't drop her. Look at her; she's not the least bit worried."

For the first time the past twenty minutes, Hayden does as requested. The deep groove between his blond brows smooths when he notices Regan's unmarred face. She's so blissfully unaware of the volatile situation surrounding her, she's without a single wrinkle or blemish. She's so peaceful, if it weren't for Hayden's demand that we move her into her room, I wouldn't budge an inch. I'd keep her nestled in my chest for eternity.

Rather than allow Hayden to make his own decision, Sally forces one on him. "Hayden, get your ass inside before the workers see you making a fool of yourself. He's a grown man, for crying out loud. He won't drop her like you did when she was a baby."

My quiet snickers cause Regan to stir in my arms. I shush her as if she's a baby I've only just laid down for a nap, praying she remains asleep. I love Regan's sass, and her sharp tongue is even more fire-sparking than her beautiful body, but I also like being the man she can rely on when things get tough. She's struggling tonight, so I want to be there for her.

Hayden's words are delivered via a sneer. "If you drop her—"

"I won't. I swear to god, I'll never let her go." I lower my eyes to his chin, praying he'll miss the possessiveness in my tone. From the way his bottom lip curls into a snarl, I doubt it.

With Hayden guiding my every move, I curl out of his truck and start the sixteen stair climb to Regan's childhood bedroom. Her room is as expected; there are just more dairy cow ornaments than I imagined. It's glamorous, pink, and smells like fresh flowers. . . and perhaps a hint of cow dung?

I'm reasonably sure the last reference is compliments of Hayden. He was so pedantic about directing my every step, he refused to remove his boots—much to Sally's dismay.

"On the left," Hayden instructs me when I move toward Regan's bed on the back wall of her room. "She prefers sleeping on the left so she can see the meadow when she wakes."

Keeping my eyeroll on the down-low, I head for the left side of Regan's bed. Her pasty white skin looks vivid against the hot pink sheets covering her double mattress. Even her platinum blonde hair appears more intense.

I let out a little chuckle when I notice her feet dangle off the edge of her bed.

Hayden doesn't find my laughter appealing. "Something funny, boy?"

I'm saved from explaining myself when Sally enters Regan's room. "Leave the man alone, Hayden. Regan wouldn't have invited him into our home if he was up to no good."

She taps my shoulder in support before dropping her focus to Regan. "She'll be out until morning, so why don't you two go and grab some supper and a shower. It smells like horse manure in here."

My jaw falls open when Hayden murmurs, "That's straight up shit, and it ain't coming from me."

He shrugs as if he never said anything when Sally shoots him a dirty glare. I can understand his defense of ignorance. I use a similar argument when subjected to Regan's intense glare.

While carefully tugging out a cow-printed blanket from beneath Regan's feet, I ask, "Should we wake her for tea? Excluding a few olives, she hasn't eaten since breakfast."

I never knew you could hear a jaw tick until now. Hayden proves you can. Apparently, his daughter's failure to announce her hunger is somehow my fault.

"You didn't feed my girl?"

"I tried. She wouldn't accept anything I offered." My words garble at the end, choked by the fear clutching my throat. From the way Hayden's nostrils are flaring, anyone would swear I just told him I attempted to feed Regan my cock . . . *Oh.*

"I meant food. She's picky about what *food* she consumes."

The redness on Hayden's cheeks doubles. "Of course you meant food. What else would you be talking about?!"

I swallow—harshly. "Condiments?"

Someone file a missing person report, as I'm fairly confident I just signed my death certificate.

"Condiments? Are you sure of that, *boy*?" He says the term usually spoken in a positive light as if it's a derogatory term.

"Hayden. . ."

I stare at Sally, stunned. She utters one word, and Hayden's anger is subdued in an instant. I so much as breathe, and he mentally sharpens his ax.

"Go grab some fresh towels from the linen closet. I forgot to lay them out when you left to pick up Regan."

Hayden stands frozen for a minute, unsure if he's coming or going. He isn't the only one confused. I don't want to leave Regan, but I'm not sure she'd consent to a sleepover. We worked through some issues on the roadside over an hour ago, but we've still got a shit-ton to weather.

Once Hayden leaves—after a silent threat of dismemberment directed my way—Sally's carefree eyes lift to mine. "Are you hungry?"

Her lips tug up in the corners when I shake my head. "Your stomach too twisted with worry to eat?"

My shake turns into a nod.

"If you think it's hard on you, imagine being him." She jerks her chin in the direction Hayden went. "He doesn't just have one woman to take care of; he has three. Four if you include his momma." She's discreet, but I don't miss the faint crinkle of her nose when she mentions Hayden's mom. "Regan is our eldest. She's the one we cut our teeth with. That's even more reason for her daddy to be extra-protective of her. Things have been tough with them since Luca's accident. They both take blame for what happened."

Before I ask how either of them could be blamed for an accident, Hayden reenters the room. The towels in his hands are as girly as Regan's sheets, ensuring I can't miss his silent message. He didn't fetch these towels for me. They are for his baby girl.

Regan's mattress squeaks when Sally stands to her feet. "We'll let you get some shut-eye. Things start early around here, so the earlier you head to bed, the easier you'll rise."

Hayden doesn't announce a single protest with his eyes before Sally curls her hand around his elbow to lug him out of the room. Considering there's a good foot difference in their heights, it's no easy feat for Sally to do, but she manages—somewhat. Her determination proves what I knew from the moment I laid my eyes on her. Regan got her fiery core from her mother.

"If you need anything, we'll be just down the hall."

"Uh-huh. That's right. *Just* down the hall. As in two walls. Six steps. One level," Hayden adds on before his words are swallowed by Sally shutting the door behind them. "I also have a shotgun under my bed!"

I hear them bickering in the hall, but once my focus returns to Regan, their voices fade into the background. Regan looks so peaceful when she's sleeping. Beautiful. Calm. Controlled. *Mine.*

I'm not as surprised by my last admission as I should be. Coming here was a bad idea because the more time I spend with Regan, the deeper I want to sink my hooks into her. I brought her here under the guise we needed to investigate the incident in her apartment last night, but in all honesty, that was a ruse. The conversation I had with Brandon while Regan packed guarantees I can't use evidence-seeking as an excuse for our getaway.

A sick, demented section of my brain wanted Regan alone so I could show her the real me away from the prying eyes of those watching her every move—not just my colleagues, but men like Isaac as well. But instead of doing that, I thrust her into a real-life nightmare by forcing her to face truths she isn't ready to face. I barely know this woman, so what gives me the right to force her to do anything?

I should come clean and admit everything, but if I do that, I not only sacrifice my career, I run the risk of losing Regan. That scares me more than anything. This weekend is my only chance to show Regan who I really am. Then perhaps once I unveil the man behind the job description, she won't be so quick to judge my deceit. Then maybe—just maybe—she'll grant me both items on the top of my wish list.

I can have her and also arrest Isaac. It will truly be a win-win.

CHAPTER TWENTY-TWO

I wake up disoriented and confused. Where I'm waking up is nothing out of the ordinary. I was born and raised on my family ranch, so my childhood room is burned into my retinas. It's the scent surrounding me that's brand new. It's virile and sweet, an intoxicating mix of a manly sexiness and fresh flowers. Considering I know the scent is emanating from an extremely alpha man, it should be odd admitting he smells flowery, but for some reason, it isn't. Floral shampoo and body wash are scents Alex wears well. It's nearly as devastating to my senses as his body curled around mine.

While picturing his enviable lips, chiseled cheekbones, and a jaw that shouldn't be covered with wiry blond hair, the circumstances of our night crash back into me. He comforted me—a man with an impenetrable shell calmed me in my hour of need.

The spell he has had on me since we bumped heads should have lifted, but instead, my quest to bed him is even more ravenous. A weasel of a man would have run for the hills at the first sign of moisture in my eyes. Alex didn't. He bunkered down and rode out the storm. That doesn't just make him admirable; it gains him my respect.

After what he did for me last night, it might not seem like much, but the list of men who have my trust is very slim. The tally now sits at four—sometimes five when Isaac's right-hand man doesn't annoy the shit out of me. Otherwise it was only my dad, brother, and Isaac's names on my list. Now Alex is listed right alongside them.

Does that mean I'll go easy on him when his panties get in a twist? Hell to the no! Gaining someone's respect doesn't mean boredom. I don't care what Alex says, he loves receiving lip as much as he enjoys dishing it. It keeps us on an even playing field and assures no hesitation when I jerk my elbow back to slam it into his ribs.

"What the fuck?" A smile creeps across my lips from the way Alex gasps the words. "Did you just hit me?"

"No," I lie, shaking my head. "I was merely stretching. If you weren't all up in my business, you wouldn't have got hurt."

"Up in your business?" I can't see his eyes, but I don't need to see them to know they're burrowing a hole in the back of my head. "I'm sleeping—"

"With your arms wrapped around my waist and your cock digging into my ass." I grind against him to prove a point.

Mainly.

Not even.

I was merely seeing if my memory was stacked with fact or fiction. It's fact. His cock is as thick now as it was when I was grinding against it Friday night. It's just a pity I couldn't assess its rigidness without my ego being bitch-slapped.

Friday night—a mere two days ago that seems more like a lifetime.

Friday night—the night he dissed me without a word escaping his lips.

Friday night—a night I'd give anything to experience again even with a psychotic stalker and brutal blow to my confidence.

If it weren't for Friday night, Alex and I wouldn't be in my childhood home, spooning like an old married couple who bicker as much as we do. I also wouldn't be tackling issues I should have confronted years ago.

It hurts coming back here, especially this week, but with Alex by my side, the bite is similar to Clancy's warning gnaw. It cautions of impending danger, but it isn't painful enough to stop you looking past the storm clouds for the rainbow sitting on the horizon.

I'm returned to the present by Alex's winded remark, "You didn't complain about me being 'all up in my business' when you were drooling on my chest last night."

My smile widens from his impersonation of my voice, but it doesn't halt my retaliation. "I don't drool."

"Uh, yeah you do. And you talk in your sleep."

I rib him harder this time. "Better to talk in my sleep than snore as loud as you do."

"I do *not* snore!" He sounds more mortified now than when I confronted him about his cock getting friendly with my ass.

I flip over to face him. Bad move. He's not wearing a shirt. "Yeah, you do." The dip in my tone reveals I've noticed his shirt-less torso, glistening tattooed pecs, and a stomach that should be featured in every men's fitness magazine in the state. "You were so loud, the pigs oinked back, grateful for your mating call."

A stretch of silence passes between us, blistering with unbridled lust and excitement. I am consumed by it, utterly defenseless to it. I struggle to breathe through the thickness, but my mouth only opens and closes—no air is sucked in.

Before I can act on one of the many inappropriate thoughts running through my head, Alex throws his head back and laughs. My ability to leave this room without assistance is lost when his deep, husky chuckle vibrates through my body. It's manly and hot and makes me incredibly horny.

Is it possible to come without knowing it? If so, the undeniable wobble of my thighs has me wondering if the thrill from his laughter was just a figment of my imagination. The joy strumming through my veins matches the sensations I experience after I've O'd.

Once Alex's laughter settles down, he lowers his glistening baby blues to my face. They are darkened with undiluted heat.

When he attempts to speak, I beat him to it, "Why are you sleeping in my bed?"

"Ah." He stops talking, seemingly conflicted about whether to tell me the truth or not. He goes for the former when he stammers out, "Your mom thinks we're an item."

I cock a brow. "That's not surprising. She's an old romantic at heart. She believes she can spot a couple from a mile out. My dad, on the other hand. . ." I leave my question open for Alex to answer how he sees fit.

He doesn't keep me waiting long. "Warned me about the shotgun under his bed."

A smile creeps across my face. "You know he's joking, right?"

"About the shotgun, no. I'm certain he has one. About shooting me with it. . .I'm hoping for some leniency," Alex answers without delay, his grin as intoxicating as his confidence makes me. "But even if I'm off the mark with your dad's protectiveness, I know I don't snore."

I roll my eyes. "I might have elaborated on that part of my statement, but I'm sticking with my original complaint. Even if my mom thought we were hot for one another, what gives you the right to share my bed without asking? You could have slept on the floor."

A bucket of water is thrown over my fire-hot attitude when Alex removes a strand of hair from my face. It isn't his caring nature causing my heart to stutter; it's what he says while doing it. "I know. But just like I'm aware I don't snore, I wasn't joking when I said you talk in your sleep." My throat dries when his eyes dance between mine. The lust holding them hostage earlier has dissipated, leaving nothing but respect and understanding. "You called out for Luca a few times last night. That settled once I hopped into bed with you."

I try to deny his assumption. I try to fire off a witty remark that will have him chewing his words like Clancy chomped on his hand yesterday. But with nothing except integrity beaming from his eyes, I'm void of a comeback. I dream of Luca often, so Alex's revelation isn't surprising. There's just one piece of the puzzle he failed to notice. Last night's dream also included him.

After settling my heart rate, I murmur, "So you used a dead boyfriend as an invitation into my bed? Not very diplomatic of you, Mister Fancy Pants." I use his loathed nickname in the hope of easing the tension between us.

It works—somewhat.

"I don't need to use Luca to get to you, Rae." Alex says his comment without the jealousy usually present when I mention Luca. "Apparently, I only need to sidestep these."

The seriousness fueling our conversation is doused when he yanks open my bedside table. "You weren't joking when you said you had a lot of free time when you were younger. I don't even know what half these gadgets are. Like this one. . ." He grunts as if he's lifting a car with his pinkie. "It looks like an unopened tulip, although I'm fairly certain it isn't."

He holds a six-inch clitoral vibrator with fluttering tips an inch from my eyes. I want to pretend my flaming red cheeks are because I'm mad his snooping ways unearthed my extensive collection of sex toys, but it has nothing to do with that. I'm hot from having his body pressed so intimately close to mine.

He seems more concerned with evading our second deep and meaningful in less than twelve hours than maintaining a respectable distance between us, to the extent that we've practically become one. He just needs to insert his extremely large column throbbing against my thigh into my aching column holder, and we'd be perfectly aligned.

Happy to use his skirting skills to my advantage, I say, "That's a multicombination vibrator. It's perfect for vulvar, clitoral, and nipple play. Do you want me to show you how it works?"

The vital organ in Alex's body, which I'm striving to ignore, flexes halfway through my question. He stares down at me with a range of emotions in his eyes. *Excitement. Envy. Lust. . .and remorse?* I don't know why the last one bothers me as much as it does. I'm accustomed to the pity stares, and the "oh, look, it's that poor Myers girl Luca left all alone." I just hate seeing it in Alex's eyes.

"I meant a store clerk demonstration—not an in-depth

rundown on how it works. Look. . ." I snatch the plum purple vibrator out of his hand and switch it on. Shockingly, the batteries are still fresh. "See. The tips flutter to boost arousal and sensitivity."

If I ever have kids, can I please be excused from giving the birds and bees talk? I'm a grown woman who has used sex toys as long as I've been sexually active, yet I'm stammering like a sixth grader who took his mom's butt plug to school for show and tell.

I'm not the only one riding the uncomfortable train. Alex's Adam's apple bobs up and down as his eyes continuously dart between the vibrator and me.

I realize I still have a lot to learn about the man pinning me to a bed for the second time in under twenty-four hours when he asks, "Does this device get you off?"

"Most of the time," I answer with a concealed smirk.

The plump curves of Alex's mouth are showcased in a brilliant light when he licks his dry lips. "Most of the time? Why only most of the time?"

"Well, nearly all the time. It has only failed once."

Something in my tone must give me away. Either that or Alex is a mind reader. "By any chance, was that one-time failure on a Friday night? Say earlier this week?"

His smug tone makes me want to punch him in the stomach. Regrettably—*and thankfully*—it's plastered too close to mine for me to act on my desires.

With a wink exposing he's a mind reader, Alex places my vibrator back in its rightful spot.

Incapable of letting him think he has won, I say, "Hold on a minute. Don't put it away. I need it."

"You *need* it?" When I nod, Alex chokes out, "Right now?"

I breathe through the fire roaring through my midsection from his cock dangerously thickening against my thigh. My struggle for air is evident when I breathlessly quote, "They say an apple a day keeps the doctor away, but all I need is an orgasm."

With a wink as daring as the one he awarded me mere seconds ago, I shove him off me, throw my legs off the bed, then dart for my attached bathroom. When I slam the door shut with me and my fully charged vibrator on the other side, Alex's groan vibrates through both the door and my core, making the need for any gyrating equipment unnecessary.

CHAPTER TWENTY-THREE

My steps out of Regan's bathroom are slow and sluggish. It's barely 5 AM—I kid you not! With all the blood in my body rushing to my lower extremities, I had no clue my interaction with Regan this morning was happening before the sun had even risen. Who bothers looking at a clock when you're awakened by a woman as beautiful and captivating as Regan? Not anyone sane.

I've barely crossed the threshold between the bathroom and Regan's bedroom when a sing-song voice halts my steps. "Whatcha doing?"

Although Regan's voice is missing the angst it held last night when she was gripped by a nightmare, its mischievous edge raises my skepticism. "Showering. You?" I pretend I can't see her sitting on her bed, eating cheese puffs for breakfast.

"Eating cheese puffs," she answers, stating the obvious. "It's what I always do while waiting for the show to begin."

"Show?" My brows lift as I scan the bed she's sitting on, seeking the clothes I laid out before entering the bathroom.

My eyes return to Regan when she drags out, "Yeah. *Show.*" Her face doesn't give anything away, but her eyes' appreciative rake over my body reveal every sordid detail of the "show" she's waiting for.

"Rae. . ."

My words fall short when she stands to her feet to mosey my way. She has her killer *I'm going to destroy you with nothing but my eyes* look down pat. Her hair is sitting on the top of her head in a messy bun only someone as gorgeous as she could pull off, and her face is void of makeup. She's a fucking knockout, and I'm utterly defenseless to her allure.

"It's only fair we even the playing field, right? You've seen mine; now I get to see yours." She slants her head to the side as if to say, *don't worry, I won't kill you just yet* before her eyes stray to the towel sitting dangerously low on my hips. "If it makes you feel any better, we can pretend you're unwell, and I'm the nurse checking your vitals."

After returning her eyes to mine, she pops a cheese puff between her lips and seductively pushes it into her mouth. You'd think comparing my cock to a cheese puff would kill any chance of me getting a boner. It doesn't. I'm so fucking hard, I have no doubt Regan can see the outline of my cock through my towel. Or even worse, I'm pitching a four-person tent.

I could glance down to check, but that's the equivalent of tapping out to a woman as fierce as Regan. I've been called many things, but there's one I'll never be accused of: being a quitter. I'll walk from Texas to Florida butt-naked before I announce defeat in our latest game of tit for tat. Don't get me wrong; I'll happily fall to my knees in front of Regan. But once I'm done with her, I won't be the only one legless.

"Do you always eat cheese puffs for breakfast?" I whip off my towel and dump it at her feet as if I am oblivious to the challenge in her eyes. "I thought you country folks were all about the protein. How are you supposed to have strong bones if you start your day with chips created on the floor of an animal feed factory?"

"Protein doesn't make your bones strong. Milk does," Regan replies, trying her hardest to keep her eyes above my waistline but miserably failing. "Amongst *other* things." Her eyes drop to my crotch when she stutters over the word "other."

Ignoring the way her prolonged stare increases the thickness of my cock, I scan her room once more, seeking my bag. "Have you seen my clothes? I swear I left them right where you were sitting."

"Nope," Regan replies with a shake of her head. "Haven't seen them."

She's a terrible liar. Not only did she blink three times before she tried to pull the wool over my eyes, her lust-filled gaze unintentionally darted to a set of drawers on my left. She's as bad as a drug addict hoping to hide her stash from her parole officer. She just gave away her loot without a single word seeping from her lips.

If it wasn't 5 AM—and I wasn't hard enough to drill through the equator—I'd head straight for the drawer she glanced at. But since I'm working off minimal sleep and a sudden lack of blood supply to my brain, I play along.

"What am I going to do if I can't find my clothes? Your dad threatened to milk my gizzards with a bucket last night, so I don't think he'd appreciate me wandering around his property with my junk hanging out."

Regan's smile makes my idiocy even more perceptible. "I can think of a few things you can do without clothes."

I wait for her teeth to finish raking her lower lip before asking, "Oh, yeah. Like what?"

I wish I had listened to the dirty side of my brain when it demanded I stroke one out in the shower earlier when Regan proceeds to fill the last ounce of air between us. I can't think with this many pheromones pumping through my veins. I can't even talk.

Touch, on the other hand. I have no issues with touch. My fingers weave through Regan's hair to unknot her bun before she's even come to a stop, and my mouth inclines toward hers just as quickly, stealing any chance of a protest.

Well, that *was* my plan.

"Nuh-uh." Regan's lips are so close to mine, her devastating rejection vibrates my mouth before nicking a vital artery in my chest. "We've been there, done that." Her wide-with-need eyes lift to mine. "You left me hanging—twice."

"Twice? When?" Her eyes answer my question on her behalf. "Hell no. I'm not accepting blame for the incident this morning. You weren't the only one left hanging. My cock hasn't stopped pulsating since you left me high and dry. It's fucking distraught after your effort."

I expect Regan's showy personality to illuminate from the devastation in my tone, but for some unknown reason, it has the opposite effect. "Ha! Thanks to you, I haven't climaxed in over two months!" she shouts, clearly peeved.

I wait for her comment to finish stroking my ego before assuring, "I'll make it up to you."

That didn't come out as I had intended, but I'm glad when the anger in Regan's eyes fades to lust. "I'm sure you will. . . but until then, how about we even the playing field?"

I glance down at my cock. As anticipated, it's thick, veiny, and pulsating as much as the little blood vessel in Regan's neck. "I think we're even."

Her cheesy breath fans my lips when she releases a deep exhalation of air. "I think we can do better." Not giving me a chance to seek clarification, she shouts, "Daddy! Can you come up here? I need your help with something."

I take a step back, mortified as fuck when she bobs down to snag my towel off the ground to toss it down the stairwell outside her room.

"Are you insane?! He *will* kill me!"

She laughs even louder at my panicked tone when I dash for the drawer she glanced at earlier. I throw it open with so much force, it sails into the air. I'm not superman; the drawer is just as bare as my backside.

As feet stomping up a set of stairs boom into my ears, I toss open the remaining three drawers in Regan's room. There isn't a single article of clothing to be found—not even a dress I'd happily wear for the remainder of the weekend.

I can only hope Regan dug my grave as efficiently as she cleared her room of apparel because things are about to get messy. I swear to God, my heart is thrashing against my ribs, and just because my stomach is empty hasn't prevented it from trying to empty itself repeatedly. Men like Hayden don't joke when they say they have a shotgun. They usually have many, in very convenient places—such as outside their daughters' bedrooms.

I realize Regan has everyone fooled with her nice girl act when her bedroom door swings open a few seconds later. Mercifully, it isn't her father coming to disembowel me. It's her mother reminding her that her father left to milk the cows over two hours ago.

"Is there anything I can help you with . . .?" Sally's words stop halfway out of her mouth when she spots me standing just left of Regan. I tried to shelter myself behind Regan. Although she's tall, her petite frame has no chance in hell of hiding a man with shoulders as broad as mine.

"Sally," I greet, dipping my chin as my hands lower to cover my deflating crotch. "Pleasant morning."

"So it seems," Sally replies, her voice picking up right alongside her smile. "Did you sleep well?"

With words eluding me, I nod.

"Good. I'm glad." With a wink, Sally pivots around to face Regan. "You were right. Decades change nothing."

I wait for Sally to leave before shifting my eyes to Regan. I want to yell at her for embarrassing me—*not as much as I want to kiss the impish grin off her face*—but before I can do either of those things, she snags my duffle bag from the hallway, tosses it into my chest, then exits her room.

"Meet me downstairs in five minutes. I've got some stuff I want to show you today."

Gobsmacked, I shout, "Really, Rae? That's it?! Who's leaving who hanging now?"

When she fails to reply to my taunt with her usual quick wit, I sneak a glance out her bedroom door. Her gallop down the stairwell stops halfway, but her eyes remain front and center.

Her unusual quietness causes precum to pool at the crest of my cock. She's not speechless because she's void of a retort. She's struggling to ignore the sexual tension teeming between us. It's nice knowing I'm not the only one straining to maintain a rational head.

"If I did any of the wicked things streaming through my head right now, my dad *would* kill you," Regan warns after a short stint of silence.

"I know," I reply. "You'll be worth it." My last sentence is barely a whisper.

I can't see her, but I know she's smiling. I can feel it deep in my bones.

My intuition is proven spot on when she cranks her neck back to peer at me. Her smile is one I haven't seen before. It's carefree and untroubled, as relaxed and beautiful as the person she embodies when she's on home turf.

"Meet me downstairs," she requests with a jerk of her chin. "There's a whole day waiting for us."

With a wink to finalize the words she can't express, she finishes galloping down the stairs.

CHAPTER TWENTY-FOUR

I stop picking at the grapes on the kitchen counter when my mom chokes on her words. Her emotional response has nothing to do with the tale she's sharing, and everything to do with Alex's unexpected presence.

Taking a page out of my book, he has dressed more casually than I've seen him. He still has on the beloved JC Penney jeans he's worn the past two days, but the light blue coloring has been swapped for a dark-washed pair, and his dress shirt and blazer have been replaced with a plain white T and a devastating smile. He even trimmed his scraggly beard, bringing it an inch closer to his ravishing jawline.

His Viking look shouldn't pair well with a cheap suit and polished dress shoes, and his casual look matches his sleek appearance just as fittingly. The contrast between his attire and his handsome face should seem odd, but the only word I can conjure to describe him is "yum!"

Unsure of the cause of our silence, Alex gestures his head to the stairwell. "Too casual?"

Not waiting for me to answer, he takes the first two steps at the speed of a bullet.

"No!" my mom and I shout in sync.

"You look perfect. Come eat." Mom guides him to the vacant stool next to me, her cheeks inflaming when she catches a whiff of his seductive scent. "From what Regan's told me, you're set for an adventurous day, so we better fill your belly."

When she spins to load his plate with the pancakes, bacon, and eggs she prepares every morning, Alex shifts his eyes to me.

"We'll head into town later today. Nothing opens until 11 AM on Sundays," I inform him after reading the silent questions streaming from his eyes. "We'll get a few items crossed off your list before Luca's memorial this afternoon."

He's worried I've forgotten why we're in Texas. I haven't. But with a massive hole in my chest in desperate need of filling, unearthing my stalker's identity isn't my utmost priority right now. That's what my whole "you've seen mine; now I get to see yours" routine was about. Alex saw me at my most vulnerable last night. I wanted to even the playing field.

It isn't that I don't appreciate the comfort he offered me; I'm just not exactly sure how to handle it. Excluding my family, I haven't relied on anyone like I did Alex yesterday. Not even Isaac has seen my vulnerable side.

I'm grateful Alex didn't remove all his beard when he leans in to whisper in my ear. The wiry hairs on his face tickle my earlobe as his manly scent stimulates my libido. "I don't think your mom will ever look me in the eye again after the stunt you pulled."

A groan rumbles in my chest when a coffee cup steals the dedication of his lips. He takes a generous gulp of my lukewarm brew as he peers at my mom over the rim of the mug. Although he isn't a fan of my unsweetened with a dash of milk concoction, with the coffee pot sitting on the counter just to the left of my mom, he's willing to sacrifice taste if it keeps awkwardness at bay.

It's a shame I'm not as diplomatic. "My mom isn't avoiding eye contact because she's embarrassed about what she saw." Alex's eyes drift to mine. They are brimming with confusion. "She's too busy reimagining the image to worry about what your face is doing."

My laughter snags halfway out my throat when a dishcloth smacks me in the face. I was so caught up relishing Alex's inflamed cheeks and wide eyes, I failed to notice my mom rejoining us at the breakfast bar. She heard everything I said, and she isn't the least bit humiliated.

"I can't be mad at her. It's true," she mutters under her breath as she slips a plate of food in front of Alex. "I just haven't decided what to tell Hayden yet. Should I make out it was an accident, or pretend you got a little cocky while the men were away?" Her smile switches to a half-smirk, half-sneer. "I should probably phrase it better. Little and cocky can't be used together to describe what I saw."

"Mom!" I grab the dishcloth from my empty plate to toss it over to her side of the counter. "Daddy would have a coronary if he heard you say that. Or worse. . . he'd take you over his knee!"

Alex looks a little unwell when my mom whispers, "Oh god, I hope so."

Confident she's locked my libido into a deep, dark cave far, far away from here, my mom exits the kitchen.

Five minutes later, I can still hear her laughing.

I stop glaring at her through a wall when Alex murmurs, "You could never be accused of being adopted."

I laugh. "No chance in hell. Although, I'm reasonably sure at some stage in my childhood I wished I were."

Alex sets down the strip of bacon he's in the process of consuming to interrogate me without words.

"It wasn't anything bad, just the standard stuff every family goes through. At the time, I didn't understand why I couldn't have a two hundred dollar party dress and a tennis bracelet for my thirteenth birthday. It was only when I started paying my own bills did I understand all the issues that came with being an adult."

"Such as, money doesn't grow on trees?" Alex asks with a smile.

"Precisely! It was a disappointing blow when I learned that one."

He laughs before he returns to chewing on a salty strip of meat produced on the very land we're standing on.

"What about you? How many times did you threaten to run away when you were a teen?"

He dabs away the grease pooled in the corner of his mouth with a napkin before twisting his torso to face me. "None."

My elbow and his rib become friendly for the third time this morning. "Come on! Every teen believes they deserve better than they're getting. It's the way they're wired."

Alex's shoulder touches his ear when he shrugs. "I'm not saying that isn't true; I just knew my threat would do me no good, so I didn't bother."

When I peer at him, utterly confused, he adds on, "My father works in a similar industry as me. If I skipped so much as half a lesson at school, he knew it, and I paid for the consequences of my actions that very afternoon."

I screw up my nose. "That must have been tough? Just like unrealistic expectations, every teen deserves to skip a period or three. It's a rite of passage."

Alex shrugs again. "In some ways it sucked, but in others, it was beneficial. It made me the disciplined man I am now."

My nose screws up even more. "You say that like it's a good thing."

"Are you saying it isn't?" He asks his question without the angst I expected. He's enjoying our conversation as much as I am. "Discipline has its place in every environment."

I wait for him to dump his napkin onto his half-consumed breakfast before halfheartedly shrugging. "I guess, but a less disciplined man would have kissed me by now."

What the hell? That was not what I was planning to say. I'm glad I couldn't hold back when my honesty causes a blistering smile to stretch across Alex's handsome face.

"Is that so?" The crinkle in his lip as he struggles to rein in his ego exposes a set of dimples I hadn't noticed before.

"Uh-huh," I reply, unconsciously bringing myself closer to him. "A less disciplined man wouldn't have eaten a heart-clogging breakfast to start his day the right way." I lift my eyes to his, the desire unmissable. "He would have eaten me."

Any chance of harnessing my rampant horniness is lost when Alex groans, "You're more dangerous to my heart than anything I've ever eaten."

He hooks his finger in the loops of my jeans to tug me closer. His yank is rough enough to bring our mouths within an inch of each other, but not strong enough to answer every silent plea pumping from my eyes.

"You play dirty, Rae."

Our breaths intermingle when I jest, "Only because that's the way you like it—"

I take a fumbling step backward when a deep, barreling voice grumbles, "Do I need to call the vet? The amount of testosterone pumping in this room reveals someone needs neutering."

When Alex's hands dart out to catch me midfall, my dad's eyes narrow even more dramatically. His eyelids are so close together, I can't see a smidge of his green irises that are identical to mine in every way.

"Daddy, what are you doing back here so soon? You're usually milking the cows for another hour." With my dad's dislike of Alex well known, I had planned for us to be out and about before he returned.

My dad heads for the fridge, the sneer on his face as muddy as the boots he failed to remove. "You don't come home often. Figured I'd spend some time with you while you're here."

"Ah. . . that's real nice of you—"

"More like utterly ridiculous. She's a grown woman, Hayden. She doesn't want her dad tagging along on her date," my mom interrupts, entering the kitchen too quickly for someone who wasn't spying.

"Date? I thought they were *friends?*" my dad retorts as his even more slitted gaze drifts between Alex, mom, and me.

When the room falls into silence, my dad's grip on the orange juice carton tightens. "Rae—"

"Mom's right. I'm a grown woman who doesn't need her dad rushing in to save her." Ignoring his disgusted gasp, I seize Alex's wrist and pluck him from his seat. "I'm going to give Alex a tour of the farm. . ." When my dad steps closer to us, as if he's ready to join in on our escapades today, I quickly add on, "Alone."

I watch his anger rise from his stomach to his cheeks before he growls, "You've got no means of getting around. The tracks are bogged with mud from the recent rain."

He looks two seconds from taking my mom over his knee as she was hoping when she throws a set of keys in my direction. "I filled the Jeep last week. She's good for at least two hundred miles."

"Sally Wilcott-Myers—"

"Oh, don't you dare Sally Wilcott me. You were moody for a week when I said I wanted to hyphenate our names. Now you're using it against me. *Please.*"

My mom shoves my dad out of the kitchen, her strength inspiring.

The smile making my cheeks ache fades when I hear my dad's faint whisper, "What if she gets hurt?"

The worry in his voice isn't the only thing dampening my joy; it's my mom's reply. "He won't hurt her any more than she's already been hurt, Hayden. Look at her. I haven't seen her smile like that in nearly a decade."

Up until now, I thought I was doing a good job of hiding my pain from the world. Clearly, my acting skills aren't as top shelf as I thought.

My eyes stray from my feet when a pair of white sneakers pop into my peripheral vision. Only someone as slick as Alex could pull off Van shoes in a country environment. Just as he did last night, he offers me comfort without strings attached. He cups my jaw, his fingers so long they weave through my hair and caress my whitening cheeks at the same time. Within a few strokes, the color returns stronger than ever, the heady lust bristling between Alex and me ramping up my libido.

"Are you ready to head out?" Alex asks, watching the worry vanish from my eyes. "I'm dying to find out if a roll in the hay is as appealing as it sounds."

I laugh at the humor in his voice. He's confident enough in his own skin, he can pull off any act. This morning, he was an eat-you-alive alpha. Now he's the jokester who'll spear your heart as effectively as he'll have you in stitches.

I was apprehensive about coming to Texas. I shouldn't have been. There's an immense amount of healing occurring, but for once, I don't feel as if my heart is being shredded in the process.

Alex and Luca are nothing alike—but in some ways, they are identical. Both whittled their way into my heart in an extremely short amount of time. They are both confident, alpha-oriented individuals. There's just one difference. Luca destroyed me. Alex hasn't been given the chance yet.

That thought should fill me with fear. It doesn't—not in the slightest. I'm not the same girl I was eight years ago. I'm fierce, and I am strong. But more than anything, Alex can love me like Luca couldn't. I just have to decide if that's what I want.

Realizing I'll never summon an appropriate response with Alex's hands on me and my parents' spying eyes watching my every move, I take a step back from Alex. "You should reconsider your shoes. They won't look so gleaming once I'm done with you."

Hearing the challenge in my voice, Alex's brow quirks. "We'll see. I'm quite nifty at sidestepping dirty situations."

His flirty tone brings back the sexual tension my dad's overbearing presence snuffed. It also reveals that he noticed the crinkle between my brow I haven't been able to smooth since Friday night. If the friction between us continues growing at the rate it has been the past two days, I'm sure it won't be long.

After gathering my coat off the kitchen counter, I pivot on my heels and head for the door. "When your shoes go to shoe heaven, don't say I didn't warn you."

My heart does a funny flippy thing when Alex murmurs, "I'm not worried about my shoes. Me, on the other hand. . ."

CHAPTER TWENTY-FIVE

Alex

"I'm not doing it. Fool me once, shame on you; fool me twice. . ."

My quote falls short when Regan clutches her stomach to laugh hysterically at the terror in my tone. She has done the same thing multiple times this morning. The most notable was when she convinced me a bull was a dairy cow and the area she wanted me to tug on was its udder. Thank god the bull didn't take kindly to my cold hands, or I would have marked bestiality off a list I never wanted to make.

"They're chickens, Alex. What harm can they do?" Regan asks, still laughing from her post outside the hen house.

I shoo away a big black beast eyeing me with its beady eyes before replying, "I'm stealing their babies. Poultry or not, they will be pissed."

"They're not their babies; they're eggs. The same eggs you were munching on this morning."

I shush her so loudly, half a dozen chickens pecking seed

outside their nesting boxes stop what they are doing to peer at me. "If they smell their offspring on me, they'll pounce."

Regan laughs even louder, assuming I am joking. I'm not. I'd rather be inappropriate with a bull than have my eyes gouged out by an angry mother hen.

When I fail to move for nearly a minute, Regan shouts, "Come on, Alex; stop being a pussy. Get the damn eggs!"

Barely holding back what I intend to do to her for her constant ridicule, I gather the last four eggs in the far corner of the nesting box.

I think I'm scot-free.

I'm terribly mistaken.

There's a chicken I didn't notice upon entering.

Except, he's not a chicken.

He's a rooster.

Coming between a mommy chicken and her babies is bad enough, but this makes matters ten times worse. A rooster is an alpha in the animal world. And from one alpha to another, I know he isn't impressed I've made his women sad.

With my hands raised in the air, I step away from the big white beast. My cowardly retreat makes the situation more volatile. He's seen the eggs I'm holding. He knows I have his babies' lives in my hands.

"I'm just gonna place them right there." I point to a fresh bundle of hay next to my mud-covered shoes that are so dirty, I can't remember what their original color was.

When I set the eggs down, the rooster feathers himself, ignoring the invisible white flag I'm waving. When he leaps down from his perch, I spin on my heels and run. I dart past the chickens glaring at me as if I am an idiot. I run and run as if I'm being chased down by a grizzly, not stopping until I'm safe on the other side of the chicken coop.

Regan finds my cowardice hilariously entertaining. She's laughing so hard, tears stream down her face as her body shudders in humor. She can laugh, she didn't have a flappy maniac pecking her heels as she raced across poop-covered dirt that's extremely slippery. I barely make it out of the hen house with my life intact.

"They can have their fucking eggs. I'll buy you some when we go to town," I say, winded.

My lungs stop sucking in air like I've run a marathon when Regan pats my back. Her gesture is one I use on rookie agents many times after their first raid. "Let me show you how the pros do it."

With a grin that makes me wonder if I've died and gone to heaven, she rolls up the sleeves of her long-sleeve shirt and heads for the realm of hell I just escaped. I straighten my spine when she slides into the stinky space without so much of a bead of sweat on her nape.

When the life-gnawing beast fluffs his feathers in the same manner he did with me, she splays her hands across her cocked hip and glares at him.

I don't feel so stupid about my telepathic conversation with a rooster when she snarls, "Really, Pat? You're going there? I thought we were friends?"

Believing her angry sneer has Pat subdued, she heads for the wooden hatch in the far back corner of the pen.

"Watch out!" I shout in warning when Pat chases after her.

Regan jackknifes quickly but not quickly enough to catch Pat in the act. He pecks at some seed in front of him, acting like he isn't on a murderous rampage. He's good. Even I'm suspicious of his motive, and I interrogate criminals for a living.

After a vicious snarl stern enough to scare a tiger into becoming vegan, Regan returns to her mission. She makes it into the hen house without a single incident, proving Pat's issues are male-oriented.

When I say that to Regan, she laughs. "So what are you saying? Only women can gather eggs?"

"Yup," I reply without pause. "It makes perfect sense in both the animal kingdom and real life. Two alphas should never cross paths, much less be in the same realm—unless one is planning to take out the other."

My tongue thickens when Regan glares at me. If given a choice, I'd rather have her see me as a coward than be subjected to the look she's giving me now. She seems as if she wants to gut me just like her father does.

"What did I say?" My sentence comes out in a hurry from shadowing her thunderous steps to her mother's Jeep.

I barely make it into the passenger seat before she floors the gas, sending droplets of mud spraying over both of us. Every puddle she dangerously careened for earlier today was done with laughter and jubilation, but this feels dirty—and not in a good way.

"Rae. . ." I grip the roll bar when she takes the hairpin corner at the bottom of the meadow at a speed too fast to be deemed safe. "Slow the fuck down. You're going to get us killed."

She lowers her speed—somewhat. It's enough to quell my anxiety, but not enough to loosen the tension clutching my throat. I don't know what I said that's got her so worked up, but I do know one thing: we need seatbelts—both of us.

After tugging on my belt, I lean across Regan's thrusting chest to secure her clip into a latch that's so sparkly I doubt it's ever been used. The clench of Regan's jaw reveals she's frustrated by my distrust, but her annoyance isn't enough to overshadow whatever the fuck I did wrong this time.

We drive for several minutes before Regan finally reveals the reason behind her anger. "I'm an alpha. You know that, right?"

I'd laugh if I wasn't in fear of my life. I'm not scared of her excessive speed. It's the glare she's giving me causing my heart palpitations.

Realizing ignorance won't get me anywhere fast with a woman as stubborn as Regan, I say, "The term 'alpha' is only used when referring to the male of the species. I sure as hell know you're not one of them."

She forcefully yanks on the steering wheel, forcing my head and the roll bar to become friendly. "An alpha is the dominant one of the group. That's me. I'm the alpha."

She says her last word with so much power, I'm certain her parents heard her—if not half the state. I wonder if that's why she's driving us away from her family home? She doesn't want any witnesses to my murder.

"You took what I said out of context. Your spitfire attitude and take-no-shit personality are two of the things I love most about you, so if you think I'm going to fight you for the position of top dog, Rae, you're wrong. You're already so far above me, I'm afraid I'll never reach you."

Regan's foot slips off the gas pedal as her eyes connect to mine. It takes me replaying what I said four times before the reason behind her dilated eyes and gaped jaw smacks into me. I just told her I loved her. It was in a roundabout way, but I still said it.

I attempt to fire off a half-assed comment about loving her

feistiness as much as I love tacos, but Regan beats me to the task of talking. Her question isn't laced with the wit I intended to use. It's fueled by hope. "Did I take that out of context as well?"

I should say yes. I should act oblivious to what she's asking, but with my ability to lie to her dwindling with every second we spend together, I shake my head instead. I ought to be ashamed of how profoundly she's crawled under my skin in such a short period of time, but I'm not. I've been longing for change for years. She gives me the change I've been seeking without any worry entering the equation. I want this—*I want her*.

Unfortunately, Regan misses my wordless reply. She's too busy striving to avoid a herd of cattle to hear my unverbalized declaration of love.

I'd give anything to tell her how I truly feel. Even more so when we veer off the muddy track, and the Jeep's tires lift off the ground.

CHAPTER TWENTY-SIX

"Please. Oh, God, please don't do this to me again."

Even barely audible through the sob she's struggling to contain, I recognize the voice of the woman praying on repeat. It's Regan. She sounds distraught and panicked—like her worst nightmare is being played out—*again?*

When she presses her cold fingers to my neck to check for a pulse, a mangled groan rolls up my chest. Her hands are freezing—as cold as death itself. Although my unexpected response to her touch scares the living daylights out of her, the relieved breath it comes with is strong enough to force my eyelids open.

It takes me several long, tedious seconds to recall our location. It isn't because I'm disoriented. I'm striving to work out why the grass is blue and the sky is green. We're upside down, still trapped in the wreckage. . . and I can smell gasoline.

Fuck.

I crash to the ground with a thud when I unlatch my seatbelt. Although my shoulder is unappreciative of its hard contact with the roll bar that saved our lives, registering pain is the last thing on my mind. Regan's safety is my absolute priority. Pain, anger, and any other stupid neurosis can wait.

"Careful," I beg when Regan's hand follows the trek mine just took. "I'll catch you, but go slow."

Her lips wobble as she weakly nods at my suggestion. While her hand continues creeping toward the silver clip holding her hostage, I scan her body, checking her for injuries. Excluding her wide eyes that are brimming with tears and a small graze on her thigh, she appears unharmed. *Thank fuck.*

If only I could do something to quell the absolute terror radiating from her eyes.

Recognizing I can't achieve that while stuck in a dangerous environment, I command, "When you're ready, unlatch your belt. I'll catch you—I promise."

With the Jeep not tall enough for me to stand in, I brace my back against the roll cage and open my arms, ensuring her fall won't be as impacting as mine. Her eagerness to escape the mangled wreckage has her landing on me sooner than I anticipated. Her knees' brutal connection with my stomach winds me, but she fails to notice. She's too busy scampering across the rain-sloshed ground on her hands and knees to pay me any attention.

Her wish to flee isn't surprising, but the name she murmurs numerous times under her breath while doing it is. She keeps referring to Luca.

With my shoulders double the width of Regan's, it takes a little more effort for me to exit the roofless Jeep. The roll cage that protected our heads as we cartwheeled through the air has crumbled inward, making the distance between the floor and roof noticeably different.

Before I can squeeze my torso through the tight opening, a set of tiny hands grips the collar of my t-shirt and yanks me backward. Regan's tugs are so strong, before my mouth can drop in awe of her strength, she pulls me free from the wreckage.

We scamper back far enough any impending explosions won't harm us, but not far enough for the seriousness of our crash to avoid hammering into me. Regan's mom's Jeep is totaled, destroyed beyond repair. No one should have survived that carnage, much less two of us.

I shift my eyes to Regan. Hers are holding the same surprise as mine. They also reveal her remorse.

"Don't you dare," I warn when she attempts to apologize. "Nothing that happened was your fault. It was an accident— nothing more."

She shakes her head, disagreeing with me. "I shouldn't have argued. I should have continued our plan of attack as we had discussed." I only realize she isn't referring to our accident when she adds on, "I just couldn't back down as Luca wasn't being fair. I didn't date to keep up appearances, but he never once stopped. That's why I was so angry the night of our accident. His list of men was endless."

She snaps her lips shut so fast, it sounds like the noise the Jeep made when the hood hit the ground during our collision.

"*Our accident?* As in, you were in the car with Luca when he crashed?" I don't know if the pulse pounding my eardrums is affecting my hearing, but my voice is so low, I barely heard my question.

Mercifully, Regan's hearing isn't as damaged as mine. "I . . . I . . ."

Hating the pain in her eyes as she struggles to conceal a truth with a lie, I tug her into my chest. I'm certain she can hear my heart racing a million miles an hour, but I don't give a fucking shit. I saw the tree that claimed Luca's life. His impact with the trunk was so brutal, the tree is permanently scarred. How Regan survived the carnage, I will never know.

There's only one thing I do know, thank fuck she did. If she had perished with Luca. . . I can't consider it. It makes me sick to the stomach just thinking about it. The pain tearing at my chest is too much. I will forever live with guilt of what happened to Dane, but it will never be as strong as the gratitude I'm feeling now that Regan's life was spared that night.

For once, I act on the prompts of both my heart and my head. Regan's glistening eyes lift to mine when I peel her off my chest. I cup her jaw as I did in the kitchen earlier this morning so I can assess every detail of her beautiful face. My eyes drift across her forehead, taking in the scar from where we bumped heads. I absorb the crinkle in her nose as she struggles to hold in her tears, the furl of her lips. I take it all in, then I do it again just to make sure I didn't miss a single thing.

When our eyes meet, Regan says, "No one knows."

"It's okay, I won't tell anyone." Relief darts through her eyes. "I don't care about anything that happened in your past, Rae. All I care about is that you are okay and safe."

My eyes dance between hers that are glistening with so much moisture, they look seconds from bursting. They nearly do when I ask, "Are you okay?"

She nods, then shakes her head, then nods again. I shouldn't smile at her confusion, but when the person you're trying to console is on the verge of cracking, you use anything available. If my smile frustrates her enough to dry her tears, it will be worth the wrath spawned by it.

I expect Regan to react negatively to my grin, so you can imagine my surprise when it has the opposite effect. Her lips curl in a similar fashion before they do something I never anticipated: they seal over mine.

She could be kissing me to shut me up, but it doesn't feel that way. The little moans ripping from her throat aren't noises expelled when forced to do something against your wishes. She's kissing me because she wants to. Just like I'm returning her boldness with as much esteem as I want her mouth on mine even more than I want to wipe the hurt from her eyes.

Regan's tongue duels with mine before she draws it into her mouth. She suckles it gently, nursing it in her mouth with playful nips and prolonged licks. I cradle her jaw and kiss her back, the movements of my tongue and lips hungry and needy. I usually take control in situations like this, but the evenness of our exchange has me holding back the urge. This isn't about banging my chest and acting macho. It's a mutual admiration that calls for a balance of power. A give and take.

We kiss for several minutes, slowly and lazily. We aren't rushing for the prize at the end. We're savoring each other, the leisured strokes of our tongues pleasing enough to diminish any need to sprint for the finish line.

That all changes a few seconds later when Regan murmurs breathlessly against my lips, "Are you as talented with your hands as you are with your mouth, Mr. Rogers?"

The sass in her tone awakens a side of me I haven't seen in years. I've always been cocky and self-assured, but some of my pigheadedness disappeared when Dane was shot. He will never walk again, much less have a lazy Sunday afternoon hookup in a meadow with the woman of his dreams.

I pause for a moment, waiting for the usual negativity that overcomes me when I think of Dane. It never comes. Regan's exploring hands as she returns to kissing me have rendered my mind blank of any thoughts that don't include her. Furthermore, Dane lives with his *happily ever after*—I've just now found mine after years of searching. I deserve to savor the moment.

As my fingers dive deeper into Regan's messy locks, she swivels her tongue around mine while her hand drops to grind my cock bulging against the zipper in my jeans.

We continue going at it for several minutes before Regan unfortunately pulls back. "Why the hell did we wait so long to do this again?" She asks her question as if it has been months since we kissed instead of two days.

Smiling, I meld my tongue along hers, kissing her in a way that electrifies the air between us with buoyant energy before moving my lips to her ear. "Because you wanted us to play farmers instead of playing with each other."

When her fist lands in my stomach, my lips furl against her sweet-smelling skin. "If I recall correctly, you're the one who stopped our last foray—not me, Mister Fancy Pants."

I nip her earlobe, causing an excited squeak to vibrate her lips. "Stop arguing or I'll be forced to bite you some more."

My cock throbs with need when she murmurs, "If bickering compels your mouth on *any* part of my body, sign me up, Scotty."

I bite her for the second time, this one a little harder than the first. "I don't know who the fuck Scotty is, but if you mention his name one more time while my mouth is on you, severe retaliation will be necessary."

Ignoring the excited thrust of her chest, I wrap my hand around her nape and pull her mouth back to mine. This kiss is hard and violent, a representation of what our relationship could be if we let others dictate our emotions. Being involved with Regan in any way could end catastrophically for me. But for now, I don't care. It's just us, two crazy people trapped by a wild, mutual attraction.

When our kiss ramps up even more, we fall to the ground, our lips never breaking. Hands go in every direction as months of sexual frustration surpasses fear and unachievable goals. We roll around the grass amongst the cow dung and bugs as stunned by our arrival as I am of Regan's kissing skills. Regan can kiss. Precise strikes, skilled bites, and an adventurous tongue confirm this without uncertainty. She has the perfect combination of speed and skill, which entices endless recklessness from me.

While grinding my cock against her thigh, my hands sneak under her shirt. Her skin is smooth and silky, quivering under my touch. Not in a bad way. She likes my hands on her. She enjoys me cupping her breasts and tweaking her nipples so much, she whips off her shirt and bra not even two seconds later.

Most men would find her confidence threatening. I don't. I love that she's aware of her beauty, and she knows how to use it to her advantage.

When she glances up at me with needy, wide eyes, our exchange turns borderline violent. We nip and claw at each other as we tackle the only thing standing between us becoming one.

Why I thought it was a good idea to wear jeans today, I'll never know. The effort required to remove them adds to the sexual frustration infusing the air. It also makes the torment almost too much to bear. Knowing the one thing I want to devour more than anything is right there, yet still out of my reach is pure torture. There are no other words.

While catching one of Regan's pert nipples between my teeth, I jerk at the silver fastener causing my frustration. I expect my aggression to make Regan uneasy, but all it does is fuel her desire. She tugs at my jeans violently, her wish to unearth the throbbing member behind my zipper blinding her with rampant lust.

When her possessive yanks somehow free my cock, our mouths break. "It's about time," she murmurs breathlessly, her lungs as depleted of oxygen as mine when her eager eyes take in my thick, hard shaft. "Now the real show can start."

Motivated by the yearning in her tone, I pull her skin-tight jeans and tiny panties to her knees. Too impatient to fully remove them, I roll her onto her back, then attack her mouth. I kiss her until her clit pulsates and swells against me, its want uncontained.

Its frantic rhythm triples when I drag my nose down the throb in her throat. The country setting hasn't overpowered her scent in the slightest. She smells seductive and sweet, and more like me than the muddy conditions we're wrestling in.

Her fingers weave through my hair when my mouth moves down her body in teasing licks and painful bites. Her stomach muscles tense when scraped by the bushy beard on my chin, but every bite, suck, and lick intensifies her seductive scent.

The scent of her pussy is intoxicating, as devastating to my perception as the carefree smiles she's been giving me all morning. No wonder why I've given in—her pull is too strong for any man to resist, much less a man as smitten as me.

What I said earlier was a slip of the tongue, but I've always believed people are most honest when placed under pressure. This woman crawled under my skin years ago. Now she's weaving herself through the veins in my heart.

A mere inch from the gem I am excited to taste, Regan yanks on my hair, returning my mouth to hers. "Not yet. We don't have enough time," she murmurs over my mouth before spearing her tongue between my lips.

The "yet" part of her comment swells my chest with pride, grateful she's already planning a second expedition, but her saying we don't have enough time pisses me off. I've dreamed about this moment for years; I don't want it threatened by something as woeful as a time constraint.

My demand she rethink her comment rams into the back of my throat when she purrs, "Usually, a fuck without foreplay is like a martini without olives, but your kisses already have me on the verge of climax, so additional stimulation isn't required."

Although skeptical some of her comment was issued with the hope of moving us onto the next stage more quickly, my conceitedness stops me registering it. If she wants me to hurry up and fuck her, who am I to deny her every desire? "Brace yourself, Rae. Fucking doesn't come with niceties."

Regan smiles a grin that nearly has me coming on the spot before squealing, "Thank god for that!"

I grin, loving the country twang in her reply. Taking her husky response as approval to get our show on the road, I dig the tips of my shoes into the sloshy ground we're using as a mattress, then rock my hips forward. Sweat drips off my body onto Regan's when I impale her in one ardent thrust. The fit is snug, but the feeling is out-of-this-fucking-world good.

Her pussy ripples around me, pained by the sudden intrusion, but also swelling with anticipation for what's about to come. When the crest of my cock slams into her cervix, she jerks her head back and lets out a grunted moan.

"Do you need me to stop?"

She shakes her head before all my question leaves my mouth. "I'll kill you if you do."

Smirking at the threat in her tone, I wait several long beats for the pain fettering her face to diminish before reluctantly withdrawing my cock. I've barely pulled back three inches when Regan digs her boots into my ass to demand my cock's immediate return.

While fighting through the tightness gripping my sack from her feisty enthusiasm, I withdraw to the tip. Before a single protest can escape Regan's lips, I lunge forward. My thrust is so hard, her cervix and my cock become friendly once more.

"That shouldn't feel good, but it does," Regan voices through heavy moans.

I pump in and out of her another two times before replying, "Tell me something I don't know. Has anyone ever taken you this deep?"

My response was supposed to be more of a statement than a question, but I'm grateful for my lack of brain capacity when Regan shakes her head.

My inflated ego doesn't linger for long when she utters, "I was so afraid of being snapped in half, I never signed up for the ride. If I had any idea what I was missing, I would have boarded the train years ago."

Jealousy wraps itself around my heart before weaving down my stomach to clutch my cock. The thought of Regan with anyone but me should fill me with black hatred, but instead, it has the opposite effect. It makes my cock harder, thicker, and determined as fuck to ruin her for any man after me.

After a quick adjustment of her hips, I slam into her harder. Our bodies slapping together sounds callous, but the more brutal I am, the louder Regan screams. That alone increases my speed.

With an arch of her back, Regan tilts her pussy forward, giving me unhindered access to the object I am determined to destroy as much as I want to devour. Her change in position gives me an unimpeded view of her beautiful body glistening in the mid-morning sun and tightens the knot low in my gut.

While my hips jackknife on repeat, I shift my gaze to take it all in. The visual is unlike anything I've ever seen. My cock commanding every inch of her swollen-with-need pussy as her teeth gnaw on her bottom lip so fiercely lipstick is not required, ensures my campaign to abolish any of her thoughts not associated with me is in full swing.

But that's not the only truth it exposes. It reveals what I've always known. She can play me like a fiddle.

Realizing her ruse has been exposed, Regan murmurs, "I've heard jealousy fucking is the best there is. Would have never believed it if you didn't prove me wrong."

The cocky glint in her eyes fades when I modify the swivel of my hips. Within minutes, my pump and roll routine has the slickness of her pussy matching the mud coating her back. She purrs my name on repeat, making my existence in this world whole and complete. She might have badgered me into fucking her like a deranged man, but the man claiming her now, the one possessing her like he wanted to five years ago, he's not commanding every inch of her body because he's jealous. He's dominating her in a way any alpha man would. *I'm making her mine.*

As evidence of Regan's excitement coats my shaft, her nails scour my back. Although I want to bang my chest and claim victory, not all Regan's wetness can be attributed to her excitement. For every hoarse cry she emits, spurts of precum shoot from my shaft, adding to the wildly wet conditions.

As my hips piston at an uncontrolled pace, Regan's nails dig into my back. Her endeavor to hold on to my sweat-slicked body adds to the chaos. We fuck like wild animals, the country setting perfect for our crazy, uncontrolled romp.

"Yes," Regan moans, spreading her thighs wider. "Fuck me, Alex. Fuck me."

My hips slam against hers as I struggle to ignore the orgasm demanding my surrender. I pound into her on repeat, loving the cries shredding from her throat as much as my cock loves her tight pussy milking it.

When she arches her back to release a throaty scream, my balls slap her ass. I rock my pelvis faster, bringing her squeals up another two decibels. Not wanting our impromptu gathering interrupted before we've found release, I seal my mouth over hers. Our kiss amplifies the insane heat between us, as needy as the frantic cries Regan releases between breaths.

After a few minutes of commanding her mouth as well as I am controlling her pussy, Regan pulls back. "I'm. . . I'm. . ." Her throaty cries are loud and without constraint—as is her pleasure.

I feel her getting tighter, firmer, her voice huskier before she shatters in the most brilliant way. She squeals my name in a breathless purr as her shoulders relax and her eyes glaze over. A shuddering sensation takes over every inch of her body, forfeiting to the madness without an ounce of protest.

I position myself better so I can watch the extravaganza

unfold. The slight gap between her lips, the hue on her cheeks, and the perfect arch of her back as her limbs give way to the uproar surging through her is a fascinating sight.

Regan's orgasm sucks out all her energy, leaving nothing but satisfaction. Aiming to have her once again enslaved to the brilliance of our exchange, I dig my fingers into her hips to adjust them upwards, giving me unrestricted access to her still-quivering pussy and beautiful face. Her pleasure-hazed features have me coming undone. She's beautiful and free, finally rid of the restraint she's had since the day we met.

With my eyes locked on hers, I continue pounding her, taking every contraction of her pussy as approval for cum to rocket out of my cock. While groaning her name, I give her every drop of my spawn, holding nothing back.

I begin to wonder if you can die from an orgasm when mine continues ripping through my body for the next several minutes. My sack is empty and content, but my cock refuses to surrender. He likes Regan's heat surrounding him so much, he's not willing to give it up. Not now. Not ever.

He's not the only one suffering separation issues. Regan's second orgasm arrives in such quick succession, they're virtually conjoined. Sweat dribbles between her breasts as her lips part to suck in much-needed air.

Her angelic face screwed up in the throes of ecstasy hands me the final piece of the puzzle I've been working on the past two months. It makes everything clear and resolute.

Regan doesn't have the ability to destroy me.

She already has.

CHAPTER TWENTY-SEVEN

I fight to catch my breath when Alex rolls off me. That was amazing. Phenomenal. Better than I could have possibly imagined. And it all happened in a field with animals watching on. I would laugh at the absurdity if every muscle in my body wasn't aching.

My achy joints have nothing to do with our accident. With the exception of the memories it induced, our car crash was pain-free. All I remember is sailing through the air before waking up strapped in the wreckage. It was what occurred after that caused my greatest pain.

I spilled Luca's secret.

Although that's mammoth, it isn't the sole reason remorse is stabbing my chest. Seeing Alex like that, in the same position as Luca, his head hanging just as low. . . *god*. Tears prick my eyes just at the thought of him being hurt.

I put him in that position. My inability to place myself second put Alex's life in jeopardy—just as Luca had done to me.

I thought Luca loved me. It wasn't as profound as I had hoped, but I thought our friendship was the best thing he had of non-monetary value, but the more I evaluate things in the leadup to his death, I realize it wasn't.

Don't get me wrong, I was at least in the top three; I just wasn't his priority. Even with my life in his hands, Luca always held the top spot.

I guess that's why I'm so pigheaded and strong-willed? I'm doing what Luca did to me for years. I put myself above anyone and anything. I closed myself off. . . until Alex. He sees through the mask I wear to warn others to stay away. He knows the hair, smile, and expensive clothes are just tricks to hide my ugly insides. And despite all that, he still likes what he sees.

I should call him crazy and quit while I am ahead, but who am I to preach sanity? I fucked a man in a field after I ran us off the road in anger. If anyone needs a trip to the psych ward, I doubt it's Alex.

I stop staring at a fluffy white cloud in the sky when Alex asks, "You okay, Rae?" He expresses his question in the same manner he did before I kissed him, except this time, I hear a bit of reservation in his voice.

"I'm good." The honesty of my reply rings true in my tone. Usually, I'd be scratching at hives by now, the memory of Luca's accident too great for me to ignore. But the pain isn't as intense today, the guilt also not as strong. "How about you? Are you okay?"

Alex waits for me to roll over and face him before jerking his chin up. "I'm good. Reek of cow dung, but fine nonetheless."

I smile, loving the mirth in his tone. He does smell like manure, but more than anything, he smells like me. "I guess we better head back and get you showered. I can't have you wandering around town smelling like cow poop; the locals might confuse you as one of their own."

Alex's shit-eating grin matches mine. I'm glad our roll in the grass didn't change anything between us. He's looking at me with as much admiration as the past two days. *Thank god.*

"I'm sure if your dad has his way, that won't be an issue."

Not wanting to lie, I don't reply.

"Is that. . . ah. Did I cross the line?" Alex asks when I gingerly rise to my knees.

Following the direction of his gaze, I spot the cause of the apprehension in his tone. Cum has dribbled down my thigh to puddle near my knee. With how many brutal pumps his cock made while shooting his seed inside of me, I'm not surprised my pussy isn't able to keep it inside. Apparently, I'm not the only one who fell off the orgasm train two months ago. Alex was as backed up as me.

"It's fine. I had the depo shot a few months ago."

I swipe at the cum before slinging it on the ground in an extremely unladylike manner. It's not like I have any other option. It's either use my hand or the shirt Alex is holding out for me. Considering he smells like sex and me mingled together, having him turn up to my house shirtless would spell disaster. The image of him shirtless in a grassy field is a rather enticing visual, but his ability to breathe without aid should be my utmost focus. *Dammit!*

Alex's eyes snap to mine when I ask, "You're clean, right?"

"Do you really need to ask that?" His angry tone should raise my hackles, but my anger seemed to pack up and leave town after our wrestling match in the mud.

"Don't get snippy with me. I don't know how many women you've fucked in a field with angry bulls looking on."

A smirk cracks my lips when Alex cranks his neck to assess the cows behind us. None of them are bulls, but I can't help but tease him. My rile paid dividends when he got jealous. My god—the chatty baker in Ravenshoe was right. Jealousy sex is pure heaven!

"If it makes you feel any better, my test was as recent as last week."

Alex returns his eyes to mine. "It doesn't make me feel better," he grumbles under his breath as he stands to his feet to yank his jeans up his thighs.

They're even muddier now than they were when he outran alpacas chasing him for their feed. If you overlook the little mishap of our accident, today has been the most extraordinary day, and it's happening on a day I usually hide away from the world. I knew from the moment I met Alex my life was set to change, but I never would have guessed it would be this profound.

Don't get me wrong; I'm not saying a romp in a field equals a lifetime commitment. But the freedom that came with it, I can't put a value on it. Every day of the past decade was planned and scrutinized to ensure I was living the life I was supposed to live. Today was the first time I've just lived. No rules. No expectations. Just one fucked-in-the-head girl showing a city slicker how things are done in the country.

When Alex hands me my shirt, the deep groove between his brow smooths upon seeing the high arch of my lips. My smile doesn't linger for long. It drops into a pout when Alex tucks his cock into his jeans before I get the chance to thank it for my back-to-back orgasms. His quick dressing skills also steal my ability to organize another hookup without the blow flies and hay-filled patties.

Worry about being left in the lurch for another two months

LADY IN WAITING   269

rolls off my back like water on a duck when Alex mutters, "If you keep looking at me like that, Rae, we'll never leave this field."

I give him a sassy wink. "You'll be worth it."

After clearing a smidge of dirt from my neck, he hooks his arm around my shoulders, tugs me into his chest, then we begin our two-mile walk home. Although he doesn't say anything, I know he heard the words I didn't express. *I'd rather wrestle you in a muddy field than cross off the next item on our to do list.*

"Come on. Once we face this, we'll be clear of obstacles. Right?" He sounds as hesitant as I feel.

I've given every excuse you can imagine the past eight years to miss the event occurring this afternoon. Once, I even cancelled with the excuse of an ectopic pregnancy. It wasn't the brightest idea I've had. Gossip spread through my hometown like wildfire. Half the old biddies were planning the wedding of the century with the supposed father-to-be, whereas the other half were arranging his funeral. After coming clean to my dad the week following Luca's memorial, I realized he was on a rampage to discover who had "knocked me up out of wedlock."

As we move away from an image responsible for both the highest and lowest day of my life, the firmer Alex's grip on my shoulder becomes. His manly clutch intermingles our scents as well as our roll in the grassy field did. It's an addictive smell—potent enough to bring my thoughts back into positive territory.

I thought the crazy chemistry brewing between Alex and me like a potion in a witch's cauldron would have disappeared the instant we fucked. I was so wrong. It's made it more crazy—slightly unhinged.

I guess I shouldn't be shocked. I came twice—*twice!* That has never happened before. And excluding Alex's scrumptious V muscle I've sketched into my memory for eternity, it was done without additional stimulation.

That's unheard of.

I'm not joking. I don't have a lot of female friends, but the ones I do have wouldn't hesitate to call it as they see it. No mention of back to back climaxes has ever been discussed at any time during our girly get-togethers. Vibrators. Clit stimulators. Strap-ons to take their husbands for a ride were discussed without a single qualm. A stranger giving you the best fuck you've ever had in the most unlikely location on the most unlikely date—nope. Not once.

If I had the means, I would have recorded our romp, as I'm reasonably sure that's the only way my girlfriends will believe me. It was so out-of-this-world fantastic, even I'm having a hard time separating fact from fantasy.

"We did just fuck, right?"

Alex lowers his eyes to mine. Confusion is slashed all over his face. "I guess that's what two people having unexpected sex is called."

"Are you regretting it?" I ask, surprised by the unease in his tone.

"No," he answers without delay.

"Then what's the deal with the dipping tone and sweaty brow?" I run my finger along his brow to emphasize my question. "I'm shocked you have any liquid left after your effort."

My underhanded compliment wipes some of the hesitation from his eyes, but it doesn't wholly erase it. After licking his parched mouth, Alex vows, "I'll never have any hesitation about you, Rae. *Ever.*" He waits for me to nod before adding on, "I'm just trying to figure out how we're going to explain that. . ." He drops his eyes to the wet patch in my crotch. "And this," I follow his gaze to the big muddy rings circling his knees, "to him."

His last head nudge launches my stomach into my throat. My dad's truck is making its way down the track Alex and I traveled nearly an hour ago. The look in his eyes is murderous, and they're locked on Alex.

"Accidents happen, right?" When Alex halfheartedly nods, I say, "Then that's what we'll go with."

I break away from his side, stealing his chance to reply. I'm not saying our romp was a mistake; I'm merely giving him an out. If he accepts it, I'll cherish the memories and pray they're strong enough to bring my self-pleasing mojo back. If he ignores my suggestion, I'm open to extending an olive branch I don't usually offer. I'll look at a second, possibly even a third round of action.

I scan the horizon when Alex nips at my heels. For how quickly he closed the distance between us, my need for an olive branch may be required earlier than predicted.

Have you ever tried to fool a man who knows you better than yourself?

I bet it didn't end well.

Although Alex and I didn't get busted doing the deed, in my dad's eyes, we may as well have. Our cattle farm borders a parcel of land stolen from my family decades before I was born. My dad has been in negotiations with the local parish for years to have the title put back in our family's name. Today his surveyor had an important meeting with the opposing land owners. Even though Alex and I were a good distance from the fences bordering our property, allegedly my pasty skin illuminates in the sunlight—as does Alex's glowingly white backside.

My father was glad I wasn't injured in our crash. He didn't hold the same esteem for Alex. I'll be eternally grateful my mom came along for the ride when my father caught wind of our adventurous morning, or Luca's memorial wouldn't be the only one held on this day every year.

It was interesting watching Alex go toe-to-toe with my father. I knew a man as assertive as Alex wouldn't back down without a fight, but I never anticipated his protectiveness either. He didn't just go to bat for himself; he defended me as well. Nothing he said to my father was different than things I've expressed numerous times the past thirteen plus years, but hearing them conveyed by a man who took me to the brink of insanity was a mind-blowing experience. He wasn't just respecting my integrity; he was honoring our relationship—a relationship I didn't know existed until he expressed it.

I'm honestly a little lost on how to handle Alex's confession. My first response was joy—which is utterly ridiculous since I haven't dated since high school, and even then, I was never interested in a second date. Then I grew worried Alex is keeping something from me. Although I'm fairly certain his dishonesty is more a requirement of his position than his inability to tell the truth, I have enough secrets weighing me down. I can't handle more baggage.

After gliding my hands down the fan of my black skirt, I turn to face the mirror. I look the same as I did when I attended Luca's funeral eight years ago, just older and wiser now.

Luca and I shouldn't have argued. We were adults who should have discussed our concerns in a respectful manner, but as Alex said, accidents do happen. I didn't set out to hurt Luca the night he was killed. If I knew the consequences of my actions, I would have never gone into our argument so headstrong, but I was young and heartbroken. He was my light—the man I looked up to as much as my father, so seeing him as I did didn't just break my heart, it shattered my faith in him.

I didn't care that Luca was gay. I loved him no matter what. But his inability to see the worth in both himself and me fills me with anger. He wanted it all, and when he thought he couldn't have it, he found the closest exit and opted for it. I'm not angry he killed himself. I'm devastated he didn't think he could overcome his depression, and that he couldn't see the impact his life had on many.

Even now, years after his death, church bells ring in the distance in memory of him. You can't love somebody that much and not accept them for who they are.

Luca should have come clean—just as I am going to.

CHAPTER TWENTY-EIGHT

Awkward. It's only one word but extremely impacting. It's also the perfect word to describe the twenty-mile trip to Regan's hometown. Regan's mother is glaring at her father, who is glaring at me, and Regan is utterly oblivious to the tension surrounding us. She hasn't spoken a word since she climbed into the back of her dad's truck. She didn't even flinch when her father growled upon spotting my hand curled over hers in comfort. She's once again locked down, trapped by her memories, and I fucking hate it.

With Hayden ensuring a minimum two-room gap between Regan and me all afternoon, I've had a lot of time to think. Most of my focus centered around the incredibly unbelievable connection Regan and I shared in the field, but some thoughts were more bitter than sweet.

Regan didn't just confess to being in the car that claimed Luca's life when it crashed into a tree; she divulged much more profound secrets—ones I doubt she's ever confessed. She said Luca had an endless list of men.

At first, I thought she was a little jumbled, but the more I played our interactions through my mind, the clearer her confession became. She admitted she loved Luca in a way he could never love her back, that she has kept his secret for years. That can only mean one thing. Luca was gay.

Although surprised by the revelation, I'm not entirely stunned by it. It was obvious from the outdated posts on Luca's Facebook wall that he was a man who craved attention. He sought it in any fashion he could get it, whether positive or negative. He cared for Regan, but not in an all-encompassing way a man besotted with her would.

That should have raised my first suspicion.

Why would you crave attention from nobodies when the absolute cream of the crop was directly in front of you, striving for your devotion? Luca did because Regan couldn't give him everything he needed. Luca knew it; I know it; Regan is just a little slow receiving the message.

It's understandable. Her entire life was wrapped around Luca's, so everything she thought she knew perished with him.

I can't wait to show her it didn't.

A flurry of buzzes, dings, and a cow mooing sounds through the truck in quick succession when we enter the outskirts of Colendale, Texas.

My hand delves into my pocket to dig out my phone when Sally laughs, "Everyone knows when the Myers are in town. Our cellphones light up like a Christmas tree. The joys of having sporadic service on the farm."

While smiling to hide my grimace, I punch in the four digit code the salesperson at the Ravenshoe airport had me select when setting up my new phone. I can't believe I didn't check if I had service when Brandon failed to make contact. I assumed the forensic team still combing through the evidence was the cause for his lack of contact. I'm a fucking idiot.

After scrolling through the email alerts updating me on Isaac's whereabouts and upcoming schedule, I stop at an email from an encrypted server.

Forensics found a partial match from the glove, sending details to mainframe. Theresa wants to be kept updated. BJ.

Forgetting that I can't access the FBI's database from a cell, I store Brandon's details into my contacts before opening up my Safari app. It takes me attempting to log in three times before I remember mobile connectivity isn't viable.

"Fuck!"

It dawns on me that I said my curse word out loud when Hayden growls, "You'd do best to tone down that language before we arrive at the church. Do you hear me, boy?"

After swallowing the brick in my throat from his deep snarl, I dip my chin. I'm in two places, torn between being a man and an agent. If Regan's safety wasn't involved, I'd shut down my phone and devote all my attention to supporting her during this difficult time. Instead, I reply to Brandon's email.

Can't access data. Forward dets to this number.

I jot down my new cell number at the end of my message.

Like all good technicians, Brandon's reply is almost immediate.

What happened to your original phone?

My teeth grind out the string of profanities I can't say since Hayden is watching me like a hawk as my finger punishes the screen of my phone.

Shit breaks. Get the fuck over it.

I don't know Brandon any more than the woman who sold me my latest fandangle cell, but I can imagine him laughing at my reply. . . or dying, once I read his message.

Anger management is always an option. . .?

Thankfully a second message quickly follows the first.

I'm joking. Forwarding the information now.
The file is big, so may take a little to download.

"Not as long as it will take for your teeth to grow back after I ram them down your throat," I mumble to myself.

My wish to kill Brandon fades when a text message pops up on my screen a few seconds later. He wasn't joking about the file size. Before I've even clicked on the blue folder icon, my phone announces its storage is near capacity.

Not interested in the life history of the assailant, I scroll to the attachments responsible for the slow download speed. With the spotty reception, it takes several long minutes for the accused's hair color to be exposed. It's mousy brown and longer than mine, which is curling around my ears after twelve months of growth.

After another few minutes, I observe that he or she has three freckles on the left brow, one of which is large in size. He or she is sporting a curly hair you'd expect to find on a witch's chin. With the structure of their forehead being more feminine than masculine, I assume the suspect is female.

Just as portions of her murky blue eyes come into view, my phone is snatched from my hand. I'm about to rip Hayden a new asshole until it dawns on me that I'm the only traveler left seated in his truck. Regan, Sally, and over two dozen guests are standing at the stairs of the church, waiting for me.

"Shouldn't have expected any better. If you can't treat your woman like a lady, how will you ever act as a gentleman?"

Although pleased he called Regan my woman, I don't get a chance to respond when he heads for the church with my almost crushed cell in his hand.

Pissed, I take off after him. *He has no clue how idiotic he's being right now.*

My turbines cool when I enter the church an inch from Hayden's heel. The number of patrons outside was nothing compared to the number of mourners filling the pews, but that's not the cause of my sudden loss of temper. It's the looks everyone is giving Regan. They're not sympathetic ones.

While returning their dirty glares with the silent promise of retaliation, I race down the aisle to catch up to Regan. My quick steps have me beating her father to the task of consoling her. She startles within an inch of her life when I curl my arm around her waist and tug her into my side, but my chest swells when she shakes her head at her father's attempt to usurp the nurturing role I'm fulfilling.

"I can't believe after all this time they still hate me," Regan murmurs when we are halfway down the aisle.

"Nobody hates you, Rae. Grief makes people stupid, but

instead of recognizing that, they blame the person they believe is responsible for their confusion. Luca isn't here, so that only leaves you."

I feel her pulse rage through her body when her eyes stray to mine. "So what's your excuse? You didn't even know Luca, but you still give me the same wary stare the locals do."

"My cagy look has nothing to do with Luca, and everything to do with you, Miss Fancy Pants."

Her smile reveals she took my comment how I meant it. I wasn't ridiculing her. I was complimenting her. This woman scares the shit out of me, but in a way I can't help but encourage.

After aiding her into a pew at the front of the church, I take the seat next to her. With a stern glare warning me to behave, Hayden hands me my phone before demanding the man sitting next to Regan find another spot to sit. I slide my cell into my pocket without glimpsing at the screen. My chivalry makes Hayden's eyes widen. Not by a lot, but enough to reveal I finally got a check in his ledger instead of an X.

Luca's memorial is the standard one every church hosts at least once a week. If you've been to one, you've been to them all. There's just a slight variance. This one has Regan stepping up to the podium. The confidence she exudes while mourning is inspiring. The dirty glares haven't decreased the past hour, but she's brushed them off. Remembering her friend is more important to her than retaliating to belligerent criticism.

Silence falls over the church when Regan removes a tattered piece of paper from her pocket. From its condition, I wouldn't be surprised to discover it was written around the time Luca passed. She coughs to clear her throat before introducing herself to the assembly of people staring at her as if they are meeting her for the first time.

"I met Luca when he arrived in town with a city-slicker attitude and a spotlessly clean pair of boots. As my daddy always said, only a man with something to hide keeps his boots clean. . ."

A flurry of black in the corner of my eye pulls my devotion from Regan. Black isn't an unusual color for a patron at a memorial to don, but the bright red splashes covering the diminutive lady's shoes catch my eye. Outside of this state, I'd be suspicious the droplets were blood, but since I am surrounded by over a dozen farmers with muddy, bloodstained boots, I don't think much of it at first.

While Regan's charismatic personality changes some of the snarls directed at her to smiles, I twist my torso to more vigilantly assess the lady gliding down the side of the church. Since Regan has captivated the crowd as well as she does every man and woman when she enters a room, I am the only one noticing the brunette's stealthy approach. She walks cautiously slow, as if her three-sizes-too-large jacket is hiding more than a petite frame.

My heart rate kicks up as my hand instinctively moves for my gun. I curse the air when my hunt comes up empty. I couldn't clear my gun through customs without exposing that I am an agent, so I traveled without my weapon of choice. It was stupid of me to do. How can I protect Regan without adequate equipment? I can think of a few ways, but none of them are legal.

I watch the brunette like a hawk, praying Regan's ability to wipe my senses has all my receptors askew. Perhaps the unnamed brunette can't afford a better-fitting jacket, so she opted for what she had? I'm not from money, so I understand not being able to keep up with the latest trends.

When the female crosses a large-paned glass window at the side of the church, her face becomes exposed. She's pretty but in a plain, unsophisticated way. Her eyes are murky blue in color, and her bushy eyebrows barely conceal a large mole sitting on the top of her left brow.

I jump to my feet when I spot the wiry hair protruding from the middle of it. Although surprised by my sudden lurch, Regan continues with Luca's tribute, none the wiser that the woman who threatened to hack her into pieces is sneaking up on her.

I step to the left, gaining the brunette's attention since she can no longer see Regan hidden behind my shoulders. I jerk my chin to the exit doors on her left, requesting she leave quietly or face my wrath. The deep descent of the lump in her throat reveals she believes my threat, but for some inane reason, she continues moving toward Regan.

When she pushes off her feet, I mimic her movements. I reach her just as she barges through a cluster of people huddled at the end of my pew. I move quickly to apprehend her, but not quickly enough to stop the carnage.

To be continued. . .

Man in Queue is available NOW!

If you want to hear updates on the next books in the Infinite Time Trilogy, be sure to join my **readers group**: Shandi's Book Babes

Or my **Facebook Page**: www.facebook.com/authorshandi

Isaac, Hugo, Hawke, Ryan, Cormack, Enrique & Brax stories have already been released, but Brandon, Grayson and all the other great characters of Ravenshoe will be getting their own stories at some point during 2019/2020.

Join my READER's group:
https://www.facebook.com/groups/1740600836169853/

Subscribe to my newsletter to remain informed:
http://eepurl.com/cyEzNv

If you enjoyed this book please leave a review.

ACKNOWLEDGMENTS

This is always the difficult part, thanking people. It isn't that I'm ungrateful, I just hope they already know what they mean to me. This community is awesome. It has its ups and down, but I've grown so much the past three years. People come and go. Readers come and go. Even characters come and go, but one thing in my life is always constant: the love I have for my husband. He's my rock and number one supporter. He inspires my great characters, and occasionally, my not so great ones, but, without him, there wouldn't be *any* stories to share. For that alone, he deserves his own mention.

I love you, boo.

When I started this adventure, I never in my life thought it would grow to what it has. I was bored, I needed a hobby. I found one. This industry doesn't just consume you whole, it gives back too. I love it, but just a smidge less than ***you,*** the reader. Thank ***you*** for supporting me. Thank ***you*** for reading my books and writing reviews, because without ***you***, I wouldn't be here either.

Until next time,

Shandi xx

ALSO BY SHANDI BOYES

Perception Series:

Saving Noah

Fighting Jacob

Taming Nick

Redeeming Slater

Saving Emily (*Novella*)

Wrapped up with Rise Up (*Novella - should be read after Bound*)

Enigma:

Enigma of Life

Unraveling an Enigma

Enigma: The Mystery Unmasked

Enigma: The Final Chapter

Beneath the Secrets

Beneath the Sheets

Spy Thy Neighbor

The Opposite Effect

I Married a Mob Boss

Second Shot

The Way We Are

The Way We Were

Sugar and Spice

Lady in Waiting

Man in Queue

Couple on Hold

Enigma: The Wedding

Silent Vigilante

Bound Series:

Chains

Links

Bound

Restrained

Psycho

Russian Mob Chronicles:

Nikolai: A Mafia Prince Romance

Nikolai: Taking Back What's Mine

Nikolai: What's Left of Me

Nikolai: Mine to Protect

Asher: My Russian Revenge

Nikolai: Through the Devil's Eyes

RomCom Standalones:

Just Playin'

The Drop Zone

Ain't Happenin'

Christmas Trio

Falling for a Stranger

Coming Soon:

Skitzo

Trey

Made in the USA
Monee, IL
07 August 2023